Goodbye Boys

BORIS BALTER

translated from the Russian
by Felicity Ashbee

HARVILL PRESS
London

Printed in Great Britain by
Northumberland Press Limited
Gateshead
for the Publishers
Harvill Press Limited
30a Pavilion Road
London SW1

BOOK ONE

Three from One Town

1

---◦◦❦)❦(❧◦◦---

The tourist season in our town started at the end of May, when the beaches dried after the winter storms, and shone golden in the sun. This is why our beaches were called 'golden'. Our beach was supposed to be second only to one other in the world. The first was said to be in Italy, on the Adriatic. No one knew where the competition had been held at which this order was established, but I was quite sure the jury had cheated. I believed our beach to be the finest in the world.

The town looked different in winter and summer, its winter life was quite unlike its summer one.

In winter, cold North-Easters came bursting into the streets, driving the inhabitants indoors. The town looked desolate, and the angry roar of the sea could be heard even in the remotest suburbs. Only one cinema was open—it gave three shows a day, and closed at ten. We spent all our days and evenings at school and at the Pioneer Club, we were rare guests in our own homes.

The town was divided into three: New Town, Old Town, and The Siltings. Our school was in New Town. There too, was the Spa with its beach, sanatoria, and Spa Hall. Visitors to the Spa were astonished to discover that we had a Siltings in our town. They imagined that there were only Siltings in Odessa. Nonsense! It isn't only in Odessa that the sea shifts the sands and builds up dunes far from its edge. And the settlements, built on such dunes, are called Siltings in all southern towns.

7

Vitka lived on the Siltings; Sashka and I in New Town. Sashka's and Vitka's girl-friends were Katya and Zhenya, who were in our class at school; mine was Inka Ilyina, who was two years younger than the rest of us. We all lived at different ends of the town, but this didn't prevent us from getting together after school. We weren't seeking solitude—we felt freer and more at ease when we were together.

On fine Sundays we went to the Spa. The deserted beaches seemed wider than usual. The 'Floating Restaurant' towered on its black metal piles, its doors and window frames, as well as the small bridge, removed for fear of damage by storms. Birds perched on the veranda balustrades, and the roof. The pale green sea with its white crests was cold and hostile. The birds called, and their cries were full of sadness and despair.

We roamed in the bare and chilly parks, where the sanatoria buildings, with their boarded up windows, showed white between the trees. We couldn't stand the silence and the desolation for long, so we'd start singing and shouting. Sashka Kriger would run up one of the long, wide stone flights of steps, and turning to us, recite:

> 'When I walk
> Or look through the window
> There are flowers and blue sky,
> The stink of magnolia's in my nose
> The wisteria's blue hits my eye.'

Of course, he'd recite other poems too, but for some reason or other, I only remember that one. Probably because, though the sky was blue, and the sun shining, it was cold, and there weren't any flowers.

On the front steps of the Sacco and Vanzetti sanatorium we often held our own impromptu concerts. Katya danced, Zhenya sang. To us, the only difference between her and a professional, was that she wasn't scared of getting laryngitis. We all had talents of some kind. Except my Inka. But this didn't bother her, or at any rate, it never affected her spirits.

8

The teachers had nicknamed Inka 'the windmill'. We were mildly condescending about her ceaseless chatter, and about the way she could laugh without the slightest reason.

We were all doing extremely well at school. Except again for Inka. It was a rarity for her to get top marks, and when she did, she would announce it to all her friends and acquaintances. She would hide her less good marks even from us, but we always found out, and shut her out from all our activities. Neither her eloquence, nor her solemn promises that this would be the last time, helped her. We were relentless. Each of us was out to make his mark in life. We never talked about it, it just went without saying.

Vitka took on the job of coaching Inka and it was a test of his capabilities as a teacher. I volunteered to be his consultant —true, Vitka didn't need my help, but I couldn't do without seeing Inka for long.

We didn't avoid other companions of our own age. Each of us had friends outside our group. But the six of us were inseparable.

In autumn and spring, the top classes went off to Collective Farms. Our school had very good workshops. Two yachts that we'd built with our own hands were used on the Sebastopol and Yalta run. All the year round we never really got the callouses, horny and yellow as the local stone, off our hands.

In May the acacias blossomed. They were in bloom for a long time, scattering white petals all over the town. And their blossoming coincided with the opening of the Spa season.

Like the announcement of a big event, word went from mouth to mouth: 'The Mainaki has opened . . .' 'The Dulber' . . . 'The Klara Tsetkin . . .' These sanatoria were always the first to open. Then the first summer-visitors began to appear on the Front, and every day the streets of the town were fuller.

The summer-visitors got the best rooms. They became Sove-

9

reign Lords of the town. The town changed its face, becoming noisier, sprucer, more cheerful. Shops, pavilions and restaurants opened. Celebrities from the capital gave performances at the Spa Hall. They appeared, dashingly bright and disturbing, and then vanished again. All over town signs were hung out exhorting everyone to create the right conditions for Healthy Holidays for the Workers. And these conditions were created.

But for some reason the grown-ups didn't like the summer-visitors. Probably it was because their livelihood depended on them, and by comparison, their own lives seemed uninteresting and dim. We treated the visitors with indifference though our indifference was only on the surface. They didn't exist for us as separate individuals; our interest and curiosity was only stirred by them as a varied and colourful mass. Women who, it seemed, were only concerned with appearing on the streets as nearly naked as possible; men who spent their entire days in the wine cellars and at the kiosks. We met them all in the streets, and on the trams. They filled the beaches. Old and young, fat and thin, beautiful and hideous; all gluttons for the sun. We saw them in the Spa Hall, smart, clean, scented, with a special freshness of their own, and condescendingly kind. That's how people look when they're free of their everyday cares. Among them were well-known engineers, scientists, white-collar workers, simple labourers. We lumped them all into one—just 'summer-visitors', and it never entered our heads that, in the towns they came from, they were ordinary people, with ordinary, everyday lives. They lived among us not noticing us, and not caring what we thought or said about them. But the town saw all their failings, and because of this, our mothers and fathers felt themselves to be superior. But at the same time, the carefree pattern of their behaviour was not without impact on our way of life.

In Bazaar street, not far from Sashka's house, was the

metal Co-op workshop: 'Metallist'. Here you could get primuses, kerosene lamps, and bicycles mended, or saucepans soldered or tinned. It was all done by one man. Presumably he had a real name, among ourselves we called him 'Mr Tinsmith'. He lived in the workshop so as not to pay rent, and always went around in the same, clumsily-patched boiler-suit. There was an all-pervading smell of fish, as well as of kerosene and rusty iron in the workshop, because 'Mr Tinsmith' was always eating fish for economy's sake. He used his joiner's bench as his bedstead, and by day stowed away the pile of rags which was his bedding on a shelf under the ceiling.

When the Spa season began, 'Mr Tinsmith' scoured his hands with white-spirit, locked up the workshop, and booked the most expensive room at the 'Dulber', the town's best hotel. In a white flannel suit, and foreign shoes of thin, plaited leather, 'Mr Tinsmith' was transformed. He didn't appear in the workshop again till the autumn, and spent all day long on the beach. In the evenings, you would meet him at the Spa Hall, or after the concert, in the company of beautiful women, and brazen-faced men on the verandah of 'the Floating Restaurant', or in the restaurant of the 'Dulber'. He used to pass himself off as the captain of an ocean-going liner, temporarily in port. And the women melted when his calloused hands fumbled their waists as they danced. At the end of the season, 'Mr Tinsmith' returned to the workshop.

But once he went back to it in the middle of summer. This happened after an affair that set the whole town talking.

A famous ballerina came to our town on her return from a foreign tour, for three days she appeared on the open-air stage of the Spa Hall. And on each of those three days we saw 'Mr Tinsmith' in the same seat in the front row. Every evening, when the ballerina finished her last dance, the usherette came up the gangway in front of the stage with a basket of roses as blue as the evening sky. These rare roses were grown by a gardener on the Siltings, who injected something into their roots to give them this unusual colour.

When the ballerina came to the front to take her bow, the usherette laid the flowers at her feet. Then 'Mr Tinsmith' would get up and go out along the gangway, tall, elegant, imperturbably calm. At the last performance I saw his eyes. Usually colourless, they were shining bright and cold, as though they had absorbed the roses' colour. He walked past us like a blind man. I nudged Vitka and he stared at me. I tapped my forehead, and then he realised it wasn't me he was to look at. Walking beside 'Mr Tinsmith' was the usherette, saying angrily:

'And what about paying? That's the third basket I've lugged for you!'

'Later, later . . .' answered 'Mr Tinsmith'.

But the usherette went on walking beside him. We knew her capacity for making rows, and stuck to their heels so as not to miss anything. But we were in for a big disappointment. There was no scene. At the exit, behind the railings, 'Mr Tinsmith' pulled a banknote out of his hip-pocket, and pressed it into the usherette's hand.

That evening 'Mr Tinsmith' didn't leave the concert alone, and the next day he and the ballerina disappeared from town.

In a month's time he was back. . . .

Vitka and I were waiting for Sashka at the corner of Bazaar street. Sashka was late. None of us was ever late. We used every swear word we knew as we waited. At last he appeared, announcing from far off:

'I've got news!'

'To hell with your news! Why are you late?' asked Vitka.

'I like that! I come running to him a piece of news, and he couldn't care less! Doesn't know what it is yet, but to hell with it just the same!'

'Sashka, don't beat about the bush,' I said. 'Why are you late?'

'I'm telling you! "Mr Tinsmith's" back.'

'You're lying!' said Vitka.

'Absolutely first-hand! From an authoritative source!'

We didn't believe Sashka. His news was always 'first-hand' and from 'authoritative sources'. This time the authoritative source was Sashka's mother.

'Shall we check?' I asked Vitka.

'I've already checked,' said Sashka.

'Never mind, this time we'll do the checking,' I said.

The workshop was just round the corner, and when we got there we took a quick look in at the door. 'Mr Tinsmith' was standing behind the bench in his boiler suit, taking an order, and having a long haggle with an elderly woman.

'What did I say?' said Sashka. 'And now look at this.'

Sashka pulled a newspaper out of his pocket. In the local news was a paragraph saying, that, after a short interruption, the ballerina was resuming her fairy-tale progress of the seaboard towns of the Caucasus.

We forgave Sashka for being late. 'Mr Tinsmith' was our personal enemy, why—we didn't know. He'd never done us any harm, we'd never even exchanged a word with him. But he was our enemy all the same. We felt he was, and despised him for his double life.

It was Vitka who hated him especially and, though there were no open hostilities between us, 'Mr Tinsmith' must have sensed our hatred of him. Whenever we met him with some woman or other, Vitka couldn't resist saying:

'Parasites! Nowhere in town to get a primus mended, and they just saunter around. . . .'

But neither by look nor gesture did the self-styled Captain ever give himself away. We positively longed to follow him, and show him up. But to be honest, we were afraid of his unseeing eyes and his powerful hands. I think this made us hate him even more.

The summer before, we'd often seen 'Mr Tinsmith' on the beach with a young and very beautiful woman. Then we met her by chance, in town, alone, coming out of the drapers. Vitka stepped up to her and barred her path.

'The man you go to the beach with is deceiving you,' Vitka said, and blushed terribly, because the woman was looking at him with her green eyes, and smiling.

'And how is he deceiving me?' she asked.

'He's not what he makes out he is. . . .'

'Oh, my dear, there are worse ways of deceiving a woman than that! I know he's not a Captain, but what business is that of mine?'

Vitka came back to us, red and angry. The woman looked at us, laughing.

'You can't do more than throw a drowning person a straw!' said Sashka loudly, and we stalked off, proud and misunderstood. The woman laughed, and the sound of her laughter followed us for at least two blocks.

Of course we never thought that from our childhood up, we too had been affected by the carefree life of the resort. For instance, till I was thirteen, I ran around town in bathing trunks, and felt as free and easy in this primitive get-up as African natives are said to. And then one day, a young woman noticed me. I was having a mineral water as she was passing by with a man, and they too stopped at the kiosk for a drink. Out of the corner of my eye, I caught their reflection in a shop window. With a jerk of the head, the woman drew her companion's attention to me, and said:

'Do look at that boy—he's a living Apollo!'

I knew my mythology well enough to get the flattering allusion. For a moment, I studied my own reflection, then suddenly saw the woman's eyes in the glass. She smiled. I wasn't going to leave my drink unfinished, so I drained it, but without pleasure. I didn't need to look at the reflection again to know the woman was watching me. I put the glass down on the counter, and ran. I ran right home, and the familiar stretch seemed twice as long. I tried not to look at the passers by, I was so ashamed of my nakedness.

There was no full-length mirror at home, so I looked at myself bit by bit in a hand one. Legs, stomach, chest. Till then, I'd simply never noticed or thought about my body. It served me excellently for games, and that was quite enough. But now I felt a burning interest in it, but felt ashamed. I didn't go out again that day. I sat at the window and waited for my mother, and as soon as she came into the room I said:

'I'm not going around in bathing trunks any more!'

'What's happened?'

'Nothing. But I'm just not going around in bathing trunks any more.'

'I'm afraid you're going to have to.'

My mother wasn't cruel. It was just difficult for us both to live on her wages, and my categorical statement had taken her by surprise. Her pride wouldn't let her admit that she couldn't give her son what he really needed. I usually told my mother all my daily doings at supper-time, but that evening I was silent. I could only have told my father what had happened, or Sergei, my elder sister's husband. But I hadn't had a father for a long time, and my sisters were working in the Far North.

Next morning I waited till my mother had gone out, then got my trousers and cotton velvet jacket out of the drawer. This was what I went to school in, in winter. The trousers turned out to be hopelessly short and worn at the knees. I took some scissors and unpicked the turn-ups. After this operation, at least the length was all right. True, a fringe dangled at the bottom, and the colour under the turn-ups was a lot darker, but that didn't bother me much. With the shoes it was worse. They'd dried up stiff, and I couldn't get them onto my feet. From a box of old ones, I hunted out some summer slippers of Sergey's. The uppers were almost whole, but the soles were worn through, and the shoes were much too wide. But these were trifles. My nakedness was covered by the once-black trousers, now tinged a dirty red, the brown jacket, and wide-nosed slippers in which my feet slopped about as in galoshes. I went out that morning for the first time in this get-up, and wore it in a heat of 30 degrees, till my sisters sent me a new linen suit and sandals.

The life of a resort, with its naked intimacy, which the summer-visitors hardly made any attempt to conceal, roused our interest in girls at an early age. Sashka and Vitka had made friends with Katya and Zhenya when they were still in the top class but two, but I'd only started noticing Inka last year. Or rather, I'd noticed her as soon as she came to our school (they'd come from the Far East) but at first Inka liked me more than I liked her. Katya used to bring notes from her, which I read with delight, but left unanswered. I was preserving my independence; it was bad enough that Sashka and Vitka had lost theirs. But when Inka invited me to her birthday, I went. Of course, it was a mistake, because from that evening on, I couldn't pretend any more.

The end of the school year coincided with the opening of the Spa season. We threw ourselves into the holiday hurly-burly of the town until we were absolutely part of it. From morning on, we were at the beach, then at the Spa Hall, and after the concert, bathing in the warm, black water, the spray breaking over it white and cold. But we got the most fun of all from the volley-ball games in the sanatoria. The P.T. experts there knew how good our school team was, with Sashka as captain; it pleased their guests to watch us play so they often invited us. We enjoyed seeing a notice of each game posted up outside by the entrance to the dining-room door. Many of the guests would gather to watch us six sun-burnt youngsters, making the most improbable leaps and bounds trying to get hold of a 'dead' ball. Of course our girl-friends were among the spectators, ostentatiously not part of the crowd, but sharing with dignity, both in our glory and in the bitterness of defeat.

So now you know something of our background and our town.

2

—••❈❈❈••—

That spring we finished school.

I often say 'we', because although Sashka, Vitka and I were very different, we were also very much alike.

Each of us had plans for the future, which we'd worked out with our parents. For instance, I was going to be a geologist, because Sergey was a geologist. Sashka Kriger was to go to Medical School, because his father was a doctor, and Vitka Anikin wanted to be a teacher. With Vitka's patience and kindness, it would have been difficult to think of a better profession for him.

I often wonder what I'd have done, if, when we were taking our maths exam that day, someone had told me that in an hour's time I'd be agreeing to go to a Military Training School instead of the Mining Institute, I just can't imagine! Probably I'd have taken whoever said it straight off to the psychiatrist. We had an excellent psychiatrist in our town, and people with progressive paralysis came to our town specially to be treated by him. True, people used to say he'd had a spell in a loony-bin himself, but personally, I don't think there's anything wrong with the idea of a doctor occasionally being in his patients' shoes. In short, while I was busy solving the bi-quadratic equation, nothing could have been further from my thoughts than the Army.

We knew from the papers that the Army was becoming a profession in our country. A lot had been written about it the year before, when they'd introduced military ranks and insignia. But in spite of our high opinion of ourselves, it had never occurred to us that these Army reforms would ever have anything to do with us personally.

We'd only a very vague idea of the Army anyway, because we were peace-loving youngsters. Outside the town, on the deserted shores of the bay, there was a naval air-arm flying-field. On the sandy spit of land there, an artillery unit was housed in a long barrack building of yellow stone. In June the fleet used to come from Sebastopol, and anchor in the open harbour. It would arrive unexpectedly. In the morning, opposite the beaches, there would be war-ships, which hadn't been there the night before. For a whole month we'd hear the rumble of gunfire, like distant thunder, and on Sundays, the town would be full of the white uniforms of the sailors, and the town would offer them the best of everything.

In our school we had a branch of the Air-Naval Cadets, with special groups for marksmanship and sailing. We, of course, belonged to both, and were proud of our successes. They made us feel more manly, too. But the military side of these activities was to us only an exciting game.

Of the three of us, I had the closest contact with the Services, my Inka's father being a naval pilot. All day long he'd be at the airfield, and his family's life was spent waiting for him. He was a simple, cheerful man, but his dangerous profession gave him a halo of unusualness. I often went to Inka's. Her father always treated me with a gently mocking kindliness, and called me 'the bridegroom'. He loved his work, was always telling stories about incidents during his flights, and when he heard that I was thinking of becoming a geologist, he said:

'Well, why not! Geologists are human beings too. Their job's almost like a pilot's . . . they don't get fat on it!'

I had solved the equation. Sashka was still writing. That meant I had the chance to have my answers checked first.

Then before the next exam, I could drink unlimited quantities of fruit juice and soda-water as Sashka's expense. I underlined my answer with a fat stroke, and looked up at the Headmaster. He taught our form maths.

'Finished, Volodya?' he asked.

I got up and went along the gangway. The Head took my paper and checked the answers.

'I hope all your decisions will be equally irreproachable.'

I shrugged my shoulders and laughed.

'I do my best, Victor Pavlovich.'

'You're all to go at twelve o'clock to see Pereverzev.'

The Head didn't clarify the 'all', it was taken for granted. But what did Pereverzev want us for?

I went out into the light corridor with the big windows, and sat on one of the window-sills. If Alyosha had summoned only me I wouldn't have been surprised. There were quite a few things he might have needed me for, as until recently I'd been Secretary of the school Komsomol (a new one had been elected just before the exam). But what could he want Sashka and Vitka for?

Alyosha Pereverzev was Secretary of the Town Komsomol. We knew him very well. He'd only left our school three years ago. He was a good speaker. In fact he was an efficient chap all round, but as an orator he was exceptional. He could make a speech on absolutely any subject. For instance, I remember an outstanding speech of his on the damage done by gophers! He delivered it to the top form when the whole school was just embarking on an anti-gopher campaign. He opened our eyes to the parasitic nature of this treacherous enemy of young collective farms and of the Soviet Regime in general. I could be wrong, but I really think that Alyosha's speech against the gophers decided his whole fate, for the Secretary of the Town Party Committee was at the meeting, and he liked that speech very much indeed.

Sashka came out into the corridor.

'What does Alyosha want us for?' he asked, looking at me suspiciously with his protruding eyes.

'I could just as well ask you the same question.'

'That's a nice affair! A fine secretary we've been enduring all this time. He doesn't even know what the authorities have summoned him for!'

Vitka had come out into the corridor too, and now stood beside us.

'Perhaps they want some more volunteers for work at the Stadium?' he suggested.

'In the middle of exams? Let's hope even Alyosha wouldn't think of that.' Sashka looked at me again suspiciously.

'What's the use of guessing? Let's go and find out. Incidentally, I've got a terrible thirst on me. I could drink a bucket!'

'Plain water?'

'You can drink the plain water, I'd rather have fruit juice in mine.'

Through the big window you could see the shimmering blue sea, and the white clouds floating over it. From the window to the door stretched a broad stripe of sunlight. The desk and the sun divided us from Alyosha. When the wind stirred the casement, the sunlight shifted along the floor, settling on the corner of the desk, on our legs, and our raised knees. We were sitting on the low, oil-cloth-covered sofa with broken springs. On the sofa with us sat Pavel Baulin, a sailor from the port, who was about three years older than ourselves. A broad, big-shouldered fellow in bell-bottoms and striped singlet. We hardly knew him except as a local celebrity. Pavel was boxing champion of the Crimea. We sat and listened, first to the Commissar, and now to Alyosha.

Alyosha leaned over the desk, his hands on the green cloth top.

'You understood what the Commissar said?' Alyosha asked.

Like all good orators, he always anticipated the worst. He didn't trust our powers of perception. Or perhaps the Commissar's dry and laconic words seemed to him unconvincing. The Commissar sat in the cool shadow, his elbows on the edge of the table, and studied the toes of his boots.

'We are talking about the great honour,' Alyosha said, 'the tremendous trust which the Party and the Komsomol are ready to show you youngsters, before you have even sat your School-Leavers' exams.'

Alyosha stopped. He looked at us searchingly, trying to guess what was in our souls. Not much insight was needed for this; with all our might, we were trying to look earnest, but we simply couldn't control our self-satisfied smiles, nor hide the excited light in our eyes. For Sashka it was easier. He didn't have to pretend. No one had ever seen Sashka serious from the day he was born, and his bulging eyes were always shining. He was sitting on my left, his hooked nose and sharp chin jutting forward. With Vitka it was another matter. His elbow dug me in the ribs and I glanced round. He was sitting between me and Baulin, and I saw from the look on his face that he'd only bumped into me by chance. Vitka was looking at Alyosha, his mouth open, smiling. This was just his naïveté. Vitka was very naïve. However hard Sashka tried to train him, it did no good.

'You are standing on the threshold of life,' Alyosha was saying. 'The Town Komsomol organisation is proposing that you should start on your independent way where you can be of most use to the Party.' Alyosha was getting into his stride, as though he were addressing a town meeting. 'We do not intend to export the Revolution, but abroad our enemies are dreaming of restoring the old order in our country. They are getting ready to attack us. When they do, you will be leading the armies of the first Worker-Peasant State in the world. The Army is calling more and more for young people with secondary education. The older officers, experienced in war, can no longer fully satisfy the spiritual needs of the common soldier.'

At this point in Alyosha's speech we looked at the Commissar, and felt our superiority over this elderly major, with his furrowed, roughish face, wide cheekbones, and heavy, jutting brow. A gold chevron flashed on the left sleeve of his well-pressed tunic, the gold on the right sleeve glowed dimly in the shadow.

'Yes, Comrades, modern methods of mechanisation demand a wide and many-sided knowledge of both officers and men,' Alyosha's voice rolled mercilessly on. 'The Komsomol are always to the fore on the building sites of the Five Year Plan. The Komsomol must be first in the building-up of our armed forces. That is why we turn to you, the best of the best, with our call to join Military Training School. Think of it! In three years you'll be Lieutenants!' Alyosha paused, and in the room still cut in half by the sunbeam, it grew quiet.

Easy to say 'Think!' But Alyosha was asking for something that we were totally incapable of doing at that moment.

'Now you know why we asked you here. Now it's over to you.' Alyosha said this in his usual, non-oratorical voice. He was sitting on the ancient chair with the high, carved back. The chair was so old it ought to have been thrown out long ago. I think Alyosha kept it because of its back. There wasn't another chair with a back like it in the whole town. 'They've agreed upstairs to your applications.' Alyosha threw in, almost by the way, pointing with his first finger at the ceiling. We knew what 'upstairs' meant. Just above us was the office of Kolesnikov, First Secretary of the Town Party Committee. Alyosha turned to the Commissar and said:

'Do they need their application forms now?'

Before answering, the Commissar looked at us.

'First they must agree. They can make out their applications after the exams. Their school reports are by no means unimportant. Candidates must have Top Grade assessments and marks.'

'You don't have to worry about that,' said Alyosha.

We didn't look at each other. Like all youngsters, we had the highest opinion of our capabilities, as of ourselves. We were ambitious and arrogant, and now, it seemed—rightly so. Alyosha had called us 'the best of the best', the Party and the Government needed us. Even we who were used to praise, had not expected as much as this. The Commissar and Alyosha were talking together softly, I couldn't catch the words. Actually I couldn't hear anything. I'd never before been faced with having to make so big a decision. What would Inka's father say now? And what would my mother say, and my sisters? And Sergey? But most of all I was thinking of Inka and her father. Of course, 'think' wasn't the right word. Their faces merely flashed before my eyes.

'We're waiting,' said Alyosha. 'Make up your minds.'

We were silent, ready to agree, but only dimly aware of the seriousness of what was being demanded of us, of how much our whole future would be changed by that short word 'yes', and of what new worries would come into our lives.

'Supposing I say "Yes". Then I go home, and my father and mother say "No" . . .' this from Sashka. He had been sitting down, but, after a glance at the Commissar, stood up, blocking the sunlight.

'Kriger, you're eighteen! Remember, at your age, members of the Komsomol were going off to the front. Remind your parents of that . . .' said Alyosha.

There would be no point in reminding Sashka's parents of that. They had never been Young Communists, and they had never gone off to any war. Alyosha knew this just as well as Sashka, so he added: 'What sort of a young Communist are you if you don't know how to convince your parents?'

'I'll say "yes",' said Sashka, 'then we'll all go together to persuade my parents!' He sat down, as if bent in half, and the stripe of sunlight lay on his knees.

From Sashka's tone I realised that he had grave doubts about his parents' agreeing. So had I. Not about my mother, but about Sashka's parents. I was sure about my mother, so when Alyosha looked at me, I said:

'I agree.'

'Fine.' Alyosha bent towards the Commissar and said: 'That's Belov, Nadezhda Alexandrovna's son.' The Commissar nodded and looked at me.

'How about you, Anikin?' said Alyosha.

Vitka blushed, and drops of sweat showed on his forehead.

'I agree too,' he said.

'How much do they pay a lieutenant?' It was Pavel Baulin who asked this. He had a slightly husky bass, and spoke with a drawl. Pavel sat reclining against the back of the sofa, his heavy arm lying easily on the bolster at the end. It was in this totally relaxed position, legs spread out, that he usually rested between the rounds in his corner of the ring.

Alyosha hunched his shoulders and threw out his hands in a revealing gesture. But Pavel was looking at the Commissar, not at him. Before answering him, the Commissar stood up.

'Army pay is reckoned not according to your rank, but to your duties,' he said. 'At the end of your training you will be appointed platoon commander. . . .'

'All right. What's the pay for platoon commanders?' asked Pavel.

'625 roubles,' answered the Commissar, 'and in the Army you don't interrupt a superior.'

'Suits me!' Pavel looked at Alyosha. 'Write it down. I agree.'

'Business for the day completed, as they say,' said Alyosha, and stood up. We stood up too. 'Bring your applications to the Party office immediately after the exams. Oh, and by the way, I'm going to Military Training School too!'

As an experienced propagandist, Alyosha had saved his announcement for the end. He expected us to be glad, and we really were. We were used to Alyosha, and sure that he would always stand by us.

3

—••ε)(ɜ••—

From the Party office Vitka and Sashka went to the beach
where Katya and Zhenya were waiting for them, but I had
to go and fetch Inka from school. She had a written exam.
Of course she turned out not to be there. In one corner of the
large playground some of the boys were playing volley-ball.
I went over to a girl from Inka's class.

'Have you seen Inka?' The girl was standing at the side of
the court watching the game.

'Yes,' she said, without even turning her head.

'When?'

'Oh, about half an hour, an hour ago . . . I don't
remember.'

'Where was she off to?'

'She went to the Town Komsomol office.'

It was always like that with Inka. You arranged to meet in
one place, and she'd bolt off to another. I got angry.

'Why didn't you say so straight away?'

'Why didn't you ask straight away?'

The boys on the left were the better players. Someone
'smashed' the ball down onto the ground on the right hand
side of the court. The girl turned to me sharply.

'It's no use your keeping on at me. You'd think I'd nothing
to worry about except acting as Inka's bodyguard!'

What was the use of trying to get anything out of this
creature with all the cares of the world on her shoulders!

'Don't get worked up. They'll lose anyway,' I said, and

went towards the gates. I needed Inka badly. It was absolutely essential to tell her why I'd been summoned to the Party office. But going back there again made no sense. She was sure to have left long ago.

I stood for a moment in the street. The velvet-black shadows of the acacias stood out sharply against the sun-whitened roadway. On the other side stretched the low harbour wall. Beyond the shelving line of the shore, the sea lay opalescent, motionless. And on the yellow sand, the tarred hulls of the motor-sailing boats showed black.

Still not knowing where to go, I went along the street. Inka caught up with me at the corner and, panting, deluged me with words.

'I know everything. . . . I've been running and running. I've been chasing all over the town.' She didn't have to tell me. It was quite impossible to imagine Inka walking quietly along the street when she was hunting for me. 'Our lot's down on the beach. Zhenya's making a scene. She's afraid they'll send Vitka to a town where there isn't a Music Academy.'

Inka was hurrying to get everything out before I stopped her.

'Just think of it! My father and you . . . both in the Forces! My father is sure to be made a captain. Actually they recommended him for a major, but he's sure he'll get his captaincy . . .'

There was only one way of stopping the flow of Inka's words.

'Where have you just come from?'

'From school.'

'And how did you get into school? Through the fence?'

'Well, I *couldn't* run all round the block! What do you suppose? I looked through the fence and saw Raika. She was furious because Yurka was losing. Raika said you'd only just gone out into the street.'

The teachers were coming out of the gates, and we went round the corner so as not to meet them. I walked on ahead, Inka didn't even try to catch me up, she saw very well that I was angry.

'Why didn't you wait for me at school?'

'I did! You've no idea how long I waited. I waited so long, I just couldn't wait any more.'

If I wanted to see Inka when I was speaking I had to turn my head, and each time I did this, I met her glance. I'd never seen molten gold, but I was sure it must be the colour of Inka's eyes. I've only ever seen eyes the colour of Inka's in dogs with tawny coats. Inka was tawny too, all tawny, from her luxuriant hair, and the big freckles round her nose, to the golden down on her legs.

It was impossible to be angry with Inka for long. I slowed down, and she started walking beside me as though she hadn't noticed anything.

And now it was I who was talking. Nobody could listen to me the way Inka did. I always told her everything that interested me. If she understood me, then it meant that I'd thought everything out to a proper conclusion. When she stopped listening, it showed there was some contradiction somewhere, and I'd stop and worry till I'd sorted it out. All the iron logic the teachers praised me for, I owed to Inka.

'I simply didn't know that I could be a soldier,' I said. 'The two have nothing in common . . . a geologist and a soldier. An officer has to be good at an awful lot of different things. Firstly, he has to be a teacher—an officer must instruct those under him. Secondly, an engineer: the Army is mechanised nowadays. Thirdly, he needs to know a lot about history. Who knows? Perhaps the battle of Cannae could help win a decisive action for Communism! And if not Cannae, then Verdun; or, shall we say, the military reforms of Alexander the Great might suggest new ways of Army organisation. . . .'

I talked as though all my life I'd dreamt of the Forces as a profession, and had made an exhaustive study of its every aspect. I'd argued the advantages of being a geologist in exactly the same way not so long ago. But what did that matter now? The main thing was to convince myself and Inka that there was nothing astonishing in my having decided to change my plans for the future, for above all, I was afraid of seeming frivolous in Inka's eyes. All I was saying had come to me on the way from the Party office to the school: it came because I had already seen it in the papers, and heard it from the Commissar and Alyosha Pereverzev. But these thoughts were now my own, influencing me and beginning to guide my actions.

'The training at the military school is only three years, isn't it?' Inka asked.

'Yes.'

'So you'd be quite independent after three years instead of five, wouldn't you?'

'Yes.'

'D'you know, Volodya, I must be very wicked. I asked my mother when I could marry you, and she said, that till you were independent, it was indecent even to think about it!'

Inka looked at me sideways through her eyelashes. She had to be quite sure what impression her words were making on me. I broke out in a sweat. I was beginning to understand why Inka's father called me 'the bridegroom'. I frowned. This always put Inka into a flap.

'Well, what've I said now, what've I said?' she began quickly. 'Is it my fault I get bored when you're not around? In three years time you'll be a Lieutenant. Think of it! You'll be twenty-one, and you'll be a Lieutenant already! And you'll live in Sebastopol or Kronstadt, or perhaps Vladivostok, . . . and I'll come and join you. No, better you come to fetch me . . . no it'd better be me; and you'll meet me at the station with flowers.'

'Pure fantasy!' I said, in an offhand manner, and tried hard to keep up my threatening frown, but my eyebrows wobbled and let me down.

We were walking along the main street. It was already too late to go to the beach. The street was hiding in the thick shade of the acacias, but where the sun pierced the shadow, there were blindingly white patches on the walls of the houses. The narrow pavement was crowded with people. They were strolling about, and when they called in at a shop, it seemed to be only out of curiosity. They had nothing to do with us, nor we with them. Then we went and sat on the Promenade. Our seat was right on the front, and below us, the sea rose and fell back against the sloping wall, sometimes sliding noiselessly up to it, sometimes slapping it. But they sounded like caressing slaps. Floating about in it were brown clots of last year's sea-weed, cigarette ends, and scraps of paper. They moved up and down with the swell, but stayed in the same place. The horizon was swathed in slanting streaks of whitish mist. Rain was sweeping in from the sea, but over the town the sun was still shining.

I suddenly remembered I hadn't found out the most important thing from Inka.

'How did you get on with the composition?' I asked. Inka shrugged.

'I did it. . . .'

We knew from experience that one of the subjects for composition, bound to come up in an exam in the top class but two, was 'Eugene Onegin as the Superfluous Man'. On purely educational grounds, we advised Inka to be sure and choose this subject, and Vitka had spent the whole of the evening before coaching her. You'd have to be an incredible dunce after all that, not to pull off at least a Grade Two. But you had to be ready for anything with Inka!

'Inka, tell me honestly, what sort of a life would you really

31

like? What would you yourself like to do . . . if no one was prodding you?'

'And you won't get angry again? Well, to be absolutely honest, I'd do nothing. Well, no, of course I'd do *something*, but only what was fun. I'd like it always to be summer, and always warm, and to be the prettiest girl, and things to be fun . . . and of course I'd like you to be always with me, and for the three years to be over already, and that we needn't ever be separated. . . .' Inka looked at me and burst out laughing. And her eyes said: 'I know what you're going to answer.'

'Not a very definite plan,' I said, 'but understandable, and in fact, I'd be inclined to say I even like it! What's wrong with things being fun? But if everyone wanted to live like that, who'd do the work?'

'Well, I'm working aren't I? Today I wrote a composition, and in two days time I'll be taking my maths exam. But you wanted me to answer honestly, so I did.'

Inka's legs were stretched out, and she raised them now, feet together. She always knew how to show off her best points. She wore low-heeled, strapless shoes, so as to stress the natural curve of her instep, and even when she wasn't laughing, she kept her mouth half open so that her teeth showed. She was sixteen, but to those who didn't know, she said she was eighteen. This was what my Inka was like, and I loved her very much all the same.

I looked at her legs, already touched by the sun, and at the white silk socks tight round her ankles. Inka's legs were strong and shapely. I'd always liked them. She put them down but I still went on looking at them.

'Don't look at them like that!' said Inka softly.

I don't know how I was looking at them, but I know that I wanted to kiss them, and that I'd never wanted to before.

'You said it was fantasy,' said Inka. 'But what do you think yourself? What do *you* think it'll be like?'

What could I answer her? Happiness always gets in the way of seeing life as it really is. To me it seemed as though nothing but happiness awaited me, happiness as yet untasted and unknown. It seemed to me that only beyond some imaginary barrier would our real life begin. That's how it looks when you're eighteen, and at forty, it turns out that what you experienced then was true happiness, and that the greatest joy of all lies in the expectation.

'O.K., Inka,' I said. 'I'll work for us both. You've just got to get through school, and then you can simply be my wife, and be like your mother . . .'

'But what would you honestly like? Just a wife, and nothing more?'

'No, Inka, to be absolutely honest, I *would* like something more.'

Some summer-visitors were sitting on the next bench. The man was unwrapping expensive sweets, and feeding them to the woman. She opened her mouth, and he popped one in. The woman took the sweet between her teeth, so that half of it stuck out, and drawing back her lips, turned to the man. He brought his lips close to hers and bit off the sweet. The woman said:

'What a wonderful smell of sea and of acacias!'

'Do you like that couple?' asked Inka.

'No.'

'But just now you were looking at my legs the way he looks at her,' said Inka. I blushed.

'You didn't like it?'

'I don't know . . . I felt a bit scared and a bit ashamed. If it weren't for that I expect I'd have liked it.'

The rain swept towards us noisily over the water. The first drops pattered on the leaves of the trees, and left wet spots on the sand. People ran for shelter to the trees and the awnings over the shop windows. Our neighbours went too. There was no one left on the deserted Promenade except Inka and me.

4

—••E)(3••—

I ran all the way home. My wet shirt dried on me, and no longer clung to my skin. But I still ran. Why? I'd have liked someone to tell me.

My mother wasn't in; she couldn't have been, because she never got back before eight. I went into the echoing emptiness of the flat, through the kitchen, the wide corridor, (the light fell on it from above through a narrow fan-light over the front door) and into my room. I opened the window, but out in the street too, at this hour, it was still deserted and quiet.

To this day I've never been able to understand why our flat always looked so empty. It was not that we hadn't enough furniture. For instance, in my room there was a narrow bed, a dining-room table, and a divan; the leather-cloth on it was all cracked, but it was still in one piece. We even had an unwieldy dresser, with coloured glass panes, and in my mother's room there was a little mahogany dressing-table. I don't remember my mother ever sitting down to it, but it was there. And still the flat seemed empty. Even the air in it felt somehow unlived-in, cold and echoing.

I stood for a moment in the middle of the room. There's nothing worse than when everything inside you is hurrying, with nowhere to hurry to. I went into the kitchen. There was a whole mountain of dishes in the enamel bowl. My mother only did the washing up when there wasn't a single clean plate left in the dresser. There still seemed to be some plates

34

left, but I heated the water, and washed everything up. Then I swept the flat. This was really my job, but I usually did it badly. I salved my conscience by telling myself that my mother wasn't too good when it came to housework, either. She'd cook enough for three days all at once, and when the soup went off, she'd say:

'It's really too bad! I cook till I drop, and you don't eat!'

I'd like to know how you can eat stuff that's gone bad! I did try once, but for the next three days I couldn't touch a thing except tea and rusks. They said I'd come off lightly. I don't know, I don't think it was as lightly as that!

I put out the rubbish. I even meant to clean the primus, but it was covered with such a thick layer of grease and soot, that even touching it was revolting. I did bring myself to touch it, but I couldn't clean it, just wiped it off with a bit of newspaper. Instead of the primus I got going on the letter-box. I mended the hinge and fixed the little door. Extraordinary, how many jobs you can find to do when you have to kill time. But it dragged all the same.

I went back into my room.

Across the street, the panes of the open windows were glinting. I sat astride a chair by the open window. The sills were low, and the wet street looked right into the room. It smelled of acacias and earth. I remembered the woman's words: 'How it smells of the sea and of acacias!'

Strange! I'd never noticed the smell of our town before. Probably because I'd been used to it for so long. And yet the town was simply saturated with smells; in spring it smelled of acacias and lilac, in summer of stocks and tobacco plant, and always—of the sea. I'm sure, now, that I'd recognise our town by its smell, out of a thousand others.

It would have been better if I hadn't remembered the woman's words, because straight away I thought of Inka, and then everything inside me started hurrying again. I wanted to remember what we'd been talking about, but I couldn't.

35

Everything was jumbled, my thoughts leaping from one thing to another. I was beginning to realise that something had happened on the Promenade, and that we'd never be able to go back to our former relationship. Nor did I want to go back. I wanted to discover what was coming next, as quickly as possible. But only time would tell me that. There was nothing I could do . . . except wait . . .

Now I know: waiting isn't the worst thing in life. But then my impulse was to run—no matter where, so as not to remain alone in the empty flat. I could hardly bear to stay sitting on the chair. My hands began setting up the chessmen, thrown in a heap on the window-sill. I don't remember how I got the idea of working out the game between Alyokhin and Capablanca, but I felt better as soon as the weight of the lead pieces was in my hands.

I called Capablanca my teacher. In my heart I preferred Alyokhin, but he was a White emigré. I've often found it's like that in life. I get to like someone, whom according to my theories I ought not to, so I begin trying to convince myself he's not worth my notice. Sometimes it works, oftener not.

I knew the endgame, and played it through twice. Capablanca lost. I wasn't upset. But I set myself the task of spotting the ex-champion's mistake, and proving to myself that Alyokhin's win was accidental. I tried to work out the next move without looking at the book. At first my mind, as though detached, fumbled for the possibilities which the disposition of the dead pieces on the board concealed. They weren't dead to me. The flash of insight usually came unexpectedly, and then I could suddenly guess the move in the stranger's mind and, following it easily, disentangle his crafty schemes. But this evening, the moment never came. I was watching the street more than the board. Raindrops hung on the grass between the cobbles of the roadway, and there were puddles in the potholes of the brick pavement, gleaming like blind eyes in the sunset. Now was the time when the summer-visitors, having had their rest after the beach, came out onto the Promenade, or went to the Spa Hall. Today they were later than usual because of the rain. As they walked past, I could see them from top to toe, and even before they appeared under the window, I could hear their voices and the click of their heels. They'd go by me, and only the width of the window-sill divided me from them, and their voices would come booming into the room.

That evening for the first time I felt the unlived-in emptiness of our flat. It must have been that way since my childhood, but I'd never noticed it. I simply hadn't had time. I was hardly ever really alone, and had never given our life as a family any thought, neither mine, my mother's, nor my sisters'. I hadn't thought much, either, about why my friends' mothers unfailingly sat me down to eat whenever I turned up. I always enjoyed meals in their homes enormously, and never realised that, when they fed me titbits, it was because they were sorry for me, and blamed my mother at bottom, for our disorganised way of life.

And it's true, our life really was disorganised, though I didn't realise it then. I was proud of my mother, and of her reputation in our town. I was proud that she'd been a Party member even before the Revolution, that she'd been in a Tzarist prison, and had even been exiled. I remember her as always working very hard. She was President of the Medical Workers' Union in our town. She was paid for this, but she'd lots of unpaid public duties too. For several years running she'd been on the Party Executive, and a member of the Town Council, and two years ago she'd organised the Centre for Education in Hygiene. It hadn't been found possible to include this in the town's Municipal Budget estimate, and the Centre itself had no funds to cover a salary. Nobody wanted to run it without pay, so my mother was running it temporarily.

Ever since I could remember her, my mother had gone

around in a man's soft brown leather jacket and a wide-peaked cap. Her short curly hair showed under the peak. I wore out that coat of my mother's two years before I left school, but she never parted with the cap. It had long been cracked and faded, and only kept its original colour in front, under the little strap. My mother's hair was already going grey, and her face had the same sort of wrinkles as the cap's.

There was one photograph I loved looking at, that was kept in an old file of papers. A young woman in an old-fashioned frock with a frilly hem, sat on a chair. The pointed toes of her white slippers peeped from under the frill. I could never have enough of looking at her hands, so extraordinarily slim and delicate. She sat graceful and relaxed, and her eyes looked out at me with wonder and gaiety. This woman was my mother too, but I'd never known her like that. Behind her chair stood three men in a row. One of them, with a moustache and a high forehead, was my father, at that time a medical student at Moscow University. You could see straight away that he was in love with my mother. He looked at her sideways, his head bent towards her, forgetting that he was being photographed. And somehow, it was odd to realise that this total stranger was my father, and that he and my mother and sisters had all lived together, and that I knew nothing about that life of theirs.

My father died when I was a year old. No one ever spoke of him in my presence. And I was somehow shy of asking. I only guessed that my father and mother hadn't got on, and that my sisters blamed her for it to this day. Later my mother had a second husband. We weren't living in the Crimea then. I could remember him, but very dimly. He disappeared almost unnoticed, and I couldn't remember how it happened. But his disappearance was connected with some kind of unpleasantness that my mother never spoke about either.

My sisters had long lived on their own, working in the Arctic region, and they came on holiday once every three years. Nina, the eldest one, was married. I'd got very fond of Seryozha even before he became Nina's husband, and I was very afraid that for some reason or other he mightn't marry her. They got to know each other on the beach. I didn't usually go to the beach with my sisters, but that day I went. We were all bathing together, and at first I thought it was my second sister, Lena, that Seryozha liked. I liked Seryozha at once. At eighteen he'd already been a Squadron Commander and, after the battle of Orenburg, he won the Order of the Red Flag. Then he studied at the Workers' Faculty, got a diploma at the Industrial Academy, and went to the Far North to build a new town. I learnt all this later of course, that day we were just fooling. For me, Seryozha was like a hero in a book. What I was to him, goodness knows! Later on I guessed, but all the same I wasn't offended. Only I never thought Seryozha and Nina would get married so quickly. Lena would have been another matter. Nothing would have surprised me with her! But we thought of Nina as very serious, and *I* thought her plain. I only discovered by chance that they'd actually got married. On the way back from the beach Seryozha brought up the fact that his holiday voucher at the Sanatorium had run out.

'I'll have to move in with you,' he said.

Nina and Lena looked at each other, and Lena said:

'Volodya, love, run along and get us some ice-creams.'

What did they take me for! Of course I stayed. Then Nina said in front of me:

'That's crazy! Mother'd chuck us both out!'

'No, she won't,' answered Seryozha.

After that, I myself said I'd go for the ices, and I went off. I don't know what they talked about without me.

In the evening, Seryozha came to our place with his suitcase. Till then, my mother had never even seen him. As soon as he came into the room, my sisters ran out into the yard. They took me with them, and then suggested I creep quietly into the corridor and eavesdrop. I didn't only eavesdrop. Through the half open door. I could see my mother sitting at the table, smiling. When she smiled like that, it was very difficult to come to terms with her. I couldn't see Seryozha, I only heard the divan springs squeaking.

'Nadezhda Alexandrovna, you haven't got it right. I've not come to take a room,' said Seryozha. 'Of course I should have come before, but I didn't get around to it; Nina wouldn't let me. I can't understand why they're so afraid of you.'

'Nina? *Afraid* of me . . . ?' I could see red patches appearing on my mother's face. 'Are you drunk?' she asked. 'Who gave you the right to come to my house?'

'Well yes, I have had a drop,' said Seryozha. 'Is it really noticeable? I don't usually drink. It was because of all this business. I've never proposed to anyone before. I don't know how it's done. I'll come straight out with it: let me marry Nina!'

'Get out of here—quick!' said my mother.

But Seryozha wasn't dreaming of going, and he was right. I knew my mother. She didn't really want him to go. She looked at him across the table, smoothing the cloth with hurried little movements. The divan springs squeaked louder.

'Actually . . . I've nowhere to go,' said Seryozha. 'My sanatorium voucher's run out, but I've still got another two months' leave. And anyway, why should I leave my wife? And why should you part with your daughter before you need? She'll be living so far away from you as it is. . . .'

I don't know how I came to be standing in the room, facing my mother, my back to Seryozha, but I was. She was getting up from the chair slowly, so slowly that I had time to think: 'Now she's *really* going to throw him out!'

'Seryozha, go quickly!' It was Nina shouting, but for some reason, everyone looked at me. I hadn't noticed my sisters come into the room. My mother came round the table, her deep-set black eyes glittering, her lips smiling. She smoothed my forehead and hair with her hot hand, and went to her own room.

Seryozha stayed. I told him to sleep in my bed, but Nina made one up for him on the floor.

Seryozha stayed with us two months, then he, Nina and Lena all went to the Far North. My mother made her peace with him just before they left.

Since then Seryozha and my sisters had come on holiday twice.

Seryozha was ten years older than Nina, but in my mother's view he acted like a child. Maybe he did. Personally, I saw nothing wrong in that. The day they arrived, while my sisters set to scrubbing and turning out the flat, Seryozha would go off to the beach. He didn't believe in keeping in the shade. The result was easy to imagine; a boiled lobster would have looked pale in comparison. In the evening, he would lie in his shorts on the washed floor while my sister rubbed him with sour cream. Next day, his shoulders blistered, he would be off to the beach again. My mother called it crazy and irresponsible, but Seryozha said:

'Pure prejudice! I came here to get properly baked, and I'm going to!'

All our group took to Seryozha. He was just like one of us. But Inka liked him specially. Probably because he too was a redhead. We spent all our days together. We taught him to sail, and he didn't mind if any of us shouted at him. Nina thought herself too grown-up for our company. So much the worse for her! Seryozha told her so outright. But Lena used to come with us, and I could never understand why he hadn't married her.

There were lots of things I didn't understand. For instance, I could see that my mother was a little in awe of Seryozha; why, I didn't know. She lectured him as though he was one of us, but in his case she never insisted on getting her way. As for Seryozha, it was the other way round; he made out he was a deferential son-in-law, but whenever he talked to her he seemed to be teasing her a little.

The last time Seryozha and my sisters had come, was the summer when my mother opened the Centre for Education in Hygiene. I rather suspected she was hurrying to get it open in time for their arrival. All the local papers wrote up my mother and her Centre. When we all gathered for supper, it was the chief subject of conversation. Only Seryozha didn't talk about it. It was obvious at once that the Centre didn't interest him. When Nina once said: 'We really ought to go and have a look at it,' Seryozha immediately thought up an excursion to Tortoise Island. Actually, we never got to the island that time, but neither did we go to see the Centre.

Finally my mother could contain herself no longer.

'Sergey Nikolayevich,' she said. 'Isn't there anything that interests you in our town besides entertainment?'

'I'm on holiday, Nadyezhda Alexandrovna. Having a rest isn't all that easy either.'

My mother was hurt. When she went to bed, Nina said:

'Now look, you summer-visitor, whether you like it or not, tomorrow we're going to look at the Centre.'

We'd been planning to go to Tortoise Island next day in the yacht. Seryozha was coming too. He looked at my sister with mournful eyes.

'Bear up! You'll get over it!' she said.

'I'll have to,' Seryozha answered.

I couldn't have got over it. But Seryozha never argued if Nina asked him for something seriously, and I liked him all the more for this. In the morning we went without him.

That evening I asked him:

'Did you like the Centre?'

We were alone on the porch where he'd gone out for a quick smoke before bed. He didn't answer right away.

'Did you like the Centre?'

'It was all right. Lots of photographs. And beautiful dia-

42

grams—in colour. Is there a good sandy beach on the island?'
We'll still get there together one day.'

Seryozha's face glowed red in the light of his cigarette.

'You talk to me like you do to Mother.'

'That's only how it seems to you.'

'What did you say to her about the Centre? Why d'you always tease Mother?'

'Same as I said to you.'

'And you say it only seems that way!'

'You're an odd one, Volodya! It's just that she's my mother-in-law! Perhaps it's different with the Chinese. But in Russia from time immemorial, sons-in-law and mothers-in-law have fought like cats and dogs.'

Seryozha threw away his cigarette end and stood up.

'No, wait a bit,' I said.

'Bed. It's high time . . .'

The relationship between my mother and Seryozha had completely deteriorated. It seemed to me to be worse now than it was when he and Nina got married. My mother and he hardly ever spoke to each other, so if they happened to pass a remark at table, I pricked up my ears at once. I was afraid they'd start to quarrel and I'd be forced to take sides. And I simply didn't know whose side I was on.

Seryozha and my sisters stayed with us till August. As before, we only all gathered together for supper, and the short time we sat at table, seemed to me unendurably long. Once, Lena was telling us of how Seryozha had fought off all attempts to be made Party Secretary of the new town in the Far North. I don't know who asked her to bring it up. It always had to be Lena! She wanted my mother to understand how highly Seryozha was respected at work, but my mother got it all back-to-front. A half empty glass of tea stood in front of her. She stopped drinking and listened attentively, half closing her eyes. This worried me more than anything. I could always tell her mood at once by her eyes.

'I wouldn't have expected that even from you,' she said, pushing aside her glass.

'What d'you expect me to do, Nadezhda Alexandrovna. I'm a geologist. I'm keen on my work.'

'Agreed. But the Party found it necessary to use you for other work, what right had you to refuse?'

'The chaps in the Regional Committee had made a mistake. In the end they chose another engineer to be Secretary. I'd studied with him at the Industrial Institute. He's not a terribly good engineer, but he's an exceptional organiser. He got more done in a year than anyone else in five.'

'I don't doubt the Committee found a worthy substitute for you,' said my mother. She stood up. Her eyes were blazing, and her lips smiled. There was nothing worse than when she looked like that. She wanted to say something else, but looked at me and went to her own room.

I followed Seryozha out onto the porch. He was smoking.

'Now I've said the wrong thing again!' he said. I was not so much surprised by his words, as by the tone of his voice—so tired and despondent. I sat down beside him and he put a hand on my shoulder.

'You don't like Mother, do you? Why not?' I asked.

'Is it worth talking about?'

'Yes, it is. After all, I'm her son.'

'You're right. I'm sorry. Perhaps we should. "Like" isn't the right word, Volodya. You see, you, and Nina, and Lena, you're close to me. But she's not. That's all there is to it.'

'Maybe Mother feels the same way. . . .'

'Maybe she does.'

'It's such a pity! You're both Communists. Both of you have fought for the Soviet cause.'

'Ah, that's another matter, Volodya. We'd stand together now if it came to it. It's just that neither I nor Nadezhda Alexandrovna can be any different. It sometimes happens that way in life. You mustn't let it upset you.'

Seryozha's hand squeezed my shoulder. I said nothing, but leant closer against him.

I could see that he and my mother were different sorts of people without his telling me. But that didn't stop me from loving them both, though it seemed to prevent their liking each other. I wanted to ask Seryozha why this was, but I didn't. I guessed he wouldn't have been able to tell me.

From us, Seryozha and my sisters were going to Moscow, and from there to Leningrad, and then they were thinking of seeing his people in Orenburg.

The day before they left, they went into town to shop, promising to be back in an hour. I waited for them for two hours. Of course I could have found them easily, but what was the point? I went to the wild beaches outside the town on purpose not to meet them.

I had to run to be back in time for supper. They were already at table, eating in silence. It had never been so depressing at home as it was that evening.

My mother went to her own room, but my sisters went on sitting round the un-cleared table, saying how sleepy they were and not going to bed. When I was smaller, and they'd wanted to talk to my mother, they used to hound me into bed. I'd have liked to see them try it now. I kept glancing at them maliciously, and then realised that going to bed would be the best way of finding out what they wanted to talk to my mother about.

The light in the room was switched off. My sisters moved about, listening to my breathing, their dresses whitish in the darkness.

'I don't believe he's asleep,' said Nina in a whisper. 'You can't hear him breathing at all.'

'On the contrary,' answered Lena. 'It's just when he's asleep that his breathing is so quiet.'

They lingered by my bedside. I didn't care, I had pretty capacious lungs. Then Nina called Seryozha, and they went into my mother's room and shut the door. As if that was any good! Even through the closed door I could hear perfectly, I only had to lie on my back.

'Mother, let Volodya come with us.' It was Nina speaking.

'At last,' said my mother. 'I was beginning to think you were completely hardened. But if I let him go with you, he must be home a week before the beginning of term.'

'Mother, we want Volodya to come to us for good . . . to live with us. . . .'

'You're mad! You must be out of your mind!'

'Mother, do listen a moment. It would be better for Volodya with us. What does he see here? We've got a new town going up, an enormous industrial complex, all sorts of interesting people are working there.'

'Obviously, this is Sergey Nikolayevich's brilliant idea!'

'You're wrong, Nadezhda Alexandrovna. Not mine—Lena's. True, I've thought about it a long time, but I couldn't bring myself to be the first to speak about it. But I've been thinking about it for ages. The boy's going to have to choose which way of life he wants to follow; but what does he know of life?'

'He's already chosen, and not without your help! He's decided he wants to be a geologist, and I've agreed. What more do you want? There are small things as well as big things in life, and someone has to do them too. They aren't less necessary, and demand all your strength. You're for things on a big scale, and so am I. But I want my son to understand and learn to respect people who stick to a hard, inconspicuous manual job, day after day, year after year, and who go on doing it as if it were work of vital importance to the State.'

'A thing can be on a big scale and still be no use to anyone,' said Seryozha. 'It isn't a question of scale, but of *use*. Maybe it really was I who fired him with the idea of being a geologist. But now let him meet *other* people too. The more you know, the easier it is to find out what you really want.'

'Mother, you're only reacting this way because you're offended. You shouldn't.' Lena said this. As long as she hadn't said anything, everyone had spoken quietly. Extraordinary creature, Lena! She only had to put in a couple of words, and a storm arose at once. I didn't have to strain my ears any more, I could hear everything, as though they were right beside my bed.

'Offended? Who says I'm offended?' asked my mother. 'You don't imagine I could be offended because someone thinks the Centre is a useless undertaking?'

'Mother, don't pretend!' it was Lena who spoke again.

'That's that, my dear girls. Now go to bed. I'm tired.'

'Mother, you're wrong! You shouldn't only think of yourself, of your own feelings,' said Nina. 'If *you* don't want to live with us—that's your affair. But Volodya ought to go. He's growing, and he needs good, regular food.'

'Very touching, I'm sure!' said my mother. 'I managed to bring *you* up, clothed you, fed you, taught you; but I'm past it when it comes to Volodya . . . Let's stop talking about it. Volodya needs me, and I need Volodya . . .'

'You don't need to be sarcastic. You know perfectly well what Nina is talking about. Remember Father!' This was Lena again.

Seryozha came and stood by the window. The door wasn't quite shut and a narrow strip of light fell across the room, cutting off the window and Seryozha. I couldn't see him, but I could hear the box of matches in his hand.

'I remember all right!' said my mother, and through the partly opened door I could hear her breathing. 'And what am I supposed to remember specially? His drunken scenes of jealousy? Come on, tell me, what am I supposed to remember?'

'You remember only what suits you.'

47

'Stop it, Lena,' said Nina. 'Mother, you're in the wrong, too. Father was a talented and gentle person. Can he be blamed for loving you so much? He loved us all, but you most of all. He chucked up the clinic, his friends, his chances for the future, and took me and Lena to come and join you in exile. And what happened then? All the burden fell on him. He had to earn a living and look after us, and constantly stand between you and danger. You can't blame him if he broke down and took to drink. He was too gentle for such a struggle, but he was always a good and true friend to you and father to us. And you often neglected him. Still, we're getting off the point. We don't have to talk about Father now.'

'Yes we do! So I was a bad mother. I neglected my children, my husband, myself. You can blame me for that! But first of all, answer me, in the name of *what* did I do all this?'

Seryozha crossed the strip of light and shut the door tight. In my mother's room there was a sudden silence. I held my breath so as to hear better, but a rushing began in my ears because of holding it for so long.

'Are you asleep, Volodya?' asked Seryozha.

'Yes!' I answered angrily. 'What will you think up for me next? I won't leave Mother!'

5

I was thinking . . . it would be a good idea to write to Seryozha and my sisters to tell them about the change in my plans for the future. But I didn't want to get up, and sat on, astride the chair at the open window. My shirt and trousers were still damp, and I was shivering, but I went on sitting there just the same.

The sun had set, and outside the dusk was sad and grey. Only over the rooftops, the sky was still showing blue. The squares on the chessboard merged into a single dark patch, and you could no longer distinguish the colours of the pieces. I didn't even try. I was listening to the footsteps of the few passers-by.

'The weary sun
Said a tender farewell to the sea . . .'
a woman was singing.

Her voice came nearer, and as she passed one of the open windows, the words of the song boomed into the room, then grew fainter again as she moved on past another bit of wall.

'It was then that you confessed . . .' she sang softly.

A man was walking beside her, his arm round her shoulder. They were happy, the two of them together, not hurrying anywhere. The woman looked at me, and said in a singsong:

'That there isn't any love. . . .'

The way she looked at me made me feel uncomfortable,

49 D

and I realised, from the gay light in her eyes, that she didn't believe what she was singing.

In the room behind me, the light went on.

'How did you get on with the exam?' asked my mother. I hadn't heard her come in.

'I got a Grade A.'

'Was it difficult?'

'Not very.'

My mother put some parcels on the table and went into the kitchen.

'Now look at that! If he hasn't done all the washing-up! You're an absolute marvel and deserve a sumptuous supper.' My mother was speaking from the kitchen. 'I'll make you an omelette with sausage in it.'

She began to sing. This happened very seldom. The last time was a year ago, when we'd had a telegram saying Nina had had a daughter, and they were going to call her Nadezhda after her.

I went round the table and stood by the open door into the corridor.

'The autumn wind is sadly moaning,

The withered leaves whirl round. . . .' sang my mother as she pumped the primus. She had a voice like a gypsy, a bit throaty, with a catch in it. When she sang, I could quite easily imagine her young, as she was on the photograph.

'Mother, the Komsomol have called on me to go to a Military Training School,' I said loudly.

I was looking out into the dark corridor, straining my ears to hear. The primus hissed noisily in the kitchen. My mother wasn't singing any more now. She passed by me into the room and sat down on the divan. Had she heard me or not? She took off her shoes. Black ones with straps and low heels. She took fives like Inka, but my mother's feet always looked much bigger than Inka's.

'Did you say something?' she said.

'Today I was summoned to the Party office. The town has to send the four best Komsomol members to a Military Training School.'

'Oh no, Volodya. It's not possible! I can't. . . . Your sisters would never forgive me.'

'It's not you that's sending me to the Training School.'

'That makes no difference. They won't take anything into account. Tomorrow I'll go and talk to Pereverzev.'

My mother said this uncertainly somehow.

'I think I'll go and lie down,' she said.

She walked into her own room in her canary-coloured socks with the blue edges.

'Mother, you promised me an omelette with sausage,' I said. My heart was beating so fast there was a thumping in my ears.

'Make it yourself, son. I feel . . . tired.'

I'd never seen her so bewildered before, and then I had a sudden inkling that my sisters had nothing to do with it. It was my mother herself who didn't want me to go to Military Training School. That scared me. It was difficult to talk my mother round when it was something she really didn't want. Everything came tumbling down. I pictured to myself having to look Inka in the face tomorrow; but this didn't stop me from thinking about the omelette with sausage.

I went into the kitchen, melted some butter in the frying pan, and when it was sizzling, put in some thick slices of sausage. I watched them frying, blaming myself for my frivolousness. Then I put three eggs into the pan, thought for a minute, then added another two. And while I was cooking, and then eating the omelette, I was tormented by the thought that I might be unfitted for anything really serious.

The light was on in my mother's room. I went over and stood in the doorway. She was sitting on the bed, her feet in their absurd-coloured socks not touching the floor. She

51

was leaning back against the wall, her mouth firmly shut, the top lip covering the lower one. The wrinkles round her mouth and chin showed more this way. Surely, no one could ever have loved my mother as I loved my Inka? Then I felt ashamed of myself, and I do still, now, that I could ever have had such thoughts. My mother was forty-nine. In my opinion a goodish age, but of course I knew that grown-ups of that age don't think of themselves as old.

'Mother,' I said. 'This is the first time in my life that the Komsomol has really needed me. Surely I don't have to refuse? Would *you* refuse?'

My mother was looking at me as though she were seeing me for the first time.

'Volodya, have you begun to shave yet?'

Granted, I hadn't ever shaved yet, and this was pretty obvious from the silky hair on my cheeks, and the downy shadow on my upper lip. But what had this to do with what I was talking about?

'You've grown a lot,' said my mother. 'You'd be hard to recognise, you've shot up so much this year.'

Of course she would have to pick just that moment to look at me so thoroughly! I began to get cross.

'You won't go to Pereverzev tomorrow, will you?' I said.

'All right. I won't go . . . I can't. But you must understand . . . this is something very serious. Much more serious than you think. I hope you realise what's happening in the world?'

My mother's deepset eyes glowed in their dark sockets.

'Of course I understand. I've been doing Political Studies at school,' I said. But at that moment, the fate of the world was the last thing I was worrying about. I turned, kicking the empty air behind me, and started prancing round on tiptoes in a Caucasian dance. To an outsider this probably wouldn't have looked very serious, but I didn't care how I looked.

I made up my bed, and when I shut the window and put out the light, my mother said:

'You're not in bed yet? Give me today's papers will you.'

Then I lay looking at the ceiling, exulting in my surprisingly easy victory. It would be interesting to know how Sashka and Vitka had been getting on. Sashka's mother of course would be crying, her eyes already red and swollen as if she'd got stys coming. But her tears were no indication that she was submitting to her fate. They were a terrible weapon against Sashka and his father. Sashka's mother didn't only cry. She screamed, calling on the gods, and all her relatives, as witnesses to her ruined life.

Naturally, Vitka's father didn't go in for crying or screaming. But that didn't make it any easier for Vitka. His father had only learned to read and write when he was grown-up, and he considered that teachers were the most important people on earth, and it was his dream that his son should become a teacher. Every Saturday, Vitka's father would appear at the school in his Sunday best. With a clanking of his metal-heeled shoes, he would walk along the corridor to the staff-room, where he'd talk long and earnestly with the teachers. And a routine was established, whereby Vitka had to stand in the corridor by the door, on the off chance that his reports weren't good enough, and might demand immediate retribution. But Vitka's reports were always excellent. We rather suspected that his father simply couldn't do without the pleasure of hearing his son's praises sung. He would leave the school looking pleased and dignified, and wagging a salt-corroded finger at Vitka, would say:

'Watch it!'

In fact, it was difficult to imagine how Vitka's father would take the idea of a possible change in his son's future. But perhaps things had gone better than expected at both Sashka's and Vitka's. After all, I'd thought my mother would be proud of the trust placed in me. It's always like that with parents, you never can tell beforehand how things are going to turn out. It would all only be cleared up tomorrow, and there was a whole night to get through before then! I knew from experience that the time would fly easily and quickly if I could only get to sleep. But now, as luck would have it, I simply couldn't. On the promenade, I hadn't been able to answer Inka about how I imagined our future. But now I could. Whenever I was alone, and not afraid of being thought naïve, I could imagine absolutely anything, and it was all as interesting as in books.

Outside, people were passing by again.

That meant the concert was over. John Danker, the King of the Hawaian Guitar was appearing. We hadn't seen him yet. We'd seen a lot of important artists, but so far we hadn't actually seen a King!

6

—••⊰⊱••—

In the morning I was woken by Vitka. There was absolutely no need to ask about the conversation with his father. Under his right eye was the first purple flush of a coming bruise. I pulled on my mouse-coloured cotton-serge trousers with the wide pale-grey stripes. I tried not to look at Vitka's face. The left half was his—lean, with a high, jutting-out cheekbone—but the right half was someone else's, with a wicked-looking eye, sunk glittering in a puffy swelling.

'Does it show?' he asked.

Naïve chap! Fancy hoping a black eye wasn't noticeable!

'Enough!' I said, and went to wash.

Vitka smiled awkwardly, and explored the bruise with the tips of his fingers. He was standing behind me, and said:

'My mother let me down! I trusted her, and she betrayed me!'

He thought I was going to ask him about it. Why should I? He'd tell me himself if he really wanted to. It was more important to think how to talk Vitka's father round. My mind started ticking as I dried myself, while Vitka told me what had happened.

'You see, I started by telling my mother everything, so that she could break it to him gently. And she seemed O.K. She heard me out. She gave me my dinner. Then she asked me to water the vegetable patch, and went out, I thought she'd gone to a neighbour. There I am, watering the garden. Then I see my father coming up from the gate. My mother's trying to run in front of him, but he's blocking her with his arm. So he comes up to me and he asks: "Is this true?" And I say: "Yes". And he lams into me!'

'I'll say he did.'

'My mother let me down!'

'I heard. You'll get over it.'

We came back into the room. A note lay on the table. It was from my mother to say she'd gone to the market, and that I was to wait till she got back and made her breakfast.

'See what *some* mothers are like!' I said.

But I couldn't wait for her. We ate up yesterday's sausage, and drank cold tea with it. The sugar didn't melt properly, and we scraped it out of the glasses with spoons. Vitka said:

'My father's threatening to go to the Party office and tear the guts out of Pereverzev.'

I choked. Vitka's father wasn't one to chuck his words around aimlessly. You could pretty well reckon that Alyosha Pereverzev's guts were out already.

'That's marvellous!' I said. 'There's a row going on at the Party office, and I have to stand here listening to the touching story of how your mother let you down!'

'The row won't have started yet. They're loading at the Saltworks today. My father's going to the Party office after work.'

'We'll have to warn Alyosha.'

On the back of my mother's note I wrote that I had some work to do. I'd long given up telling her all my affairs, unless they involved her directly. It was more peaceful for both of us this way. For instance, it's easy to imagine how she'd have reacted if I'd naïvely told her about my yesterday's conversation with Inka. Personally, I felt that neither my relationship with Inka, nor many other things I hadn't told my mother about, did anyone any harm, and so I kept them to myself with a clear conscience. Probably Seryozha's influence had had something to do with this, but I didn't realise it at the time.

We seldom used the front door, but we went out that way now so as not to meet my mother.

'Wouldn't it be better to wait for Aunt Nadya?' Vitka suggested.

'What for?'

'To ask her advice.'

'Better not to ask for advice, Vitka.'

'Why not?'

'Well, you know, Mother'd make a lot of fuss. We'd better try and persuade Uncle Peter on our own.'

Vitka was walking on the inside of the pavement, trying to hide his black eye in the shadow of the houses. It was still early morning, and fortunately for him, we hardly met anyone. We overtook the early beach-going mothers with their children. The mothers' arms were weighed down by their overstuffed string bags. Three years ago the comedian Vladimir Khenkin had visited the town, and he had called these shopping nets 'In-hopes-es' because at that time people took them about everywhere, in their pockets, briefcases, and handbags, 'in hopes' of picking something up. Even my mother was never parted from her 'In-hopes'. I'm sure Khenkin invented this name in our town, and afterwards, the summer-visitors carried it all over the country.

A stout woman was stumping quickly along in front of us on her short legs, the net in her hand trailing almost to the pavement. As I looked at it, stuffed with packages, I simply couldn't believe that there had been a time when I drank my tea without sugar, and when my mother tried surreptitiously to shove me her portion of bread.

The woman's son was walking behind her, a skinny, long-legged little boy in red shorts. For some reason fat mothers often have skinny children. She was in a great hurry. There are women like that who are always hurrying. Probably they're afraid of missing something. I was sure the woman in front of us could think of nothing except getting a comfortable place under an awning before someone else grabbed it. But the boy wasn't hurrying anywhere, and I understood him very well. He examined everything, carefully, walking slowly and warily, stopping dead every so often for a fraction of a second. He knew what only children know, that the most interesting things happen unexpectedly, and that the most important thing is not to miss them. Every now and then the woman looked round and called her son. The sweat was running down her round face and treble chin. The boy kept catching her up and then something new would attract his attention, and he'd stop again.

The boy saw Vitka, and though his feet went on moving, he couldn't tear his eyes from Vitka's bruise. At last he'd found what he'd been looking for all this time.

'Mother!' he shouted, and ran.

Turning round, the woman stared at us suspiciously, but of course didn't see what her son had seen. He was walking now, holding onto one of the loops of the 'In-hopes', to be on the safe side.

'That kid has decided you're a pirate,' I said. 'Only he can't work out where you got that bruise.'

Vitka smiled and turned his face away, but the boy went on looking at him just the same, and making faces.

People who didn't know Vitka took him for an uncouth, not too intelligent chap, but in fact, in spite of his stocky shape, square face and heavy chin, Vitka had the gentlest and most vulnerable of natures. Of the three of us he was the most considerate, and the most artlessly trusting. The little boy's interest embarrassed him.

'I thought my mother would help me, but she let me down,' he said. 'You always seem to know how things work out. But I never do. I bump into everything like a blind puppy. I want everything to turn out for the best, but the worst happens!'

'Never mind. You'll live and learn. The main thing is to know how to apply the dialectical method in practice.'

We turned the corner and almost ran into the boy. He was lying in wait for us, ready to turn to flight, and already worried because we hadn't appeared. He let out a screech and ran to catch up his mother. This time he only pretended to be frightened. He ran, skipping along on one foot, looking round and laughing.

The street led down to a small square. The tramlines were gleaming in the sun. People were crowded round the stop waiting for the tram. Our old friend the Tartar street-cleaner was watering the roadway with a hose. Every now and again he raised it, and a spurt of water shot up noisily onto the dense leaves of the trees, making glittering drops fall from the wet branches. The cleaner smiled, and aimed a gush of water at our feet. We took a high jump over it and he laughed, and began washing off the mud which had dried on the cobbled roadway after the rain. We went to Sashka's house on the corner of Bazaar street. He lived on the second floor over the chemist.

'You go in alone,' said Vitka, and he buried his nose in the advertisement hoarding.

At the tram-stop the summer-visitors were jammed together, several rows deep. I saw the little boy for the last time from the porch of Sashka's house. He'd lost sight of us, and was turning his head every which way, but his mother was dragging him by the hand, as she skirted the queue. I waved to him, and started up the stairs.

7

—••E)(3••—

The door banged as if a gust of wind had hit it, but Sashka didn't even glance round. I stopped several steps below the landing, and he looked down at me with wild eyes.

'It's a nightmare!' he said, clutching his head.

There was such a screaming coming from inside Sashka's flat that you could hear it out on the stairs.

'Sonia, how old are you?' Sashka's father was asking. By the sound of his voice, he must have been standing right by the door.

'What on earth . . . are you crazy? Don't you know how old I am?' Sashka's mother screamed.

'Well, suppose I *do* know. What I don't know is when at last you'll understand the times we're living in. The State needs your son. We ought to see this as both his and our good fortune.'

'I'd only wish that kind of good fortune on my enemies!' Sashka's mother screamed. Let that bandit and his Party-member mother have this sort of good fortune. . . !'

Of course, the 'bandit' was me, and the 'Party-member mother' was my mother!

'A nightmare!' said Sashka again, giving me a shove. 'She's gone absolutely off her rocker! This nightmare's been going on since yesterday evening.'

I was in no hurry to go downstairs.

'You can tell your mother,' I said, 'that she needn't try getting round me with any more of her sweet-sour roasts.

And you needn't hope I'll ever come here again, either!'

'Thanks a *lot*! And just how do *I* come into it?'

It smelt of the chemist's on the stairs, Sashka sniffed his hands and said:

'My father woke me three times during the night. He couldn't give Mother the valerian drops himself. It had to be *me* that saw her suffering! I feel sick from the smell of it.'

'O.K. Sashka. If you really want to know, my mother didn't come round straight away either. And you'll see Vitka yourself in a minute.'

We went out onto the front-door steps, but we couldn't see Vitka. He was standing behind the advertisement hoarding talking to the Tartar street-cleaner.

'Ah Vitka, Vitka,' the cleaner was saying, 'what did you have to fight for?'

'I keep telling you. I haven't been fighting. I hit it on the side of the boat!'

Vitka must've been repeating this version several times because his voice sounded hopelessly tired.

'You certainly hit yourself accurately! Very neatly,' the cleaner said, laughing. 'If you weren't fighting, then some-one must've beaten you up. What did they beat you up for? Was it girls?'

Vitka was standing in the roadway. The cleaner rolled up his hose.

'You're all in one piece, though your friend's been knocked about,' he said, when we came up to him, and his white teeth flashed wet. He slung the hose over his shoulder and went off, repeating loudly: 'Their friend's been knocked about, but they're all in one piece. . . .'

Sashka looked at Vitka's eye with exaggerated attention.

'. . . War in the Crimea . . . the Crimea is in flames. . . .'

'My mother let me down. I trusted her, and she betrayed me. . . .'

Vitka's gentle soul was more shaken by his mother's treachery than by anything else. And who wouldn't have been? We were fond of our parents, and wanted to think of them as allies and helpers. It made us sad when they didn't understand us. But we never thought that it might be we who were making them sad, and this wasn't because we were cruel or thoughtless. We were simply behaving as our parents had at our ages. And in this eternal strife between parents and children, it's the children who are always right even when they are wrong!

We were standing in the shadow of the hoarding.

'No more wailing!' I said. 'We're grown-up enough, and nothing's going to be altered just because your parents are against it. They couldn't seriously try and stop us from going to the Training School. You've got to understand; we're already grown-up!'

I was only giving voice to what had been maturing in us since yesterday, or perhaps even earlier. The moment comes to every one, and certainly to each differently, when he suddenly feels grown-up. No matter if, after this moment, there still remains in him a lot of childishness. The feeling of being grown-up, once experienced, gradually grows stronger. It was in the street, by that advertisement hoarding, that we felt grown-up.

I could see from my friends' faces that they liked what I'd said. But Sashka wouldn't have been Sashka if he'd let it go without comment.

'I just love optimists! *He* hasn't got a black eye! *He* wasn't woken up three times during the night. *He's* O.K.! *He'll* go to Training School with his mother's permission.'

'Rubbish! Vitka, d'you remember the woman with the little boy?' I asked. 'The one who was hurrying to the beach? She had a goal—to grab a place under the awning. She could see nothing beyond that. Sashka is like that woman. Our goal is the Training School. Only *I* believe the way there is going to be interesting, too. It will be something to look back on.'

I wasn't sure whether Sashka and Vitka had fully appreciated the profundity of my thoughts.

'I'd like to be looking back on it now!' said Sashka.

As for Vitka, he could not forget his black eye even for a second, and went on studying one of the advertisements. His special interest in it attracted Sashka's notice. It showed a man in tails, with a neat parting through his wavy hair. Huge red letters announced that this man was John Danker and, for those who didn't know him, just below were the words, 'King of the Hawaian Guitar.'

'I dispute that,' said Sashka. The King's real name is Peisakhovich, and before he was crowned, he was a shop assistant in Kiev, at Madame Fisher's.'

'How do you know about Madame Fisher?' asked Vitka. Naïve chap! It was always the details that struck Vitka, and this often stopped him from guessing when Sashka was making things up.

'That's a good one!' said Sashka. 'Have you never heard of Madame Fisher? You didn't know she had a fancy goods store on the Kreshchatik? Perhaps you didn't even know there *was* a street in Kiev called the Kreshchatik?'

'Sashka, stop!' I said. But it was impossible to stop him once he got going.

'Collars with Madame Fisher's trade-mark were known throughout the world. Only ignoramuses like you know nothing about them!'

Vitka looked at Sashka mistrustfully, and smiled. The collars had confused him, as though it would be harder to invent the collars than Madame Fisher herself.

The postman was crossing the road. Sashka looked at his bag as though spellbound.

'D'you see?' he clapped me on the shoulder. Of course I saw, but the postman's bag meant nothing special to me.

'Fancy putting up with a Komsomol Secretary like you for two years!' said Sashka. 'Imagine our parents' faces if they opened their newspapers tomorrow morning, and saw something in them about us! I don't know about Vitka's father, of course, but my mother would never stand up to that! Vitka, can you imagine how your father would take it?'

Vitka hadn't got around to imagining anything. Sashka always had millions of ideas, but usually only one in a hundred was worth anything. Vitka looked at me. I realised at once that Sashka's idea about the paper was a brainwave, but I didn't want to admit it right away.

'We could try it,' I said. 'Let's go to Pereverzev.'

We crossed the road. The tramstop was almost deserted. The mothers and children were already on the beach. And those who'd come to our town for entertainment only, were still asleep. Their day ended shortly before sunrise, when the restaurants shut, the sand cooled, and the sea got warmer than the cold air. The new day began when they were driven from their beds by the oppressive heat of the sun-baked houses.

By now the sun was high, but not yet hot. We were walking in the warm, damp shade of the street. The little puddles where the pavements had been watered, shone like bits of glass. Once again we felt grown-up and walked unhurriedly, though we really wanted to run. The clock in Alyosha's room struck nine just as we got to the Party office. Alyosha himself had only just arrived, and was looking through the papers on his desk.

'Welcome, Professors!' he said.

It was Pavel Baulin who had nicknamed us professors. We neither knew nor bothered to find out what he was hinting at by calling us that. We were quite happy with the straightforward meaning of the word, and ignored that special intonation with which he said it. Pavel himself had left school at fourteen, then he'd tried going to a P.T. College, but had thrown it up. His excuse was he couldn't live without the sea.

64

'Last night the Party office decided to support your applications,' said Alyosha, pushing our dossiers to the edge of the desk.

'Alyosha, this evening Vitka's father is coming to see you!' I said.

'What for?'

'To tear your guts out.'

Alyosha's long straight hair, parting naturally, fell on either side of his face. He pushed it back from his forehead.

'You snivellers!' he said. 'Where's Anikin?'

I called Alyosha over to the window. Vitka was standing on the other side of the street, needless to say, facing another John Danker poster. The whole town was plastered with them; I was convinced Vitka would remember that poster of the King of the Hawaian guitar for the rest of his life!

'Vitka!' I shouted to him. He looked round. 'Look at that!' I said to Alyosha. 'You, who like to use big words!'

'Anikin, come here!' Alyosha called.

Vitka shook his head, and turned back to the poster.

'He won't come!' I said. 'Let's decide what to do without him.'

'Ye-e-es,' said Alyosha, and came back to the table. 'It's a bad business . . . the point is, the Committee has decided, and Kolesnikov has approved. What does Viktor himself think? How does he feel about it?'

'He thinks what he thought before. So far he's not changed his mind.'

'Then everything's O.K.' Alyosha pushed his hair back with both hands. 'Let Anikin Senior come! I'll talk to him in Kolyesnikov's office.'

'Wait, Alyosha. You know what Vitka's father's like. Why let it turn into a row? Sashka, out with your suggestion!'

Sashka was sitting on the divan, carefully studying the tip of his nose. I could not remember Sashka's ever before having to be egged on to speak! This was the first time.

'D'you hear?' I said. 'Out with your suggestion.'

'Alyosha, you know us,' said Sashka. 'We're modest chaps, we don't chase after glory. But if my mother were to read in her paper tomorrow morning, that her son was "the best of the best", and that the Army couldn't do without him, she'd calm down. Well, maybe not quite; but at least it would be possible to live in the house! That's my mother . . . but as to Vitka's father. . . .'

Alyosha needed no further details. He was very quick in the uptake, and got the idea at once. As soon as he had heard the word 'newspaper', he started walking up and down the room; and now he was at the door.

'Well done, Professors!' he said, not letting Sashka finish. 'You can consider the article's as good as printed! Wait . . . I'm going upstairs.'

'Stop—' I said. 'We've no time to wait. We're going to see Vitka's father. But just in case, you'd better be out of the office at five. Just in case. . . .'

It was very hot outside. I couldn't remember it's ever having been so hot at the end of May. Trying to think in the heat of the sun isn't much fun. My head was buzzing, though the day was only just beginning. Sashka said:

'We're all right. Alyosha will see it through. I've always said "Alyosha's the tops!"'

'Vitka,' I said. 'You come with us as far as Zhenya's. Tell the girls we've got held up. Then come on to the Salt-works. Don't let your father see you till we tell you, understand?'

'I'm not going to the girls!' said Vitka.

'Nonsense! Bruises don't disappear over night! Aren't you going to sit for tomorrow's exam?'

8

—••⊷⊱⊰⊷••—

Vitka got off the tram near Zhenya's house, while Sashka and I went on to the terminus at Old Town. People were standing or sitting in the narrow strip of shade from the low, window-less wall. They picked up their sacks and baskets and went towards the tram. To me they seemed shadowy and insubstantial. They walked past me, and I looked at them as in a trance. How had I got here? Why was I here? To-morrow would be the last exam. We ought to have been sitting long ago, in the cool of Zhenya's garden, round the table fixed into the ground, the lilacs smelling faintly, warmed by the sun. When the wind touched the pages of our books their rustling became one with that of the leaves. Only we could hear the voice of whoever was reading; it could not fill the emptiness around us.

Twenty-four hours. Only a day and a night—! Till this minute, that's what I, too, had thought. But now, my faith in the stability of time had been severely shaken. Only twenty-four hours—a day and a night—separated yesterday from today, but everything we had lived by before they summoned us to the Party office belonged now to the distant past.

Beyond the tram terminus, the Siltings began. Along the wide unmade streets which had no pavements, the little houses looked even smaller.

'What are you standing there for? Let's go by the shore,' Sashka said. He thought I was standing by the tram round-about wondering which way to go to the Saltworks. The tram

67

left, and the sun's glare blended with the gleaming rails.

'All right, let's go,' I said.

We went down to the shore by the narrow path trodden between woody-nightshade bushes. The wide, wild beaches stretched right as far as the Saltworks. The morning tide had left a fresh layer of seaweed far up on the sand, already bleached and dry. Two fishermen were repairing a boat. The echoes from their axe-blows were louder than the blows themselves. Tar sizzled in a black cauldron over a bonfire, and the flames under the cauldron were transparent in the sun. We took off our shoes and carried them in our trouser pockets. The hot, coarse sand was pleasantly prickly underfoot. Since we had stopped running around barefoot, our feet had become sensitive. We walked along the wet sand, so firm that our feet left no marks, and the warm water lapped over our feet, washing them.

'Sashka, have you got it clear? The chief thing is to complain to Uncle Peter about your parents' lack of public spirit,' I said.

'I wouldn't dream of it,' answered Sashka. He'd already gone stubborn on the tram, but it wasn't a suitable place for an argument. Now we were alone, I could tell him just what I thought of him.

'Ass!' I said. 'Either you do what you're told, or you go home!'

'Leave me alone!' said Sashka.

It was very hot. Sashka was walking behind me and he was furious. So what! I didn't care what mood he was in. We took off our shirts. The air felt fresh on our damp skins, but not for long. By the middle of summer, when we had a thorough tan on us, we were quite oblivious to the sun, but now we felt its burning heat. We tucked our shirts into our belts, rolled our trouser legs up over our knees and strode under the wooden archway onto Saltworks territory.

The salt was extracted from water which flowed from the

salt lake into rectangular basins. When the water, filtering from basin to basin, had evaporated, the salt was scooped out with spades. The 'basins' stretched for about three miles along the seashore. The Saltworks was the only industrial enterprise of national importance in our town. Our dazzlingly white salt, powder-fine, was classified First Class Table Salt.

We walked on for quite a time on Saltworks territory past the moored barges. Somewhere behind the salt mounds a brass band was playing a Krakoviak. The brassy sounds swelled and faded again as if weakened by the heat.

'Out of the wa-a-ay!'

I pulled the sun-drunk Sashka to one side. A stout old boy ran past, trundling a barrow. He looked at us with round, angry eyes. His dirty grey shorts had slipped down below his round belly. His arms were wide apart straining against the barrow's handles, his bare feet kicking sideways at each quick short step. The wheel of the barrow went rattling along the plank, and the old fellow seemed to be using every ounce of strength to stop it tipping off onto the sand.

Workmen with barrows were running along the shore between the salt mounds and the moorings. To keep out of their way we walked along the narrow edge of the basin. The white salt at the bottom was covered with a film of water which reflected us, our arms outstretched, balancing. The nearer we came to the centre of the Saltworks, the better we could hear the band.

We saw Vitka's father coming back from the moorings with an empty barrow. But before we saw him, Sashka pointed to a poster. On the square bit of plywood opposite the fourth mooring was written: 'Glory to the Stakhanovite Brigade of Peter Andreyevich Anikin!'

Vitka's father's brigade was the first to be proclaimed Stakhanovite in our town. The event had taken place comparatively recently, and we well remembered all the details. Only a few days after the papers had reported the feats of the Donbas miner Stakhanov, Vitka's father and his mates had set up a staggering loading record at the Saltworks. Until then, one man in each work-gang had filled the barrows with a spade, while the other five took the barrows to the barge. While the barrows were being filled, the 'pusher' had a rest, and while they were being wheeled away, the 'shoveller' was sun-bathing. On the record-breaking day, each man in Vitka's father's team had two barrows. While one was being taken away, the other was being loaded.

There was a correspondence in the local paper. Could this properly be called Stakhanovism? The pros and cons were then considered by the Party executive. Some held that the Stakhanovite movement was only concerned with advanced mechanisation, and not with manual labour, others that it would be a political mistake not to support workers' initiative. My mother made the best speech of all. She said that Stakhanovism wasn't only concerned with mechanisation, but with the good organisation of all methods of production. After that, the majority decided to recognise Vitka's father's team as worthy of this high title. Of course we'd long regarded them as true Stakhanovites. Formalities were the last things that mattered to us. The important thing was that this movement, which was spreading throughout the country, had now started in our town as well. And it wasn't just anybody who had started it, it was Vitka's father.

Now all the Saltworks' teams applied Anikin's method. On the days when the barges came for the salt, a special Stakhanovite Competition was organised, the results of which were declared on the spot. After that the Saltworks reverted to their normal pace; new water was let into the basins, and after it evaporated, the salt was shovelled into mounds for drying.

On loading days, the brass bands and the flags flying at the moorings gave the Saltworks a festive air.

Uncle Peter was trundling an empty barrow; he gave us a

look. He had eyes like Vitka's, blue, but their blue was colder. We shouted in chorus:

'Hullo, Uncle Peter!'

But our greeting made no impression. His oilskin trousers crackled as he jogged past us in time to the music, his broad back quivering. Heavy elderly people always run that way.

'Did he say Hullo?' asked Sashka.

'I don't think so. . . .'

'Bad business. . . .'

'Did you think he'd soften up the moment he saw us?' I said. 'Come on, let's go.'

By the time we had caught up with Uncle Peter he was holding the handles of a loaded barrow.

'Uncle Peter, where's Vitka?' I asked.

Uncle Peter leaned on the handles, pushed the barrow, and trotted off with short, quick steps. Very polite of him! But if he thought he could scare us, he was wrong. We were not to be intimidated by silence.

'Let's sit down,' I said.

We sat down on the basin's edge. Sashka fidgeted around trying to get comfortable.

'Are you sure we'll get away without a couple of black eyes?'

I could not be absolutely sure. I was banking on my mother's prestige, and on Uncle Peter's respect for her. We sat on the edge of the salt-basin and watched. Another old fellow, thin and stringy, with a round, cropped head of grey hair, was loading barrows with a big, scooplike spade, never straightening up. All the time the men were bringing up empty barrows and taking away full ones. When the 'shoveller' raised his head, we could see his horse-shoe shaped grey moustache, and his tufty eyebrows. Both moustache and eyebrows looked as if they were glued onto his sunburnt face. His long thin arms moved as if on hinges. But the oddest thing was that the old boy wasn't sweating at all.

71

Uncle Peter came running back again, and with a jerk swung the empty barrow round. He had already been to and fro to the mooring stage several times, but he did not take any notice of us. We weren't upset. A fight is a fight!

'Mikheich,' he said to the old chap with the moustache. 'Zaitsev is catching up on us!'

'No wonder! It's less than a hundred yards to his landing stage, and more than two hundred to ours.'

'We'll have to give our lot a third barrow each.'

'Give 'em a third one by all means, why not! Let it stand. It's not asking to be fed while it stands there. But there's no one to load it. I can only just cope with this lot, as it is.'

Uncle Peter turned to us. Or rather, he didn't actually turn, he just moved his head in our direction. But it was enough. When Prince Andrey said: 'This is my Toulon', he must have felt as we did. We picked up shovels (there were a lot scattered round the basin), and stood watching Uncle Peter.

'Bring up that third barrow, we'll help,' I said.

Uncle Peter looked at Mikheich.

'We could try,' Mikheich said, 'but Zaitsev'll make a stink.'

'Let him! The youngsters aren't strangers. They're friends of my Vitka's. Another time we'll add a seventh man to the gang.'

Uncle Peter went off with the loaded barrow. He didn't even look at us, just called over his shoulder,

'Put something on your feet.'

We stood sideways to the salt mound. The quick way was to fill the shovel at a single scoop then, with a sweep of arms and body, sling the salt into the barrow. With no more barrows to be filled than before, Mikheich had had nothing to do. He wasn't bored. He sat on the top of the mound, smoking and airing his views on how the loading was going with the workers as they ran up.

'Look at Zaitsev . . . just look at him! How his belly

wobbles. He's been running round with a barrow for ten years, and it seems bigger than ever!'

When Uncle Peter came back with the empty barrows stacked one inside the other, Mikheich slid down off the mound.

'Andreich, it'll work! Just you see if it doesn't! So long as Zaitsev doesn't get wind of it!'

'So what! Let him!' said Uncle Peter.

The men kept glancing at us curiously, but it didn't worry us. It was not the first time we had spades in our hands. The main thing when you work with a spade is not to strain your belly. We learnt to avoid this by spreading the load and relaxing our muscles in time. The band speeded up and then stopped. All you could hear was the gritty sound of metal on salt.

Down by the moorings, a man in a linen suit was shouting the results of the loading competition through a megaphone. The figures were given out every hour. When we took up our spades, Zaitsev's gang was half a ton ahead of Uncle Peter's, but we missed the next announcement. The band was playing, this time a Gopak. Uncle Peter came running up. He had to run both ways now.

'We've caught up!' he said.

Mikheich answered:

'That's the stuff! Now Zaitsev will be having kittens.' We weren't interested in how Zaitsev would have his kittens. We were working. A cloudy drop of sweat hung from the tip of Sashka's nose. I saw it drop, but when I looked again, another one was hanging there.

'Sashka! Stop dissolving the salt! That's not what it's been dried off for!'

'Clot! How can I dissolve it, when it's salt running off me!'

'Never mind. You can't always be eating dumplings.'

'Fair enough, but I sweat when I eat dumplings, too. . . .'

73

So I wasn't going to be able to make Sashka angry. A pity! It's easier to work when you're angry. Our eyes hurt from the sunlight and the glitter of the salt. Salt settled on our backs, our shoulders, it even seeped through the canvas uppers of our shoes. You could ease the itching for a bit, by brushing it off your back and shoulders with your hands, but there was nothing to be done about the soles of your feet. All the same, we never let the spades out of our hands.

Something had happened down by the shore. A faint hurrah reached us, muffled by the distance. A red flag was run up on the mast of the barge we were loading.

'We've done it!' said Mikheich, and sat down on his scraggy bottom in the salt.

I hadn't noticed where the other old fellow had appeared from—the one we'd already seen, in shorts and the straw hat with the tattered brim. He stood for a minute or two looking at us in silence.

'Aha!' he said, and ran off to the shore. His fat legs didn't bend at the knees, his arms, while bent at the elbow, were pressed to his sides.

A crowd had already gathered on the shore. They'd come running to the moorings from all over the Saltworks. Uncle Peter was being tossed, and they were trying to get hold of the rest of his team. Mikheich said:

'I want to be tossed too!' He threw away his cigarette butt and got up. His trousers looked as if they were empty. He ran towards the crowd shouting: 'Brothers! Here I am!'

The band was hurrying down to the moorings, the drummer running behind, his drum so enormous, you could only see his head and his legs.

'Volodya!'

I looked round. Vitka's face, criss-crossed with bandage, slowly emerged over the top of the salt mound.

'How are things?'

'Nothing, so far. Wait.' I answered.

Sashka and I sat modestly on the edge of the salt-basin, in raptures over the outcome of our labours, and watched. They were all being tossed, one after another. Whoever they caught they tossed, while the band played a fanfare. The barge moved away from the mooring-stage, and the sailors ran up a sail at the prow. These pot-bellied little motor-barges ran all the way down the coast as far as Feodosia. Once there, it only took an hour to unload the salt from their holds onto railway trucks. We knew that by the end of the five-year plan, there would be a mechanised loading section at our saltworks. We knew all about the future of our town!

Uncle Peter came up to us, and with him the man in the linen suit and the fat old boy in the shorts and hat.

'Come on now! Out with the truth!' the one with the straw hat shouted. His voice was unexpectedly high-pitched and querulous.

'You must get it straight, Zaitsev. It's got nothing to do with the lads,' said the man in the linen suit. 'They've set up a new record. Get it? It's a new record. . . .'

Zaitsev, who was a couple of steps behind, stopped, as if he were going to butt someone.

'RE-CO-O-RD! I'll record you, Anikin! Just you remember! I'll bring all my seven to the next loading. And if that's not enough, I'll get the old woman along to hump barrows! I'll record you!'

Zaitsev turned and went off at a clumsy run. He was probably incapable of walking calmly.

Sashka said: 'I'd love to know! Does he always run at home!'

'Thanks for your innovation, Anikin. And thanks to you, too, boys.'

'Thanks for what, Gabriel Spiridonovich? It's not for you we're doing it, it's for the State.'

'And it's in the name of the State I thank you.'

'Well, if you've the right to do that, thank away,' said Uncle Peter.

The man in the linen suit laughed and went off. Uncle Peter turned a barrow bottom up, and started unloading his bag of its radishes, onions, eggs and smoked fish.

'A bit much for one person,' whispered Sashka.

'Shut up,' I whispered back.

The workers in Uncle Peter's team were having their dinners too, and most of them had some of this season's wine. It fizzed and foamed in the thick tumblers. They raised them and said:

'Cheers! Andreich.'

Uncle Peter answered, 'Cheers to you!'

He didn't drink, but we knew he didn't count drinking a vice.

We sat still, hands between our knees, and watched. Uncle Peter scooped a handful of salt from the mound and tossed in onto the food. Now it was he who was watching us. It was very difficult not to waver under his glance, but we held out.

'Dinner is served, gentlemen!' said Uncle Peter.

Personally, I didn't feel it was quite the thing to accept the invitation immediately, but Sashka thought otherwise. Before I could bat an eyelid, he had sat down at the barrow. I could only follow suit.

'Why aren't you revising for your exam?' asked Uncle Peter.

'Vitka's vanished somewhere. We've been hunting for him all morning,' I answered.

'Sure you were looking in the right place? They say there's some kind of a King has turned up in town. Plays a balalaika I think.'

'Hawaian guitar,' Sashka corrected.

'Hawaian, is it? Never heard one like that.'

'Nor have we, but we're planning to.'

76

'Then you've earned ten roubles just at the right time. And I'll add another five to it myself, for your help. Think that'll cover it?'

'It wasn't for the money, Uncle Peter. . . .' I began.

'Well, you won't be working for nothing even when we've achieved Communism,' said Uncle Peter. He shelled an egg, salted it, and bit off half.

Sashka was devouring smoked fish as though it was the only thing he'd come for. I nudged him. He turned to me, mouth open, put another fish in and went on chewing. I thought his jaws would never stop. But at last he got through it and said:

'Uncle Peter, I'm not an anti-Semite, but tell me, why do parents in Jewish families meddle so much in their children's lives?'

'Why d'you ask me a question like that?'

'What d'you mean—why? Because it's a nightmare! I don't know if Vitka told you about the Military Training School. I told my parents. I told Father and Mother we were "the best of the best". There's no one like us, and there can't be. It's because of this the Town Komsomol is sending us to the Training School. And what happens? My revered father reaches for his belt, while my beloved mother holds me down . . . It's a nightmare!'

'You mean, your father couldn't cope on his own?'

Uncle Peter salted his half-eaten radish.

'What's coping or not coping got to do with it? It's a disgrace to the whole town,' I said.

'So that's it, is it! If you think you've come to lecture me. . . .' Uncle Peter leant back so that he could see us both at once. Sashka put down his smoked fish and wiped his hands on his trousers.

'How d'*you* come into it?'

Naïve question! Of course Uncle Peter paid no attention to it.

77

'Don't you come telling me any fairytales about Jews. See that?' He held out his clenched fist towards Sashka. 'See that!' The fingers were white with salt, and covered with deep cracks. 'I don't need a belt. And I don't need anyone to hold you down for me.'

Uncle Peter had understood everything. In the circumstances it would have been better to have said nothing. But for this you needed a grain of common sense. Sashka had none. Instead of shutting up, he yelled out:

'When everything's going wrong, when your own parents are poisoning your life, who can you turn to?—your friend's father, a progressive man, a Stakhanovite?'

There was nothing to be done. It was heredity. Or maybe Sashka was shouting because he was scared? I had no time to decide which. Uncle Peter heaved himself up slowly, his hands pressing on his knees. Sashka didn't notice a thing. So he must have been scared!

'And if he doesn't understand you? If instead of taking your side, he backs your out-of-date parents, what are you to do then? *What?*' Sashka shouted, looking at that moment very like his mother.

Uncle Peter slowly subsided. It took as long for anything to reach Sashka's brain as up a giraffe's neck. Only after Uncle Peter had sat down again did Sashka dodge out of his way. One of the workmen said:

'Andreich, what are they trying to talk you into?'

Uncle Peter made no answer.

'Inside of an hour, everything is changed. And do they ask the parents?' he said. The corners of his mouth turned down, his heavy hands lying wearily on his knees, he suddenly looked dejected. But I was wrong. Uncle Peter had no intention of giving in! 'I didn't begin the right end, it's true,' he said. 'It's Pereverzev I ought to have started with. It's he who stirred it all up. And where will it land you? Ten years studying . . . longer than high school. And who in the old days ever wanted to be an officer after going right through school? Only fools! It was different for me after the Civil War, and I'll never say anything except "Thanks". I learned to read and write in the Army, and I'll be grateful to the people who taught me till my dying day. But there were others—our platoon leader, for instance. Two stripes he had. Nowadays he'd be a lieutenant. Deserving chap. Got some medals. But except for his name he couldn't write a word. They demobbed him for illiteracy. So what could he do then? What had he been shedding his blood for? To go back to twisting bulls' tails? He went to Moscow to see Voroshilov, and he got reinstated! He had a go at Adult Education classes, but chucked it. Our teacher, a good chap, tried to talk him round, but it was no go. "I may be illiterate," he says, "but I beat the literates. And if I have to—I'll do it again!" Now, this platoon leader's commanding a regiment. He had good reason not to get out of the Army. But what's bitten you?'

'The time has come to replace the illiterate commanders. Technology . . .' I said.

'So I've heard. I'd like to see that platoon leader letting himself be replaced! What does Nadezhda Alexandrovna think?'

'My mother understands. She says we should be proud of the trust they're showing us.'

'That's her affair. She reads the papers. But don't you go putting ideas into my Vitka's head. Call him. He doesn't need to hide from his father.'

Sashka and I looked at each other.

'Stop playing hide and seek!' snapped Uncle Peter.

'Vitka!' I called.

We said nothing while Vitka was edging sideways from behind the salt mound. He stopped a couple of paces away and looked warily at his father. Uncle Peter took more eggs and another string of fish out of his bag.

'What's the idea of going out without breakfast?' he asked.

Vitka turned away and said nothing. Tears filled his eyes and I couldn't bear to look at him.

'What are you turning away for? Upset, are you? But upsetting your father is all right, is it?'

'It's not you that upset me.'

'Well it's not your mother's fault at all. She can't go against my will. Sit down; eat something, before your friends polish it all off.'

Vitka joined us and sat down.

'Must have used up half a mile of bandage, not an inch less,' said Uncle Peter.

Vitka immediately raised his hands and started fumbling with the dressing.

'Leave it!' shouted Uncle Peter.

We still said nothing while Vitka ate. Mikheich came up and said:

'Shall we let the water in or knock off for today?'

'No time to knock off. Not with the sun as hot as this.' Uncle Peter stood up. The men hurriedly tied up their dinner bags and bundles. 'Wait for me at the first basin. And you go home and work. Come tomorrow, you'll get your money.' This was to us.

'Well, that was quite a talk. Now it's up to Pereverzev,' said Sashka, when Uncle Peter had left.

'Wait till tomorrow. Everything may change when the article comes out.'

'Nothing will change!' said Vitka.

By now we were walking along the shore past the mooring stage. The brass band was playing another fanfare, this time in honour of Zaitsev's team. It was he being tossed. He flew up into the air, his face keeping its solemn expression. His heels flashed white against his sunburnt legs. Uncle Peter was standing not far off with the man in the linen suit.

'Goodbye,' I said.

'Till tomorrow,' said Sashka, with meaning.

Vitka still said nothing, and the man in the linen suit called after us: 'Regular eagles!'

'Only chicken-breasted,' said Uncle Peter. He really needn't have said that.

We walked through the archway. A woman in blue overalls was standing on a ladder, taking down the slogans. The red material quickly faded from the sun and the salt, so they were taken down after each loading.

'Vitka, why don't you go hang yourself?' asked Sashka.

'Why should I?'

'With a father like that I'd have hanged myself five times and drowned myself twice.'

'Your mother's no better. . . .'

'My mother's another story. She's an offspring of the petty bourgeoisie. She can be excused for her out-of-date psychology.'

I was walking between the two of them. Vitka was silent but this was not the best way to get Sashka to pipe down.

'If I were you, I'd renounce a father like that publicly,' said Sashka. 'Write a detailed letter to the paper . . .' but Sashka had no time to finish. Vitka flung himself at him from behind my back, and threw him down on the sand.

'Psychopath! Neurotic!' screamed Sashka, as Vitka stood over him panting.

Then Vitka sat down on the sand as well, and said:

'I'm not going anywhere with you two.'

'Just look what a state we've come to!' I said, and sat down beside Vitka. Now we were all three sitting down. I wanted to say that one way or another, everything would work out all right in the end, that it always does in life. But I realised in time how irrelevant my philosophising would sound at that moment, and said nothing. I could see it was easier for me than for them, I didn't have to fight for my right to go to the Training School. I think it was on those empty beaches, by the sparkling sea stretching to the far horizon, that I realised, for the first time how free and easy my life was, however disorganised my home.

'Let's swim,' I said, and started to undress.

9

—••E)(3••—

The table was all scribbled over with scientific formulae and doodles. Zhenya's father had tried to plane it off, but gave up. It would have been easier planing it off than weaning us of the doodling habit.

Zhenya's mother was more sensible. She covered the table with oilcloth, and when we went out into the garden to do our homework, she would take it off. We didn't mind. On the contrary, if Zhenya's mother forgot, one of us would remind her.

I used to sit in the wicker chair with the torn back. I always sat in this chair. It was all of three years since anyone had disputed my right to it. And to be quite honest, it was I who'd torn the back. I loved tilting backwards and balancing on the back legs.

We hadn't had time at school to go through the draft of the New Constitution, but they'd warned us that there'd be a question on it in the exam. So while we'd been at the Salt-works Zhanya and Katya had gone through it all. And now Katya was giving us a summary of the special points in her own words. She was trying very hard, but I wasn't listening. Or rather, I was listening but not taking it in—because of Inka. I would never have confessed this to anyone, but I kept on looking at her.

Inka was sitting behind the lilac bush. I could see her head bent over her book, and her legs stretched out and close together. We made Inka sit by herself while we were working, so as not to disturb her. Of course she found it boring, but what else could we do? When she couldn't stand it any longer she'd move over and join us. She could always find an excuse for this. But today, she didn't budge from her place, even when we got back from the Saltworks.

I looked at Inka's knees, and thought that sometime I'd absolutely have to touch them. But even without doing so, I knew they were soft and warm. The hem of her blue dress with its polka-dots was so tight round her legs, that it was astonishing the material didn't split. Time and again I'd seen Inka on the beach in only a bathing suit, and I hadn't felt a thing! But since yesterday on the Promenade, everything was upside down. I supposed this would pass. But as soon as I saw Inka, I knew that so far it hadn't. Since yesterday, my power over her was badly shaken, while hers over me had grown out of all bounds. Inka sensed this too. She always sensed such things quicker than I did. Inka was pretending to be absorbed in her book. Her elbows were dug into her knees, her fingers in her hair. The shadow of the leaves fell on her, but where the sun touched her hair, it shone copper-coloured. The bench behind the lilac bush was fixed to the ground, and Inka must have had to sit right on the edge of it for us to be able to see so much of her. I could imagine how comfortable she must have been, but there she sat. When I glanced at her, I could see her eyes shining between her fingers.

'Our constitution will be the most democratic in the world,' Katya was saying, and then asked: 'Why?' She always had this way of putting questions to herself. 'Because in our country, all citizens who have reached the age of eighteen can vote and be elected. We will no longer have any disenfranchised persons.'

Katya was a very thorough girl. Anyone else as thorough ought to have been deadly dull. But whatever else you might think, it would not have entered anyone's head to have called

Katya boring. Her grey eyes were always shining, and her cheeks were dimpled with smiles. Now, Katya's dimples were the envy of all the girls, though three years ago, she'd been teased and nicknamed 'dumpling'.

'So that means a priest or a speculator can get into the Government? I don't agree with that,' announced Vitka. He was lying on the wooden camp bed, a cushion under his head. Zhenya had made him lie down as soon as we got back from the Saltworks. He felt a bit sheepish about it, but there he lay. It was useless trying to resist Zhenya, we knew that perfectly well. Whenever Zhenya's mother came out onto the terrace and looked at us, Vitka felt particularly awkward, grinning and blushing foolishly.

Katya had stopped talking. She was always so happy, and enjoyed herself so much explaining things, yet now, believe it or not, she was flummoxed by one of Vitka's questions! She always got lost if you broke her train of thought. Katya looked at Sashka. Who else could she look at? Sashka always came to her rescue at moments like this, and so he did now.

'Look at that, he doesn't agree,' said Sashka. 'He doesn't like priests.'

'And do *you* like them?'

'No, I don't either . . . In theory, you can elect one— but in practice, who'd want to? Not you, I hope.'

'Everything's so simple,' said Katya. She didn't like it when people argued.

'You see, Vitka,' said Zhenya. 'To get elected, someone has to put you up as a candidate. Now who, for instance would put up "Mr Tinsmith"? But he's not disenfranchised. See?'

I'd never have expected Zhenya to speak to Vitka so gently. She always treated him as her personal property, and shouted at him. In fact, she hadn't really a very kind nature. You only had to look at her thin lips to realise this. She had a long face with a velvety skin looking almost as though it had been powdered, and eyes as black as night. When my sisters first

85

saw her, they said that in time she'd be a beauty. I don't know. It seemed to me enough time had gone by already! Personally, I thought even Katya was more attractive than Zhenya, not to mention Inka. We used to tell Zhenya she was unkind, but she didn't agree.

'I've just got character,' she would answer.

She reckoned character was essential if she was to become a singer. Rubbish! Character has nothing to do with it. What matters is a voice. And Zhenya had a voice. Nobody doubted that.

Zhenya was leaning over Vitka and talking to him as if nobody else were near, though what she meant by this it wasn't clear.

'A touching sight,' said Sashka.

'It's none of your business!' Zhenya answered.

Vitka said: 'All the same, I don't agree. If in practice you can't elect whom you want, it's no use putting it in the Constitution that you can.'

That's where condescension gets you! At any other time, Vitka wouldn't have dared utter a word of opposition to Zhenya.

'Just look at that!' said Katya. 'Volodya, why don't you say something?'

She couldn't do without me. But just at that moment I glanced round at Inka. After that when I looked back at Katya, nothing made sense. Sashka laughed. He was sitting on my left, and he looked me straight in the face and laughed.

'As Socrates used to say: I've never seen anyone look so dumb,' said Sashka.

'You didn't exist then! . . .'

'That's fixed you!' said Zhenya.

'We shan't have time to revise anything at this rate!' This of course was Katya.

'Let's talk seriously about what's serious,' I said. 'It's as simple as two and two make four. Socialism means complete freedom for everyone. Everyone has an equal right to build the Communist Society. . . .'

'I'd like to know just how priests are going to build Communism!'

It was always that way with Vitka. You'd have thought he'd been having dealings with priests every day. But in the whole of our town there was only one priest at the Greek church, and he went around just like anyone else, in an ordinary suit, and even hid his hair under his hat: in summer a straw one, in winter a felt one.

'Priests are a class on their own,' I said. 'The Church is separated from the State, so how could you elect a priest to a Government body?'

'O.K. To Hell with the priest. But can "Mr Tinsmith" get elected?'

'Well, look, Vitka,' I said, 'D'you think your father could be elected to the Supreme Soviet?'

'He wouldn't agree to be.'

'What d'you mean, he wouldn't agree?'

'He'd say he wasn't literate enough.'

'Rubbish! Every cook has got to know how to run the Government! But there's another reason why they'd never elect your father. Only the most progressive people will be elected to the Government.'

'Oh come now, that's a bit much . . . my father and "Mr Tinsmith". . . .'

I'd rather have bitten my tongue out than have coupled Vitka's father with 'Mr Tinsmith'.

'Don't interrupt,' I said. Just as I'd got everything perfectly clear in my head, Vitka had muddled it all up. 'I only took your father as an example so that you could understand. Not everyone will be elected. The *right* to vote and to be elected will be the same for everyone. But only those who have earned the confidence of the people will be elected.'

'Any questions?' asked Sashka. 'There's logic for you! I've always said: Volodya's got brains!'

What a discovery! Way back in school, our history teacher had said that I had an exceptional understanding and feeling for our modern age. Of course she put this down to my mother. What rubbish! My mother didn't come into it at all. It was just I myself who could grasp things so well. I glanced round. Inka was looking at me. She smiled, and bent over her book again.

'People like "Mr Tinsmith" ought to be drowned, not given rights,' said Vitka.

First the priest, now 'Mr Tinsmith'. But I could see from Vitka's face he was saying this for the sake of saying something. No one likes to admit defeat.

'You don't need to drown him; he'll die of his own accord,' I said.

'Well, that's fine. Now we're all agreed,' said Katya. 'Let's get on. Further on it's for you, boys. Another reason why our Constitution will be the most democratic is that even the Armed Forces will take part in elections. In Capitalist countries soldiers can't vote. There, the Army is outside politics,' Katya was talking as if she were reading. If she did look at one or other of us, she simply wasn't seeing us. You could tell this from her eyes. Katya had a marvellous memory. Once she got going, she could recite page after page—so long as you didn't break her train of thought. I looked sideways at Sashka.

He was sitting with his eyes shut. He had peculiar eyes; bulging, with short eyelids. Even when he was asleep Sashka's eyes were not absolutely shut. An outsider might have thought he was watching someone. Sashka was pretending to doze, but I could see through this. He had not forgiven me for Socrates, he was sure to be thinking up another crack, and only waiting for me to look at Inka again. I wasn't such a fool. I wasn't dreaming of looking at her again. Why should

88

I? I could imagine her, and I could imagine her thinking about me.

On the other side of the fence Zhenya's neighbour was watering her garden. The water was hissing. The woman kept calling out monotonously: 'Shura, don't touch the tap!'

Shura wasn't touching the tap, the woman just kept shouting as a precaution. I knew that young imp. Whenever the woman started shouting, he'd turn up somewhere quite close to her.

Sashka opened first one eye, then the other. But he wasn't looking at me. His nose was pointing at the terrace of Zhenya's house. Sashka's nose was very odd too. It was large and thin and could turn like a ship's rudder. When we were smaller they used to call him 'the Rudder'. Sashka took offence, so in time we learnt to leave his nose alone.

'Dumplings!' said Sashka. 'They're going to feed us dumplings today!'

However hard I sniffed, I could smell nothing but lilac and wet earth. Yet Sashka could smell dumplings.

'Now you've interrupted again!' said Katya.

'Go on, go on,' Sashka looked at me with his bulging eyes. We understood each other very well.

'Go on, go on,' I said to him.

The corners of Sashka's mouth smiled. He imagined I couldn't hold out, and that sooner or later I'd look at Inka. I'd have liked to know what he was hatching, but it wasn't worth risking. Now I too caught a whiff of burnt olive oil. Sashka's sense of smell was much to be envied. It was really simply because he loved eating. During school breaks he would never go out of the classroom. He used to sniff in a leisurely way round the girls' satchels, identifying what they'd brought for lunch. Sashka was very scrupulous, he didn't take things at random, and he never took more than half. Once when someone had gone off with the whole of one of the girls' lunches, it was Sashka who was more indignant than anyone else.

Sashka's friendship for Katya had really started on a lunch basis. Sashka adored french rolls with butter and liver sausage. As soon as Katya noticed this he began to find special little parcels for him in her satchel. You'd have had to be a hardened egoist not to appreciate Katya's kind heart. Sashka did appreciate it. The one thing we simply couldn't make out was what happened to all the stuff that Sashka devoured? He was half a head taller than Vitka and me, but so scraggy it was absolutely shaming being seen going to the beach with him. Vitka explained it by the 'law of diminishing returns'. Vitka didn't often hit on a witty remark, but when he did, he kept on repeating it. Sashka was livid. But as no one could think of another explanation, Vitka's stuck.

Next door, Shurka had at last got at the tap. The hiss of water on the other side of the fence was cut short, and the woman gave a heart-rending scream:

'*Shurka!* I'll tear your ears off!'

10

—••E)(3••—

Zhenya's father came in at the gate, but I'd already seen his uniform cap beyond the wooden fence. He had an odd way of walking. First his heels jerked off the ground, then his toes, with such force that he seemed to be bouncing, his cap jumping up and down above the fence. His momentum carried him a few paces through the gate before he stopped.

Our relationship with Zhenya's father was very complicated. He worked as an agent for the housing office. In the mornings he went to the station at train arrival times, and ran up and down the platform shouting: 'Best rooms in town! For all tastes and means!'

Of course he wasn't the only one, there were about ten other agents running up and down too. But Zhenya's father was the nimblest. He had all the addresses written down in a fat notebook. He did the letting, but we found him the addresses. We ran, with no thought of profit, all over town too, finding out where there were suitable flats to let. On particularly successful days Zhenya's father would give us money for ice-creams.

At midday, all the agents gathered at Popandopoulo's wine shop. By the bar they looked like bosom friends who had just dropped in for a drink. But we didn't only see them at Popandopoulo's, we saw them at work at the Station, so we knew they weren't really friends at all. With our help Zhenya's father earned more than anyone else. He often stood the other agents a drink, so they somehow put up with him. It was us they hated. But we didn't care two hoots. Looked at from the State's point of view, what difference does it make which agent lets more rooms? The main thing was that the summer-visitors should be sure of somewhere to stay. We looked at it from the point of view of the State, so our consciences were clear.

When we were smaller we had got on very well with Zhenya's father. But once he'd guessed about her friendship with Vitka, everything changed. In his opinion, Vitka wasn't cultured enough. Zhenya's father used to be a comic actor. People who are failures are usually difficult. But failed actors and writers are absolutely unbearable. Zhenya's father never said anything openly against Vitka—he was afraid of Zhenya. But we could see quite clearly that he couldn't stand him. As soon as we realised this, we stopped helping him at once. Vitka tried secretly to get addresses out of us, but we didn't hold with such grovelling. Zhenya's father was angry with all of us. That was his business. We accepted it— children are one thing, parents another! Pavlik Morozov's heroic feat proved this point.

Zhenya's father stood on the path, looking at us. Under the tall peaked cap with its wide, cotton-covered top, his narrow face seemed tiny, and was deeply wrinkled all over. It was impossible to understand how he ever managed to shave. He looked at each of us in turn, then fixed his eyes on Vitka. Vitka put his feet down from the camp bed, but Zhenya held him by the shoulder, not letting him get up. She turned towards her father, shielding Vitka behind her. It was just like a scene from 'The Inspector General', everything stopped dead. Only Katya noticed nothing. She was sitting with her back to the gate, saying:

'The Supreme Soviet of the USSR is divided into two chambers; the Council of the Union and the Council of Nationalities.'

She only saw Zhenya's father when he'd already run up onto the terrace.

'But we haven't finished yet!' said Katya.

Sashka calmed her down.

'We do *know* it all.'

And we really did know all about the proposed Constitution. But we'd made it a rule to go through everything before each exam. We usually went on working till six in the evening, and got it all done by then. After six, none of us had the right even to mention exams. Everyone looked at me.

'What a day!' I said. 'One long parental demonstration!'

Zhenya got up and ran into the house. Sashka said:

'Nice manners some fathers have adopted! They don't even say "good-day"!'

'Shut up!' Vitka was still sitting on the camp bed, his head turned towards the house. He couldn't bear it when Zhenya was teased, then he really got dangerous. Indoors everything was quiet. Only once, we heard Zhenya saying: 'You have no right!'

We could pretty well guess what kind of conversation was going on. But we were tactful people, and the best proof of tact is to pay no attention to what doesn't concern you.

I put my hands on the arms of my chair and got up. As I went over to Inka, she looked at me, and smiled. I smiled too, goodness knows why! I felt as though I'd never had a real talk with her. I felt as I did when I answered her note and went to her birthday party. And yet, then it hadn't been quite like this. True, I'd smiled at her then, too, without knowing why. But then, I'd been excited in a different way.

Inka was sitting right back in the seat. I looked at the open textbook on her knees. When we'd come in from the Salt-works it had been open at that same page—I remembered perfectly well.

'It's the wind!' said Inka. 'The wind turned the pages back!'

In the garden next door the water was hissing again. Shurka was bellowing by the fence.

'Feather-brain!' I didn't feel like scolding Inka, and only said it from habit.

'But it's true, it's true! D'you know how much I've read? That's how much!' Inka simply couldn't lie. She hurriedly shuffled through the pages, then covered them with her hands and laughed. 'I've still got the whole of tomorrow,' she said, 'and you yourself said—"What a day!"'

Shurka wasn't bellowing any more, probably he was eavesdropping.

Inka got up, and the book slid from her knees to the ground. She didn't even think of picking it up. She just looked at me and smiled. I think she knew why she was smiling. She clasped her hands behind her neck and stretched. I squatted down and my face brushed past her warm legs. I was in no hurry to pick up the book, but you can't sit on your heels for ever, and I'd no idea how long I'd been squatting already. At moments like these you are never aware of the passage of time.

I looked round. Zhenya's mother was bringing out a dishful of golden dumplings. Sashka hurriedly grabbed the books off the table, and shoved them at Katya without looking. Sashka could do several things at once, like Caesar, but he couldn't look at me and at those dumplings at the same moment. Sashka was looking at the dumplings . . . I got up.

'Thank you,' said Inka softly, but she didn't take the book from me. She turned and went over to the table.

I followed her, like the world's biggest idiot, carrying the book.

'Where shall I sit?' asked Inka, running up onto the terrace. 'Aunt Vera, shall I take this chair?' she called out. Inka felt at home everywhere.

11

---•◦❈◦•---

'Come along, help yourselves, help yourselves!' Aunt Vera kept saying. 'He had a bad day at work.' She smoothed the oilcloth with her plump hand. 'But you just help yourselves. Take no notice.'

'We will, Aunt Vera. Don't worry!' said Sashka.

'You have to cope with all kinds of situations at work. It can't have been anything much,' Vitka said.

'That's right. Is the jam sweet enough?'

'Get on with you, Aunt Vera! The dumplings are marvellous! They simply melt in your mouth,' said Katya.

They really did. From all sides our hands kept reaching out towards the dish. Sashka was licking up a dribble of jam from his dumpling, and munching disgustingly.

'Sashka, don't champ so!' I said.

'I've been champing since I was born.'

Zhenya was sitting between Vitka and her mother, her elbow on the table, cheek resting on her hand, staring into space. When Zhenya stared like that it was better to leave her alone. Aunt Vera knew this as well as we did. But it seems most mothers are made the same way—they can't let their children be!

'Darling, why aren't you eating? Come on, have this dumpling. See how nice and crisp it is.'

'Will the happy day never dawn when I finally get away?' asked Zhenya in a tragic voice. 'Can't you understand? I'm not a baby! Get it? I'm not a BABY any more!' Zhenya was almost screaming.

I can't stand storms in tea-cups. Someone would have to intervene, but I couldn't think of a way. I had suddenly gone all stupid. It was because Inka had found my hand under the table and was gently touching my fingers. I hadn't even seen how she got there. She kept her hands under the table and, so that no one should notice, was leaning with her breast on the edge of it. She wasn't looking at me, nor I at her.

'Small children—small troubles; big children—big troubles,' said Sashka, and shoved his last bit of dumpling into his mouth.

'Too true!' said Aunt Vera.

'You can't imagine how clever my grandmother is,' Sashka went on. 'Whenever my mother does anything not quite as she should, my grandmother always says: Small children . . . small troubles . . . but my mother doesn't listen to her. I have to listen to my mother, but she doesn't to hers! Where's the logic in that?'

'Get on with you!' Aunt Vera shrugged, as if giving Sashka up as a bad job, and laughed.

Sashka scratched the back of his head with his greasy fingers, as he inspected the empty dish.

'Aunt Vera, Zhenya won't eat that dumpling anyway. Let me have it. . . .'

'Help yourself . . . you're welcome!'

Aunt Vera got up. With her stoutness this wasn't so easy, as both bench and table were fixed to the ground. When she'd gone up onto the terrace I said:

'Sashka, you're a genius!'

Sashka nodded. He couldn't answer—he was munching his dumpling.

'No need to get upset,' Vitka said. He was holding Zhenya's hand in full view of everyone. 'It was our own fault: we stopped helping your father. D'you think it's easy for him to run around town at his age?'

'You don't know what he said when we were indoors! You don't know, so shut up!'

'So long as it's only what he said . . . what's it matter? At least he didn't hit you!'

'It would just have needed that! . . . hit me indeed!'

Sashka finished his dumpling and said:

'I wonder if Pereverzev is still alive!'

'I'm going!' said Vitka.

'You're not going anywhere alone. We'll all go along with you,' said Zhenya.

'Of course we'll all go with you,' said Sashka, 'and don't look at me like that. It was only a dumpling!'

12

—••€)(€3••—

We waited for Zhenya outside the gate. Vitka half-opened it
and looked up the path.

Nowhere else in town were there poplars like those in
Zhenya's street. When they were in bloom the whole street
was covered with fluff. A layer of it muffled the steps of
passers-by. At night it was like snow lying on the ground.
And when the wind blew it was a real blizzard. From a
distance the street looked lovely, but it wasn't so nice living
there when the poplars were flowering.

By the looks of it, it was going to be a warm evening. Not
a leaf on the poplars stirred, and there was not a sound of
the sea. Yet between the sea and us, there was only one row
of houses. The trunks of the trees were already in the dusk,
though the sun still lit their tops. We were standing in the
shadow, but we could feel the sun's warmth just the same.

'This time tomorrow we'll be quite free,' said Katya. 'I'll
miss school, though.'

'You could always stay another year,' Sashka suggested.

'You're crazy!'

'See how logical she is? She's sorry to leave school, but she
doesn't want to stay on another year. What's the difference?
We've chosen your Training College for you.'

Sashka was exaggerating. It was he who'd chosen Katya's
training for her, not we. For a long time, Katya hadn't known
what to go in for. Then she'd made friends with Sashka, and
after that it somehow decided itself, that she, too, should go

to Medical School. With a memory like Katya's it was nothing to learn the names of three thousand bones and a few hundred muscles. If there'd been nothing more to it than that, Katya would have been a doctor in a week. 'With Katya's memory and my erudition,' Sashka used to say, 'I shall be a professor in five years and she'll be my assistant.' Katya didn't take offence. In fact I don't think she was capable of taking offence. There are lucky people like that.

'Nothing much happened,' Katya said. 'Everything went off very well. My sister says Army units *do* have civilian doctors. In a war, one of you is sure to be wounded, and I shall look after you.'

Katya's sister had a job as a waitress at the 'Floating Restaurant', and before that she'd worked in the pilots' canteen, so of course she knew if there were civilian doctors with army units or not.

'See how her mind works?' said Sashka. 'And as for a heart . . . did you ever see anyone so heartless? We haven't even done our final exam, and she's already dreaming of one of us being wounded!'

'That's only if there's a war.'

Inka stood, her hands behind her, studying the poplars. Her head thrown back, she crossed and uncrossed her feet. Whenever Inka looked at anything so attentively it meant that she found the conversation very interesting, but didn't want to admit it.

'Fair enough,' said Vitka, moving away from the gate. Zhenya came out and we went up the street. We usually walked this way, the girls in front, the rest of us a couple of paces behind. But it didn't interfere with our conversation.

'Now, tell us properly, where did you get to with Uncle Peter?' asked Zhenya.

'Volodya, where did we get to?'

'We've already told you, nowhere. He said we weren't to put ideas into Vitka's head.'

99

'We've heard that already. But at least, he's not going to beat Vitka up again, is he?'

'I suggest you ask Uncle Peter that himself. He certainly wanted to hit *me*. Volodya knows I'm not lying. If I hadn't stopped him with a look I'd have got myself a black eye too. I looked him in the eye, and he realised it would have been dangerous!'

I fell back a bit and inspected the seat of Sashka's trousers. He began to get worried.

'What are you up to?' he asked, trying to see what was the matter with them.

'Nothing,' I said. 'I was simply looking to see if there were holes in your trousers. You were crawling so hard, there might've been.'

'Rubbish! You can forget about my trousers!'

'I'm fed up!' said Zhenya. 'It's impossible to have a serious conversation with you!'

'I'd like to drown all serious people,' answered Sashka. 'What can I say about someone else's father? I can't even vouch for my own!'

'He won't beat me up again,' Vitka said. 'He wouldn't have anyway; it was mother who betrayed me.'

'But will he go to Pereverzev?' asked Zhenya.

'I bet he's there already. It would have been better if he'd had another go at me.'

'Oh come off it! Alyosha's been warned. He's no fool. He'll have left the Town Komsomol office long ago. And tomorrow the article will appear and everything'll be O.K. Let's drop in at Alyosha's on our way, and hear all about it.'

'What article?' asked Zhenya.

I can't think what made me blurt it out. Zhenya pricked up her ears, even her eyes narrowed.

'What article?' she asked again.

I might have talked my way out of it, if Sashka hadn't come wading in.

'I'd like to know who's the worst jabberer in our group!'
he said.

There was nothing for it, we had to tell them all about the
article. And we'd wanted it to be a complete surprise to
everyone.

Zhenya lived on the outskirts of Old Town, two blocks
from the Siltings. I envied Vitka; his was the same way
home as Zhenya's. Whenever I took Inka home, I had almost
to cross the whole town. In summer this was pleasant
enough, but it was another matter in winter when the north-
easters were blowing. It was bearable as long as we were walking together, but when I went back on my own, I used to get
angry, as though it were Inka's fault the Air-Force flats were
built in the Spa part of the town.

Inka was walking on the edge of the pavement. She looked
back, then jumped up and tore off a poplar leaf. Then she
looked back again. She kept glancing at me stealthily, as
though I'd hurt her somehow. I suddenly thought of her
walking home by herself, and in general of how much she'd
be alone during the next three years. As I looked at Inka, I
simply couldn't believe I could ever have been cross with her
for living so far from me. I caught her up, and said softly:

'Three years aren't five. . . .'

Inka listened, her head down.

'Of course not,' she said.

We came out onto the sandy wastes. The asphalt ended,
and the dusk of the streets changed to sunlight, suffusing
the whole sky.

'Look! . . . it's still daylight!' said Katya.

The tramlines at the roundabout flashed crimson. In town,
the lines were flush with the street, but here they were raised
on sleepers, with wormwood growing in between. For the
third time today I was crossing the wasteland that divided
Old Town from the Siltings.

We came out onto the wide road. In the daytime, there

was never anything there except sun, short shadows, and hens. A queue of people stood by the water-fountain. They took the water away in barrels on handcarts, whose wheels sank deeply into the sand. Friends of Vitka's kept stopping him to have a word with him, their attention drawn by his bandaged eye, and then Zhenya would wait for him. Inka was walking in front of me, peering into the courtyards. Behind the low walls the summer stoves were being lit, and there was a smell of smoke and fried fish. I had never before paid any attention to how Inka walked. She put her feet down straight, and her shoes left narrow marks on the sand.

We arrived at Alyosha's house. His sister was washing the terrace. The girls from the Siltings were known for their beauty and cheekiness, but Nyura stood out among them. She was no older than we were, but she'd already had time to get herself married to some sailor, and to leave him and come home again. Alyosha didn't have too high an opinion of his sister. Well, maybe he knew her best. After all, he was her brother.

'Is Alyosha home?' asked Vitka.

Nyura straightened herself, and pulled down the hem of her skirt which was hitched above her knees.

'That's so's not to blind you,' she said and laughed. Obviously she'd have liked longer to have a chat. 'What d'you want Alyosha for?' she asked.

'We just need him. . . .'

'Well he's not here. He's not back yet. What d'you need him for?'

Sashka put his hand on the wall and said:

'Have you got some iodine in the house?'

'Iodine? . . . yes, but what for?' Nyura looked at Vitka's face and smiled, and her eyes, changing colour like the sea, narrowed suspiciously.

'So you've got iodine. What about eye-lotion?'

'What kind of eye-lotion? What for?'

'So you haven't any eye-lotion. I advise you to go and buy some. The chemist will know what kind,' said Sashka, and came back to us. We were standing at the corner waiting for him. We were quite worried as we turned off into the narrow alley.

'Well! That's cheerful! Alyosha's still not back,' said Sashka. Nobody answered him. We came to Vitka's street. All the houses stood along one side. On the other, the ground fell steeply away into sand-dunes. Far off the sea glinted, and below, the dusk was cool over the wild beaches. The nearer we got to Vitka's house, the more worried he became. He went on ahead, and kept looking round angrily because we were lagging behind. I'd dropped back because of Inka. She was looking at the sea, and I could see the sad oval of her cheek. I know that an oval can't be either sad or gay, but that's how it seemed to me. I was sure the last thing Inka was thinking about was Vitka's father. But why she should be sad, I couldn't understand.

Vitka's house was the end one in the street. They'd started building it about four years ago, and while it was being built, Vitka and his parents had lived in a room in someone's flat in town, and then for a while, in makeshift premises. We helped build the house. All the clay used for the plastering, had been puddled by our feet. Katya and Zhenya used to join us during the day (Inka wasn't one of us then). We'd go down to the sea and swim, and Aunt Nastya, Vitka's mother, would give us an evening meal that she'd cooked in the open on a simple sandstone hearth. The food smelled of smoke, and seemed to us very good. Then Uncle Peter would come back from work with his team-mates, and we'd go into town, while the grown-ups went on working on the house till midnight.

We hadn't always felt as free as that at the Siltings. Vitka was accepted at once as one of them. But when Sashka or I appeared, there were always fights. Not that you could call them proper fights. In a fight there are two sides beating each other up. But on the Siltings, it was a one-sided attack on Sashka and me. The gang-leader was Mishka Shkura, a boy of our age, who looked good-natured at first sight. He had slobbery lips, and was always laughing. Vitka used to say of him: 'He's a fool, but cunning!' At first we tried to put up a resistance, but this only made things worse. When they caught us with Vitka, they beat us up all three, because Vitka didn't want to be just a spectator. True, they'd apologise to him afterwards. So Sashka and I tried to escape the notice of the Siltings' gang, and if we didn't succeed in making off in time, we offered no resistance. They used to give us a couple of clouts on the face, and after that, let us go in peace. This went on till Uncle Peter took a hand in the situation. He turned up one day when they'd surrounded us, and were just going to pitch into us. Personally, I think Uncle Peter had been waiting for just such a moment. Sashka and I, pale and hunted, stood encircled by the gang, now watchfully quiet.

'Do you work as a team?' asked Uncle Peter. Then he said to us: 'Each of you, choose one of your own size.' And he sat down in the cool shade of a bush.

We chose. We picked fairly; our opponents were our own height, and approximately our own strength. The outcome of the fight was predetermined by Uncle Peter's presence. All our past humiliations, all we'd suffered, went into every blow. Sashka went berserk, and even after his opponent had dodged to one side and called 'Stop!' he hit him again twice. I'd never seen Sashka like that before. Blood trickled from his nose, and he seemed to have gone deaf and blind. Vitka ran up to him. He put his arms round him, but for a long time couldn't make him understand that the fight was over. Sashka kept trying to tear himself free, yelling 'I'll kill him!' Vitka had to knock him down onto the sand. The gang watched in silence.

'If I ever catch you fighting as a team again, I'll pull your legs out of their sockets,' said Uncle Peter.

He went off to the Saltworks by the narrow path along the shore. The excitement stirred up by the fight gradually died down. Victors and vanquished stood up to their knees in water, washing. Mishka Shkura, my opponent, kept displaying the inside of his top lip, and his bloodstained teeth to all who cared to see.

'What he bashed me with to make me see such stars, I can't imagine,' said Mishka, roaring with laughter.

The event had a sequel. That evening, the fathers of the boys we'd trounced came to Uncle Peter for an 'explanation'. The whole Siltings turned out to watch the fight. The avenging fathers surged up to the attack and down again, spitting blood and sand. Uncle Peter, his shirt torn and half off his shoulders, threw them down the sand-bank.

We were just over fourteen at the time. From then on no one on the Siltings touched us. And we no longer had to make our way stealthily across the wild beaches to visit Vitka. But the chief thing was that now we could bring the girls to the Siltings without risking humiliation. The street was quite narrow in those days, but four years of stormy seas had been heaping up the sand dunes, and now it was wider.

Aunt Nastya stood at the open gate, looking out for Vitka, and doing up and undoing a button on her printed cotton blouse. Aunt Nastya was quite young, it was difficult to believe that Vitka was her son.

'Is father in?' asked Vitka.

'He's gone out. He came back from work, changed, and went out again.' Aunt Nastya kept peering at Vitka's face, seeming not to notice us. Bad sign. We moved away across the street, but we could hear everything just the same.

'Forgive me, son. I really didn't mean any harm; I'm sorry for your father, and I'm sorry about you. You got me all mixed up. Is your eye hurting? Is it?'

Aunt Nastya looked up into Vitka's face, and with quick fingers tightened the bandage that had slipped down onto his cheek.

'It's nothing! Don't fuss! Haven't I ever had a bruise before?' answered Vitka. He glanced sideways at us, gently freeing himself from his mother's hands. We pretended to be admiring the sea. The water was transfused with colours, lilac, scarlet, purple—varying in tone and density. They seemed to lie in strips, unblending; while the distance shimmered, lit by the reflection of the already hidden sun.

Sashka turned, his shoulder brushing against me.

'Uncle Peter's coming!' he said.

Uncle Peter was walking down the middle of the street in his heavy black serge suit. It was the suit he wore to school on Saturdays. He went through the gate, between his wife and son, without looking at either. Aunt Nastya and Vitka followed him. At the foot of the steps he stopped, and reached out with his left hand. Aunt Nastya went to him quickly, and he put his arm around her shoulder, and like this they went up onto the terrace, and indoors. As he climbed the steps the dry boards creaked under his feet. Before going in he stopped and said:

'Just you remember this, Nastya. If three people tell you you're drunk, you can only lie down and sleep it off, even though you may not have had a sniff of wine!'

Although Uncle Peter was addressing Aunt Nastya, we knew very well who it was meant for. We came up to the fence and Katya said:

'Aunt Nastya's not a bit like my mother.' Katya often said irrelevent things. We were used to it, and paid no attention. Vitka came out onto the terrace and said:

'I'm staying at home.'

'What's happened?' asked Zhenya.

Vitka came down the steps and over to the fence.

'I don't know myself. . . .'

'Has he said anything?' asked Sashka.

'Just what he said on the terrace about being drunk. Then he asked for his supper. Apart from that, nothing!'

'It was an aphorism,' said Sashka.

'O.K. You go. Don't be offended, Zhenya, but I can't very well go out right now.'

'D'you take me for a fool? Come tomorrow, as soon as you get up. Come at six, if you're up then. . . .'

'Won't your father swear at you?'

'Rubbish! Just let him try. . . .'

We never paid any attention to Zhenya's father's moods, and were completely uninterested in what he thought about us. Nor was I bothered by Sashka's mother's screaming. But when it came to Uncle Peter, I felt, somehow, guilty. It was no use repeating to myself that there was no question of guilt between us and him: in my heart of hearts I felt terrible just the same, as though I'd betrayed someone. And from Sashka's face, I could see that he didn't feel too happy either.

Vitka stood by the fence until we turned the corner.

'It makes me wild! The chap's taking his finals tomorrow, and they're tearing his nerves to pieces,' said Zhenya.

'A lot of things make you wild. But on the beach yesterday you were screaming at him about the Training School yourself,' said Sashka.

'Rubbish! I wasn't screaming at all. I simply said he might be sent to a town that didn't have a Music Academy.'

'Actually, where will they send you? Which town? Which Training School? We really don't know a thing!' said Katya.

'You don't know because we don't. Nobody's said a word to us about it.'

'Let's go and see Alyosha,' I said, as we came out onto the wide street. Some small boys were trying to fly a kite, a fruitless occupation on such a windless day. One of them, his shirt torn on the shoulder, was yelling heart-rendingly:

'Higher! Hold it *higher*!'

He was bending down so as to scream louder, and jumping from one foot to the other in a frenzy. Over by the next block, his buddy was holding the kite above his head, yelling too:

'*You* pull it taut then . . . go on! My hands are dropping off!'

As I watched the boys, my heart felt lighter. Even now, whenever I see kids, life seems more worth living. On the walls, well-fed cats sat looking with unblinking green eyes at the sea, and the small black fishing boats. The girls from the Siltings were coming to the tram roundabout. They always went to town singly. They, and even more their boy-friends, were set on by the Siltings' boys, but these weren't girls to get scared.

At the corner we met Nyura. She was walking barefoot in a smart crepe-de-chine frock, carrying her patent-leather shoes in her hand.

'Your boss is back. Hurry up, or he'll be gone again,' she said.

Alyosha must have seen us from the window, because when we got to the house he was already standing on the terrace, barefoot and shirtless. He tossed back his hair and said:

'Everything's O.K., professors. Don't miss tomorrow's paper.'

Obviously Alyosha wanted to get rid of us, we were used to his little jokes; but at the moment the newspaper was the last thing we were interested in. I went over to the terrace while Sashka and the girls stayed by the gate.

'So it's O.K., is it? But you just tell us what sort of a talk you had with Vitka's father,' I said, and sat down on the porch steps.

Alyosha tried to laugh it off.

'You insist on a report, do you? There's still two months till the next conference. Have patience!'

'What kind of a talk did you have with Vitka's father?'

'Must you pester me! A perfectly ordinary talk. Kolesnikov explained to Anikin: you can't ride a wave sideways in a storm, you'll only overturn.'

'But we specially asked you not to let it come to a row!'

'There wasn't a row! But we're not letting anything wreck the political campaign.'

'What campaign? What's a campaign got to do with it?'

'Have we got to have a session on basic political education? All right. Let's begin! You know about the international situation. We have to attract young people into the Army. You were the most outstanding at school. Next year others will follow in your wake to the Training School. Is that clear?'

'Perfectly. We're the most outstanding. But why hurt Vitka's father?'

'He's only himself to blame. We're not allowing anyone to wreck the political campaign. Is that clear? Now you tramp off home! I haven't even had supper yet.'

'All right, we're going. But you didn't have to hurt Uncle Peter's feelings.' I went to the gate.

Inside, Alyosha's mother asked:

'Which shirt shall I iron? The blue one?'

'One more question,' shouted Sashka. 'Which town, and which Training School are we going to?'

'We'll go wherever we're posted. . . .'

Alyosha went in. Sashka said as I came through the gate:

'Well, as a statement of the position, that's not too hot.'

Our mood wasn't improved by the conversation with Alyosha. We saw Zhenya home, and got into the tram. It was packed, and the brakes screeched as we went down the incline. We pushed Inka and Katya in, while we ourselves hung on to the footboard. Inka held me by the arm, her fingers clutching my tensed muscles as though she were afraid I'd fall off. The tram crawled slowly downhill. The lamp standards hid themselves among the trees, their lights glowing like pale egg-yolks through the leaves. The shops were closing, and shop assistants in overalls were pulling down the shutters with hooks.

We got off at the Promenade. People were sauntering up and down its whole length, sitting on the ice-cream pavilion benches, talking and laughing. A light cheerful hum seemed to rise from them and hang over the sea front, the sounds separating themselves near-to, but merging further away. Through it, muffled snatches of talk and laughter were caught and lost again. That evening, the stocks and night-scented tobacco plants were just coming out. Their strong, heady smell hung on the air like the expensive scent of a woman, beautiful, but no longer young, who has just walked by you. For some reason or other, women after they're about thirty, use a lot of scent.

We lost Sashka and Katya, and never dreamt of looking for them, we somehow forgot all about them at once. The two of us walked against the stream of people, and when we were separated, hurried to join each other again. Inka got bored walking this way, and coming round the man and woman who'd got between us, took my arm. We'd never walked together like this before, and I was afraid to look at her. I suddenly seemed to be noticing things I had never noticed before. The men we met stared at Inka. She walked calmly under their gaze, in her fashionable frock, and her strapless shoes made to order by our famous local Greek shoemaker. And I walked beside her in my crumpled cotton trousers, with blisterlike bags at the knees, and brown canvas shoes with leather toecaps, and a checked cowboy shirt, faded, and stinking of sweat. I began intercepting the men's glances, and grinned back at them brazenly. A noise started in my ears, but I didn't guess right away that it was my own heart beating.

It was still fairly light on the Promenade, but now the street lamps shed pale beams. Inka asked:

'Would you like me to be a doctor?'

'Was that what you were thinking about when we were standing outside Zhenya's house?'

'Yes. How did you guess?'

I didn't know myself. It just came. It sometimes happened to me that I could guess everything.

'You were feeling very lonely when you were looking at the poplars, weren't you?'

'Yes, but how did you *guess*?'

'It struck me then, that after we're gone, you'll be quite alone. But the rest I only thought of now.'

'So you would like me to be a doctor?'

'*I'd* like it all right. But you find chemistry and zoology so difficult.'

'You all think I'm some kind of a fool. But I'm not a fool at all. I'm very gifted really. You've said yourself that I'm gifted.'

'Yes, but you're scatter-brained.'

'No I'm not a bit! I just get bored! How many times have I said to myself: Now, I'm going to get down to it, and *work*! But then I get bored. Is it my fault I get bored? It isn't as if I wanted to be bored!'

We hadn't noticed that we'd got to the end of the Promenade, and were now walking along Stalin street. This was the main street. It used to be called Simferopol street, because the highway to Simferopol began from here. Not long ago, they'd changed the name, and for this they had to hold a town meeting. But for a long time the street went on being called by its old name—people couldn't get used to it.

It was dark. The branches of the acacias touched the roofs of the houses and hid the sky. At the corners, the street-lamps shone, but their light could hardly get through the thick leaves. Occasionally, a lighted tram passed along the roadway, then suddenly you could see what a lot of people were about. But they didn't bother us. On the contrary, we felt more free because of all the people talking and laughing round us in the darkness.

'Inka, why do you love me?'

As soon as I'd asked this, the noise in my ears deafened me.

'I don't know. Why do you love me?'

I didn't know either. Probably this is something nobody knows. But I wanted to know.

'You're so beautiful, and yet I keep nagging at you all the time. . . .'

'Am I really beautiful?' I suddenly felt the warmth of Inka's cheek on my shoulder.

'You're very beautiful. Everyone was turning to look at you on the Promenade.'

'I know. . . .'

'How did you know? You weren't looking round?'

'I only pretend I'm not looking. Actually, I notice everything. My eyes must be made that way. I look in front of me, but I notice everything . . . how everyone's dressed, and what they look like, and how they look at me.'

I touched Inka's fingers with my hand. She was still squeezing my elbow. We walked like this silently, without even knowing how long we had been walking. I only took away my hand when we passed under a street lamp, and then caught hold of her fingers again, and they were so slim and gentle that it hurt me to press them.

We went through the small square, and crossed the big one. Beyond it, the Spa part of town began. It stretched all the way to the Mainaki salt lakes. On our right in the darkness lay the wastelands. It was all of two years since they'd started to build the town Stadium there, but so far they'd only put up the football goalposts. The passing trams lit up the freshly planed cross-beams. On our left, behind low stone walls, the dark domes and trees of the sanatoria rose up into the starry sky.

We turned into Sea street. There were three more blocks

to Inka's house, and we went more slowly. From morning till evening this street was full of people. It led to the beach and the Spa Hall. But now there was no one on the street except us. Inka said:

'What is interesting for a man is his future, but with a woman it's her past. It's true, it's true, I read it in a book. What d'you think they mean by past?'

I wasn't thinking. I didn't in the least want to. But I was used to answering whatever Inka asked. The main thing was to start, then something would always come into my head.

'You've got a future,' Inka said. 'You'll achieve whatever you want. You're very intelligent, and you're good at everything. Father and Mother say so too. They say you're still a boy, but you've a great future before you. That means you're interesting in yourself, doesn't it? But what sort of past have I got? None!'

'Inka! What d'you want a past for? You've got a future too. At first you *can* only have a future, then it turns into a past. *I* think the future's more interesting!'

The leather soles of Inka's shoes tapped on the asphalt, but my footsteps were inaudible because my worn-down shoes had rubber heels. The lighted windows of the five-storeyed house shone through the cast-iron railings. A light burned over each of its three entrances. The light filtered through the dense leaves of the trees, and glimmered on the iron railings.

'Just imagine that this is our house; not mine, but *ours*. D'you see? We've been to a concert, and we've come home. But that's the future, right? And you say the future's more interesting! I want everything to be in the past already, so that you'll have finished Training School. . . .'

'You've said that already.'

'So what! I've said it already. I could go on talking about it all the time.'

At the corner a couple passed under the lamp. A man and a woman. Inka said:

'Oh I quite forgot. Mother's at home alone. My father's on night-flights, and Mother's at home all alone. You know how she doesn't like being alone when my father's on night-flying.'

I was playing with Inka's fingers and said nothing. Through the darkness the hollow light tapping of the woman's heels came nearer, and with it the heavier shuffle of the man's steps. Both were measured and unhurried.

'A night like this is made for love. Are you still angry?' asked the man.

'No, just tired,' answered the woman.

They walked along by the railings, and the light fell on them in patches. They passed us, but we couldn't see their faces. When they were only a couple of paces away, nothing more was visible. The smell of scent hung in the air.

'Let's go back to the sea,' said the man.

'No, by the sea everything seems so insignificant.'

Their voices were fading into the distance.

'And it's down by the sea that I stop feeling insignificant,' said the man. We didn't hear what the woman said, maybe she didn't answer.

'Wasn't that "Mr Tinsmith"?'

'I think so. The voice was like his at any rate.'

'Would *you* like to go down to the sea? Never mind about Mother being alone. Would you?'

'No.' It was my voice. But it wasn't me saying it. I didn't want Inka to go.

'Then come with me as far as the entrance.'

I pushed the gate with my shoulder and it opened easily. We went along the asphalt path between the flower-beds to Inka's entrance. She held my arm. If her mother had been looking out of the window, she'd have seen us by now. But Inka had thought of this too.

'It doesn't matter,' she said. With her free hand she opened the door, and gently pulled me in behind her. The door banged to. We were enclosed in the resonant silence of the deserted staircase. The stone steps were dimly lit by a light showing from the second floor. Inka was no longer beside me, but her eyes shone from behind the stairs. I didn't remember her having left me. She raised her hands—I don't know how I guessed it, I couldn't see them—and pressed the palms, hot and faintly damp against my ears. Her lips touched mine. I thought I was going to fall. And I would have fallen but the wall was behind me and my back bumped into the hot-water pipe.

'Did you hurt yourself?'

I didn't recognise Inka's voice. I didn't feel the bang—what hurt me was Inka's voice: anxious, devoted, tender. I only dimly remember what I did next. I only remember the feelings of the next moment. Inka's hands were on my shoulders, but I was unaware of their weight. I clasped her legs, and touched her knee with my lips. It was soft and warm, just as I'd imagined it in the garden at Zhenya's.

'I shall fall!' said Inka. Her lips were almost touching my ear. Extraordinary, how much more you can say with the tone of your voice, than with actual words. Inka's *voice* said: I'm afraid of falling, but you needn't pay any attention to that if you don't want to! Then suddenly everything was back where it belonged, and I felt my power over Inka again. I let go of her legs and got up. Somewhere upstairs a door banged. Inka said:

'That's on the fourth floor.'

We went towards the stairs, and she laid her hand on the banisters.

'Don't you ever dare wear such a short frock again!'

'But everyone does. . . .'

'No, not everyone. Zhenya doesn't.'

'Zhenya's got ugly legs.'

'And yours are much too pretty!'

'Is that so bad? If you don't want me to, then you must

say so, and I won't wear short frocks. Tell me honestly. You want me not to?'

I didn't know myself what I wanted. I didn't even know if I wanted Inka to obey me unquestioningly, like she used to.

'Tomorrow we're going to the Spa Hall. You revise till six, and at six I'll call for you.'

'You didn't answer my question.'

'I'll answer you tomorrow.'

'No, today.'

Inka's hand showed white on the banister and I kissed it. I can't think how the idea of it came into my head. Someone was coming down the stairs unhurriedly. He stopped, struck a match, and probably lit a cigarette. Inka, too, was listening.

'He's still a long way off,' she said.

'You go. . . .'

Inka went up one step, then another. She was going up facing me, her hand trailing on the banister. Then she turned and ran the rest of the way. I used to bound up several steps at a time, but Inka stamped on each step with both feet, and from the top to bottom the well of the staircase was full of the noise of it. Inka couldn't live without noise!

13

—••⊱⊰••—

My heart was thumping with happy anticipation.

I lay with my eyes open, not yet fully awake. I only woke up a moment later when I remembered the half-dark entrance and Inka's lips on mine. From that second on I began to be aware of time and space. The room was full of breeze and cool sunlight. A scrap of paper was rustling along the floor. The draught blew it right across the corridor, to the kitchen and out on to the brick path and the grass outside. The paper flew up, fell slantwise, and lay, white on the green. I could see the corner of the garden, and a strip of morning sky. In the kitchen the primus was hissing. A neighbour was calling to her chickens.

I felt happier with every heartbeat, and just as I thought I couldn't lie still any longer, my mother came into the room.

'Are you awake? Get up quickly,' she said.

I dressed, made my bed, washed, and at the most unsuitable moments stood stock still, gazing into the distance. I can imagine how odd I must have looked, for my mother asked:

'What's up with you?'

I stood holding my towel, the water running down my wet face onto my chest. I didn't answer, and my mother didn't ask again. She put bread and butter on the table. As usual, she was in a rush. But because I wanted to be alone as soon as possible, it seemed to me that just today, she was being very slow getting herself ready. She went to her room for something, then to the kitchen, then back to her room. She looked preoccupied, and as always when in this mood, her lower lip covered her top one. And because she neither noticed me, nor the beautiful morning, and her life seemed to be all worries, whereas mine was all pure joy. I felt somehow guilty before her, and because of it, I loved her all the more.

'Drop in and see me after the exam,' she said.

'All right.'

My heart thudded and missed a beat, and when my mother banged the kitchen door after her, it started to thud again as though I'd run a hundred yards. I swallowed some food quickly, hardly chewing it, and drank my tea standing. I drank half, and poured the other half into the bucket under the washstand. I was ready to go, but I didn't. I thought: You've got to learn to control yourself'. I controlled myself. I grabbed the bucket and began throwing the eggshells and radish stalks off the table into it, and in passing whisked a teaspoon in too. To punish myself, I stood for a minute with the bucket in my hands. I wanted to throw everything down and run, but I stood still. Seryozha used to call it 'taking yourself by the scruff of the neck'. He admitted he had to take himself by the scruff quite often. From that morning, I too, made use of this method for cultivating my willpower and self-control. As I stood, bucket in hand, there were two of me arguing: One said: 'stop bothering about all this nonsense', but the other answered: 'it won't kill you. You've got to learn to control yourself'. I controlled myself I shut the windows, checked all the bolts and latches several times, and swore. As I shut the last window I could bear it no longer, and banged it so hard the putty fell out. I think the catch wasn't properly shut, but I didn't bother to check.

I rushed out into the court, and as I locked the kitchen door my hands were shaking with impatience. I tore along the street, overtaking the beach-goers. They got out of my way, scared, and one old bird shouted after me:

'You long-legged clot!'

Ever since I'd been compared to Apollo, I'd had a pretty good opinion of my figure, but I had no time to explain this to the old girl.

Sashka was standing at the corner of his house.

'Seen the paper?'

I could see from his face that he was in raptures. That was his affair. As for me, I'd taken myself by the scruff as soon as I saw him (which I did while still a block away), and went up to him perfectly calmly.

'We get the paper very late.'

'The *Spa Visitor* won't be delivered at all today. My mother's already at the Post Office. I bet there won't be a paper left in town.'

'You can expect anything from your mother! Have you read the article?'

'Read it? . . . My mother won't let the paper out of her hands. I'm sure you didn't expect that of her! As soon as they brought it, and she saw my picture, she said: only she could have had a son like me! She read the article out aloud, and my father and I had to sit on the sofa and listen.'

We walked quickly along the street. It seemed we'd never walked so fast before. Sashka was out of breath. It's not so easy to talk while you're walking at such a speed. But we'd hurried for nothing. In the window of the newspaper office near the Town Komsomol, yesterday's number of the *Spa Visitor* was still displayed.

'O.K. You didn't read the paper, but you listened,' I said. 'What was in the article?'

'I can't tell you about the whole article. My mother only read the bits about me. First she read it, then she had to count the lines. There were five more lines about you. My mother said, "Of course, his mother's a Party member. Your father couldn't get into the Party, but his mother could!" "If all you're interested in is the lines," said my father, "count the ones at the beginning where they're all mentioned." But my mother said she wasn't interested in all of us, only in her own child.'

I glanced sideways at Sashka. His mouth was a bit turned down at the corners, as though he were smiling. The corners of Sashka's mouth were always turned down, and it always seemed as if he were laughing up his sleeve. But I didn't think he was smiling now.

'You're a real man, you're all right,' I said. I hardly know myself how the words came out; we never praised each other to our faces.

'You think so?' asked Sashka.

'I'm sure of it. If your mother hasn't succeeded in making a child prodigy out of you in eighteen years, you must have the real stuff in you!'

'You've no idea how sick I am of it! But what can I do? She's my mother.'

We said no more all the way to the school.

In the school yard it looked as if it were break-time, only no one was running about or screaming. When we came into the yard someone shouted:

'They're coming! "Here's the man, spick and span".'

I think it was Raya shouting, the girl whom I'd asked where Inka was. Yura Gorodetsky came up to us. He, too, was in Inka's class. They weren't having an exam today. But Yura assumed that no exam could take place without the School Committee Secretary. They had only recently chosen him to replace me, and he wasn't used to it. No harm in that. He soon would be!

'Hullo!' said Yura, venturing to shake hands with us. We responded condescendingly; such familiarities weren't normally tolerated from the younger generation.

Raya was standing behind Yura, although it was absolutely

none of her business. I'd categorically forbidden Inka to tag around after me like that. People kept running up to us from all sides of the yard. We'd already had some newspaper publicity, but of course nothing on this scale. They'd written us up, the year before, but that was only a short article about the work of our class for the Red Front Collective Farm. We'd even had to hold a special meeting of the Komsomol to draw people's attention to it. No meeting was needed *now*! There'd been nothing like it since two years ago when the Commander of the Black Sea Fleet had visited the school.

We'd have loved to stay a while in the school yard, but we felt this to be incompatible with our dignity, and went inside. We lost nothing by this. It was impossible to get anywhere near the notice-board in the hall. Over the heads of the crowd I could see the newspaper cutting with our five photos. They'd used the pictures from our school records. They were all the same shape and size; I couldn't recognise myself from such a distance.

Someone shouted:

'Here come the birthday boys!'

The crowd made way for us. I caught sight of Vitka's face for a second. He'd come earlier than us, and the first laurels had fallen on his head. He had a stunned smile on his face and was looking at us out of one eye: the other was covered with a black patch held by a narrow elastic which crossed his cheek and forehead. I guessed at once it was Zhenya who had concocted it—she couldn't live without drama. She must have got the elastic out of a pair of knickers. Everyone thought it his duty to bang us on the back, or catch hold of us by the hand. Questions were being hurled at us from all sides. But as everyone was shouting at once, it was impossible to make out what was being said. Sashka was making signs and shouting:

'Questions must be submitted in *writing*!'

A noisy crowd came with us up the stairs to the first floor.

The light corridor with its open windows was soon packed. Only the bell finally drove people into their classrooms.

We sat down at our desks. Their black lids were warm from the sun. A few dare-devils attempted to force their way into our class, but they were chucked out unceremoniously. People were settling down at their desks, milling in the gangways. One of the girls kept asking in a frightened way:

'When was Lenin born? Someone, do tell me, when was Lenin born?'

We loved the turmoil of the exams with its holiday mood. Firstly, because everybody envied us, assuming that we knew everything and had nothing to be afraid of. Secondly, because exams stood for the gateway to freedom. But on that day in '10A' hardly anyone was thinking of exams.

'Isn't there anyone who remembers when Lenin was born?'

Everybody did. It was just that nobody was listening to the girl. They were listening to Sashka.

Vitka shouted:

'22nd April 1870.' Smiling blissfully, he too was listening to Sashka as though he'd no connection with the affair.

Sashka stared at Vitka with his protruding eyes. Busy explaining in a voice imbued with feeling, why it was that we alone had been offered places at the Military Training School, he hadn't heard the girl's incessant plea. If any of our classmates had entertained the slightest hopes of getting into a Military Training school, Sashka's account would have left no doubt in their minds. It was useless for them even to think of it; they would not be accepted.

We didn't notice the representative of the Local Education Authority come into the classroom with Vera Vassilyevna, our history and social science teacher.

'I move that the meeting be closed!' she said.

We were fond of Vera Vassilyevna. In our eyes, she'd only one unforgiveable fault; she tried to look younger than her age. Vera Vassilyevna dyed and waved her hair, sported a frivolous curl on her forehead, and screwed up her blue eyes when she talked to the male members of the staff. Inka said she screwed her eyes up because she hadn't yet given up hopes of getting married. Whatever else she didn't know, these were matters on which Inka talked sense.

As she passed us, Vera Vassilyevna said:

'Congratulations, congratulations! I'm proud of you.'

Then she spread out the Question Cards on the examination table, looked at us, and smiled. She didn't call us out by name, she only indicated with her hand that we should come up.

'Strictly speaking, they've already passed their exams,' she said, turning to the Education Authority representative.

'Of course,' he answered.

Vitka and I were in no hurry to take a question card. Why run unnecessary risks! We looked at Vera Vassilyevna. Was she joking or not? But Sashka had already grabbed a card, and, without even reading it through, said he was ready to answer. You'd only to give Sashka a little praise and he immediately lost all power of reasoning.

We had to take cards too.

This was our last exam.

There were to be many more exams in our lives, but we wouldn't be taking them in school.

BOOK TWO

Inka, my Inka

1

---◆❳❲◆---

We were standing at the corner under the windows of the Party office. There was nothing more for us to do there, but we stood there all the same. We were free. So free that we simply didn't know what to do with ourselves. We could do whatever came into our heads. But when you can do anything you like, you never know what you want.

That day we decided to grow up once and for all. We proved the firmness of our resolve by walking out of the school building on our hands—I in front, then Vitka, Sashka bringing up the rear, though Vitka had been against this method of perambulation.

'Look at the idiots! Can't we walk out like anyone else?'

'We've been coming out of school like everyone else for ten years,' said Sashka. Sashka couldn't walk on his hands, so someone from the middle school respectfully held up his legs.

'Well!' said Sashka, and we burst out laughing. Sashka could have said anything or nothing just then, we'd have laughed just the same.

We were standing facing each other, puffing out smoke. On the way to the Party office we'd suddenly decided it was time we started to smoke. We bought a packet of Northern Palmyra—one for the three of us. We'd have done better to buy three packets of cheaper ones. I realised this later when I kept having to reach into my pocket for the cigarettes. Sashka demanded a cigarette whenever he saw a pretty girl, and on the streets of our town you ran into a pretty girl at every step. Vitka was caught up in the debauchery too, not wanting to lag behind Sashka, and it was this that irritated me most of all. Vitka made a kink in the paper holder of his cigarette—goodness knows where he'd learnt that!—and chewed at it till the cigarette was sodden. Then he'd spit it out and demand a new one.

It gave us a special kick lighting our cigarettes as we sat on the divan in Alyosha's office. But Alyosha didn't seem to notice. He must have thought we'd been smoking for ages. This annoyed us, and we puffed away all the harder. Alyosha read through our applications, and put them in a file headed 'Personal dossiers of Komsomol members selected for Military Training school.'

'What's the next procedure?' I asked.

'In a week's time, there's a Military Selection Board held in the presence of an army Commissar.'

'But what Training School are we finally going to?' asked Sashka.

'Wherever they send us.'

'But where can they send chaps like us, who've got the sea in their blood?' asked Sashka.

'We'll see, we'll see,' answered Alyosha.

'I don't much like that "we'll see",' said Sashka, as we came out of the Party office.

'Don't whine,' I answered. I didn't much care for Alyosha's evasive answer myself. But I'd made it a rule never to give way to forebodings. Not a bad rule either. You can follow it all your life, so long as too much doesn't go wrong.

Standing under the Party office windows we forgot all about our suspicions. From here we could see the harbour gates, and beyond them the sea. In the roadstead, the steamship *Georgia* puffed smoke gently. We used to love swimming out to meet the passenger boats, and sitting on the buoys, looking at the passengers on the decks. They were astonished that we weren't afraid of swimming out into the open sea. But for us it was a trifle not even worth mentioning.

The steamship lay on the water and seemed quite small. But we'd seen her more than once close to, from the buoy. You had to throw back your head to see the passengers on the top deck, but you could talk to the ones on the lower and middle decks, though it meant shouting to make yourself heard.

As I looked at the ship, I couldn't believe that even last year, swimming out to sea had given us such intense pleasure, so childish and insignificant an exploit did it seem now.

'Now don't tell me,' said Sashka again, 'that my father's saying's not right . . . "Try anything once!"'

'O.K., he's right,' I said.

It wasn't exactly easy trying to talk with cigarettes in our mouths. The smoke got into our lungs and eyes, so that we coughed till the tears came. This didn't add much to the image we were aiming at by smoking. So we talked as little as possible, and then in short sentences. Though we were facing each other, we didn't for a moment lose sight of the newspaper office windows, and would suddenly begin to laugh whenever a passer-by (there weren't many in the streets) stopped to look at the papers. The women, especially, thought we were laughing at them, and looked at themselves nervously.

'It's a pity you didn't have a bruise like that two years ago,' said Sashka. Vitka answered:

'*I'm* not sorry!'

'You don't appreciate the advantages; that's why you're not sorry. Imagine a black patch on your photograph!'

Our pictures were two years out of date—that was what Sashka was hinting at—but Vitka only shrugged and coughed.

I had still not managed to read the article properly. You couldn't very well stand in the school entrance hall reading about yourself. But I'd been able to glance through it. It was headed: 'Exploit of young Patriots'. From the article I learnt that I'd always been distinguished for my thoughtfulness and serious attitude to life. I'd been told this before. But it's one thing to be told a thing, and quite another to read it in the paper. It was only the word exploit that bothered me. In the opinion of the writer of the article, our 'exploit' was like that of the young builders of 'Komsomolsk', who'd given up a quiet and comfortable life and, at the call of the Party and the Komsomol, had gone where they were most needed! To be honest, I hadn't given up anything. Getting into a Military Training School simply seemed more tempting. But probably, the Young Communists of the First Year Plan had felt the same way. After all, the editor must know what an 'exploit' was, better than I did.

'Now, don't tell me my father's not right.'

'All right, your father's right, and I'm wrong. I was wrong to crack you up this morning.'

'Kindly explain.' Sashka was pretending; he knew perfectly well what I was talking about.

'You might at least have read the question card.'

'Vitka, have you any idea what he's talking about?'

'Vitka hasn't a clue!'

'Oh come! . . . why? Of course I understand. It's true, the business with the question card didn't turn out too well.'

Dear Vitka! Always so naïve. The thing he was most afraid of was being thought slow in the uptake. I put my arm round his shoulder and rubbed my cheek against his sweaty one.

'You still don't know everything,' I said. 'You should have heard Sashka playing the modest fellow on the way to school.'

'D'you really mean that?' asked Sashka.

I didn't know myself if I meant it or not. Most likely, half and half. I'd always had leanings towards self-analysis, and I couldn't help knowing that I, like Sashka, was inclined to be conceited. Only Vitka of the three of us, didn't suffer from that wearing and, by its very nature, fruitless feeling.

The enormous thermometer on the wall of the Party office showed 30 degrees in the shade. The women selling soda-water under the trees were throwing away melted ice by the bucketful.

'Shall we go for a swim?' suggested Vitka.

'We can swim every day,' answered Sashka.

I saw what he meant. You'd have to be the world's biggest nit not to think up something more exciting on a day like this. We'd have thought of something long ago if the girls had been with us. Our brains worked better when they were around. But Inka was revising, and Katya and Zhenya had arranged to go to Inka's mother. They hadn't said what for, but we knew they were going to alter their old frocks for this evening.

A man in a white suit from one of the Sanatoria was standing in front of the newspaper office window. For some reason, people who came to the Sanatoria were called patients. In my opinion, of all the healthy people who stopped to read the papers, this man was the healthiest! He had to bend down to read, and his shoulders hid the display. He glanced casually at the *Spa Visitor* then moved on to *Pravda*.

'I like these smart-guys who are only interested in sensations!' said Sashka.

The man glanced round, and came back to the *Spa Visitor*.

'He asked for it!' said Vitka.

We puffed still harder at our cigarettes while the man read. Then he went off, and as he passed us, winked at Sashka.

'For once your nose came in handy, he recognised you!' I said.

'D'you know what kind of a nose Spinoza had?'

Let's go for a swim,' said Vitka.

Sashka looked long and thoughtfully at him.

'Have you ever thought of having a shave?' he asked.

131

Once, the winter before, we had tried having one. But it wasn't a success. It was our own fault. Instead of going boldly into the barber's, we'd hung around outside for a long time. When Sashka at last went in, we'd lost all desire to be shaved. We waited for him in the street. It didn't take long. The door opened unexpectedly, and Sashka appeared on the threshold, gently pushed from behind by the barber Tartakovsky.

'I've enough headaches without you. Bring a note from your Mum, then we'll think about it,' he said.

'Shall we go to Tartakovsky?' Vitka said, smiling.

'Try anything once,' said Sashka.

Pavel Baulin came up to us.

'Hullo, you Professors!' Pavel shook our hands, which we accepted as our due. 'D'you know what Pereverzev wants me for?'

'To hand in your application.'

'Have you handed yours in?' Pavel, for some reason, looked at us suspiciously. 'What do they want applications for?' he asked.

'Pure formality, Pasha, pure formality,' answered Sashka.

'D'you think it'll be O.K.?' asked Pavel. He seemed to think it depended on us whether he had to fill out an application or not.

'Nothing to it! All you've got to write is: I request to be admitted to Training School—that's all.'

'But I'm not requesting anything! It was they who suggested it, I only agreed. It'll be the same as with the Technical School. They tried to talk me into it, and finally they did. Then, when I decided to chuck it, they questioned me for two weeks about why I'd applied. I don't like it! You wait for me. I'll be back soon.'

With nothing better to do, we counted up our cash. Our liquid resources amounted to ten roubles, and I put them into my pocket. Pavel came out onto the porch, looking at his inky fingers with disgust.

'They've put a halter on me! Come on, let's go to Popandopoulo's.'

That was quite an idea! Sashka's suggestion of getting a shave was eclipsed at once. And all this time we'd been debating what to do and not thought of anything! Only I wasn't sure I'd be able to drink so as not to let Pavel guess it was the first time in my life.

'Now that's real man's talk,' said Sashka. 'We'll have a drink first, and then a shave.'

'D'you think it's worth it?' asked Vitka. He smiled and looked at me.

'What's not worth it? Drinking? We *must* have a drink!'

'I don't like it when a true member of the proletariat plays the intellectual,' said Pavel. 'Trend-setting, are you, with that pirate's patch?'

'Baulin. Pop in for a moment.' Alyosha was standing at the window of his office. I think he'd been standing there for some time, and had heard the whole conversation.

'I haven't any business with you till this evening!'

'Just come in for a minute, Comrade Baulin.' Alyosha pushed his hair back from his forehead with both hands. We knew he and Pavel were friends, but for some reason he tried to conceal this friendship from outsiders.

'Oh bugger off!' answered Pavel.

He crossed the roadway and we followed him.

'Come back!' called Alyosha.

'Cheerio!' said Sashka.

'Come with us!' Vitka called out, rubbing his hands with pleasure.

We'd never before dared talk like that to Alyosha. But now our feeling of equality blurred the distinctions between us and we were enjoying the novelty of the sensation.

Pavel walked on, his bell-bottoms sweeping the dust of the street. We couldn't walk abreast because of the crowds, some either fell behind or ran on in front, feeling very sorry none of the boys we knew could see us walking with Pavel. As for Pavel, he wore his aura of glory as simply as his bell-bottoms or his singlet.

The wine cellar looked like a shell set into the wall of an ordinary house, and faced with stone. In the echoing vaults barrels of wine stood and two small marble topped tables showed white. The bar stuck out into the street, and from the dark depths of the cellar came the sour smell of crushed grapes, and a chilly coolness. You had to have special virtues, known only to Popandopoulo, to be allowed to sit inside the cellar. For instance, Pavel wasn't allowed in. He had to drink in the street like other mortals, and the passers-by had to walk round the drinkers and the bar. Yet we often saw 'Mr Tinsmith' and his lot sitting at the tables inside.

Popandopoulo used to wipe the bar-counter with a cloth and call out in a toneless voice:

'Glass of this year's vintage. . . . Adds ten years to your life!'

He wasn't speaking to anyone in particular, and he didn't try to persuade anyone to have a drink. But the promise of ten years of life acted irresistibly. Popandopoulo's porous raspberry-coloured nose seemed to be saturated with wine. It hung over his upper lip, and gave to his face a look of doleful virtue.

In days gone by, Popandopoulo had been the proprietor of the Hotel and Restaurant Dulber, lived in his own country cottage, and ridden about town in a red-lacquered carriage, in tails, a white shirt, and a black bow tie known as a 'dog's delight'. But it was only from Zhenya's father that we knew what he had once been. At that time Zhenya's father used to appear as an entertainer at the restaurant and sing topical hits.

Pavel leaned his elbows on the bar and held up four fingers. The bar was in the black shade of the acacias, but even there it was airless.

'For them too?' Popandopoulo nodded in our direction.

'So *you* don't think we're people?' Sashka asked politely.

Popandopoulo drew off some wine from the barrel into an earthenware jug and poured it into glasses without looking, but without spilling a drop.

'Sun . . . grapes . . . health!' he called out.

I felt as if I'd sat down at the chessboard to play a vital game against a strong and unknown opponent. I breathed in, and the warm, sour smell hit my nostrils. Vitka drank his in small gulps, screwing up his eyebrows painfully. But Sashka drank up as though his glass were full of soda-water, not wine. He even belched. I sipped mine first, it was harsh and set my teeth on edge. I drained my glass, and felt as though I'd eaten a kilo of unripe grapes.

'That was good!' said Pavel.

'Not bad!' I said hypocritically.

After a minute, I had an unusual feeling of lightness. It seemed to me that I could have taken off and flown if I'd wanted to particularly. But I didn't want to. I felt all right on the ground.

'Your father's made a smashing job of you!' said Pavel.

Vitka fixed him with his one eye; it was flashing.

'How did you know it was my father?'

'Alyosha told me.' Pavel was fiddling with his empty glass on the bar top. 'I just can't get what's pulling you into Military Training School.'

'And what about you?' Sashka asked.

'I've my own plans. I've a personal summons from the Frunze Naval Training School. I'm already in the team for Inter-Forces Competitions.'

This was news to us, and it somehow rather pushed us into second place. In fact, I began to feel a bit put out.

'You won't get far with your fists alone,' I said.

'I don't intend to. I'm for more freedom, and more money. I'm bored with being hitched to a tug. Another drink?'

'Why not?' I said, and took some money from my pocket.

'Stick it up. Let's drink sailor-fashion.'

'How's that?'

'The one who invites, pays.'

Two sailors from coasters came up to the bar. One of them said:

'Wait! We'll knock it back together!'

We waited while Popandopoulo poured wine for all of them. The sailor raised his glass and said:

'Let's rub them all out!' and clinked glasses first with Pavel and then with us.

'Rub who out?' asked Sashka.

'Where'd you dig this lot up from?' the sailor pointed with his glass at Sashka.

Pavel said: 'Come off it, Professors! D'you want to shame me? Drink up, and I'll explain.'

The sailor put his glass down on the bar and said:

'Nope! I'm not drinking in the dark.'

'It's like this: there's always someone trying to stop you enjoying life, Professors. For instance, he's got a skipper, sails on the *Poseidon,* who's binding away all the time. So, not to let it get you down, you drink to rub them all out.'

We got the idea at once. Sashka straightaway suggested rubbing out 'Mr Tinsmith' too. We debated the fate of Tartakovsky for a long time, but decided he should shave us first. Then we suddenly all stared at Popandopoulo and burst out laughing. Popandopoulo was looking over our heads with sad eyes like an old bull-dog's.

'Glass of this year's vintage . . . add ten years to your life!' he called out.

'If you squeezed his nose, it would squirt wine,' said Sashka.

This struck us as extremely witty, and we roared with laughter again.

Zhenya's father came up to Vitka with a glass of wine. We

136

hadn't noticed when the Housing Office agents had appeared in the bar.

'Congratulations!' said Zhenya's father, clinking with Vitka's empty glass.

Vitka had probably forgotten he was holding an empty one. Zhenya's father was smiling. It was an unpleasant smile. When he smiled, you felt he was wanting to pinch someone.

'May I be so inquisitive as to ask you when and to which town you'll be going?'

I don't think I'd ever heard Zhenya's father call Vitka by the formal 'you' before. Vitka was taken aback.

'We're going to Leningrad,' said Sashka. 'At the same time as Zhenya. You can see the courtyard of our Training School from the windows of the Music Academy.'

Zhenya's father gave Sashka a look, and went back to his own group at the other end of the bar.

'Who asked you to tell lies? Come on, out with it, who asked you?' hissed Vitka.

'What a father-in-law to have landed yourself with! Did you see the look on his face? I've a suggestion. Let's drink to rub him out too!'

'D'you want a bash on the snout?' asked Vitka.

'No, but just think! A glass of wine, and for the rest of your life you'll be rid of this menace!'

Sashka had a habit of waving his hands about when he talked. We were always trying to wean him of it, but we'd probably used the wrong tactics. He was talking now and waving his hands as though we'd never spent any time on him at all.

'Sashka!' I said, dropping my hands.

'I get you,' answered Sashka, but a second later they were flapping in the air again.

Someone was looking hard at me. I turned my head. It was Pavel, his big thin-lipped mouth smiling.

'P'raps it's enough for a first go?' he asked.

We hadn't expected such treachery from him.

'Six glasses!' shouted Sashka.

'Sun . . . grapes . . . health,' said Popandopoulo, wiping the bar.

'Six glasses!' shouted Sashka again, and his nose began to grow. When Sashka was angry, his face was all nose.

'Who's going to pay?' asked Popandopoulo.

'Don't you know me?'

Popandopoulo looked at Sashka with his sad eyes.

'I know a respected doctor in town, but I didn't know his son was growing up to be an alcoholic.'

The bar went quiet. You could only hear the footsteps of the passers-by and the buzzing of the wasps. The affair had become one of principle. I threw six roubles onto the counter and Vitka shouted:

'Six glasses!' and squeezed through to the bar, shouldering the sailor aside.

Popandopoulo didn't even look at the money. I got up and joined Vitka.

'Are you turning up your nose at Soviet money? Are you going to infringe the laws of Soviet trade? Don't forget, this isn't your own restaurant, you're in Government service! Have you forgotten that? Have you?'

I was still speaking when Popandopoulo began filling the jug.

'Sailor-fashion!' said Sashka, pushing the glasses along the bar. 'And let's rub them all out!' he shouted.

'Then we'll have some sense,' said the sailor.

'I keep telling you, they're professors.'

We went away very pleased with ourselves. The last thing I remember was Zhenya's father's venomous smile, and the sad, old bull-dog eyes of Popandopoulo.

Almost everyone has things in his life that are painful to remember. And when you do remember them, you come out in a sweat. On the whole I haven't committed so many sins that I'm afraid of digging up the past. But when I remember Popandopoulo's sad, doggy eyes, I begin to feel very uncomfortable. And someone else's eyes, too, haunt me like a nightmare.

In January 1942, near Sechovka, when the frozen snow squeaked and scrunched underfoot, I fired my revolver several times, point-blank, at a German lance-corporal. For some reason he didn't fall, just swayed, trying to raise his automatic, and looked me in the face with eyes no longer human. After each shot, scraps of overcoat and little jets of steam flew out of his back. He fell, face down, and the jets of steam faded away before my eyes.

I don't know where my guilt lies. Evidently in being human and therefore answerable in my conscience for all the baseness and the crimes committed on earth.

2

—⊷❧⊰⊱❧⊶—

We didn't go into the barber's quite the way we'd have liked. Outwardly, we were fairly brazen, but we didn't feel too sure of ourselves. We were afraid we mightn't have enough money to pay. We'd no idea how much a shave cost. And anyway, Tartakovsky was a bit of a riddle and we didn't know how to take him. Tartakovsky had come to our town from Odessa, and he arrived there from Golta, with Kotovsky's brigade. It was simply impossible to believe that this fat, bald old man had galloped about on a horse, and shaved Kotovsky himself! But you couldn't disbelieve it either. In the most prominent place in the barber's shop, there hung a Certificate of Merit, issued to 'Red Cavalryman Ruvim Naumovich Tartakovsky for Bravery and High Revolutionary Spirit in the Struggle against Typhus'. We were all prepared to love and honour Tartakovsky, for his Certificate signed by Kotovsky. But unfortunately. Tartakovsky, for all his revolutionary services, was now a disgraceful, belching speculator, a remnant of the N.E.P. The barber's shop in which he worked was his own personal property, and the best in town. The Finance Department imposed higher taxes on him every year, but this had no effect. When they suggested he should join a Co-op, he invariably answered:

'I'll wait a little.'

We knew all this, as you always do the private life of every small-town personality.

So this was Tartakovsky, and it was to his barber's shop

that we were going. Tartakovsky was sitting at a small round table piled with newspapers, reading the *Spa Visitor*. We looked at each other, while he took off his gold pince-nez and put on his working glasses with the black frames. He laid the newspaper down on the little table with our pictures uppermost.

'Come in,' he said, putting his hands on the barber's chair.

We'd already arranged that Vitka should be shaved first. There should be enough money for him at least, and meanwhile, Sashka would run home and get some more out of his mother.

'And what shall we do for you? Eh?' asked Tartakovsky.

'A shave,' said Vitka in a bass voice. Where on earth did that bass come from? Probably it was just nervousness.

'But *I* think we'll have a cut, first. I'll do you a half-boxer's. Your own mother won't know you!'

In the mirror I saw a sudden look of anguish in Vitka's eyes.

'A half-boxer's might do,' I said.

Sashka disappeared. Tartakovsky, screwing up his eyes, looked at Vitka in the mirror.

'I appreciate that the black patch suits you very well, but we'll have to take it off,' he said.

Then, having enveloped Vitka in a white sheet, he raised his hand with the clippers before attacking the back of Vitka's head.

'Future lieutenants. Well, well. . . .' said Tartakovsky, and the little instrument chirred in his hand.

'Don't you approve?' I asked.

'Why not? I only wondered why lieutenants and not ensigns?'

'The Red Army has introduced the rank of lieutenant.'

'It's just that that interests me. Why lieutenants and not ensigns? As I remember it, in the Tzarist Army, they had ensigns and not lieutenants.'

'What's the Tzarist Army got to do with it?'

'Hasn't it? Well, well . . . What is it to do with, then?'

Tartakovsky had finished the back of Vitka's head and was now clicking with the scissors. I sat at the little table, leafing through *Red News*, and quietly seething.

'So you tell me, why did they have to shoot all those Colonels in 1917?' Tartakovsky took the sheet off Vitka and flicked the hair from his neck with a little brush.

Then he went behind the curtain to prepare the shaving tackle. He did it all slowly and thoroughly, but it seemed to me he was working very fast, and that Sashka wouldn't be back in time. Vitka looked at himself in the mirror and smiled. A milky pink bit of untanned skin showed at the nape of his neck. His blue eye flashed, surrounded by the deeper blue of his bruise, but the swelling had gone down. Vitka could well smile! Four roubles for one person was quite enough. But I foresaw the possibility of unpleasantness, and this prevented me from talking frankly with Tartakovsky. I almost hated Vitka for his blissful smile. How was it I'd never before noticed that he had such big, sticking out ears?

I don't know how Tartakovsky interpreted my silence. He came out from behind the curtain with the shaving things in his hands, and began lathering Vitka's face. Tartakovsky was silent too, now, but his lips moved comically. Then it suddenly occurred to me that, if I didn't keep him talking, he'd finish shaving Vitka even sooner.

'Army ranks have been introduced to strengthen discipline. They stress the fact that the Army is becoming a profession you can have for life,' I said.

But now Tartakovsky didn't want to talk. He only moved his lips as he went on shaving Vitka.

'Shall we have a massage?' he asked.

Vitka looked at me out of the mirror with frightened eyes.

'But of course!' I said quickly, perhaps a shade too quickly.

But the massage didn't help. When I took my place in the armchair, there was still no sign of Sashka. What if his mother didn't give him any money? I broke into a sweat. We'd got to pay two-fifty for Vitka. I kept my hand in my pocket, squeezing the crumpled notes in my sweating palm. But Vitka had sat himself down at the little table, crossed his legs and was leafing through the pages of *Red News*. It was not *his* worry. He was used to accepting that, if I undertook something, I knew what I was doing. It was my fault. I'd trained him!

I don't remember how Tartakovsky cut my hair. He went behind the curtain to prepare the tackle and I whispered to Vitka:

'Run and get Sashka!'

But Vitka looked as if he'd had a bang on the head. He sat and looked at me.

'Run and get Sashka. . . .'

'Where's your friend vanished to?' asked Tartakovsky as he came out from behind the curtain.

'Gone out to have a smoke.' I looked at Tartakovsky in the mirror, trying to see if he had guessed I had no money.

A hopeless task. It was impossible to deduce anything from his face, as, gnawing at his lips, he beat up the soapy foam in a little aluminium cup.

'Just like in that old joke,' he said. 'The Officers used to say, "Learn, learn, and one day you'll be a student"; and the students, they answered, "If you don't do any learning, you'll be an officer". So I ask you . . . what on earth do you want to be officers for?'

'In the first place, there aren't any officers in the Red Army, only Commanders. And secondly, you don't seem to understand the most elementary truth!'

'So *I* don't understand. Don't I? Well, well. But perhaps it's I that would like to know if *you* understand. I suppose that never entered your head?'

Sashka flew into the shop and held up his hand. All was well.

I settled back in the chair and, catching Tartakovsky's eye in the mirror, asked:

'Did you guess?'

'Naturally.'

The hot, soapy foam tickled my skin, and I forgot everything else in the world. It covered the whole of my face. My skin itched and tingled with it, and it was very pleasant. But the touch of the razor was still nicer. It scratched and stroked my skin lightly, gathering up the foam. Then I was nearly suffocated by a hot cloth laid on my face. The steam opened my pores, and I felt the air penetrating to my very blood-stream. With quick dabs Tartakovsky put cream all over my face. Under his fat fingers my skin became as resilient as a rubber ball. After the massage, he sprayed me with eau-de-cologne, and I felt as if he'd soused me with flames that didn't burn. I'd never known anything like it before. And when, after all this ritual, Tartakovsky left my face in peace, it looked to me like a completely new one.

While Sashka was being shaved, I examined myself in the mirror. Vitka did too. Then we went outside and started looking at ourselves in the glass of the shop windows.

'Personally, I think Tartakovsky's a typical counter-revolutionary,' I said.

'What makes you think that?' asked Sashka.

'Just intuition,' I answered.

At any other time Sashka would have bombarded me with a hundred questions, but now, Tartakovsky was the last thing that interested him. Me too.

'To be on the safe side we'll drink to rub him out too,' said Sashka.

And that's how we decided Tartakovsky's fate.

We had another cigarette, though we were beginning to feel sick, and went up Bazaar Street. We might just as well have gone down it, it was all the same to us where we went. The heat was growing stronger, but the skin on my face was cool. Without touching it I could feel its velvety smoothness. After our shave, our faces had somehow, imperceptibly changed, and we couldn't look at each other without laughing. We kept forgetting that we'd been drinking, but when we suddenly remembered, we began walking a little unsteadily. We barred the way to girls coming towards us, and said goodness knows what to them! The girls laughed, and not all of them told us to get to hell out of it!

But it was a bad idea going to Bazaar Street. Near the chemist's, Sashka's mother swooped down on us. I think she'd been lying in wait. People say of good football goalkeepers that they know how to choose their place. Sashka's mother knew this too, she could intercept him anywhere in town. He and I had time to throw away our cigarette ends before we met her, but Vitka still had his in his mouth. Luckily, Sashka's mother had eyes only for her son.

'Oh! Aren't you my beauty!' she said, patting him on the cheek. For this she almost had to stand on tiptoe. Of course, we had been much improved by our shave, but to call Sashka a beauty was going a bit far. Sashka had been left with side-boards, and this made his long narrow face even longer. With his bulging eyes and large nose, he looked like a billy-goat.

'Do let me have a look at you. What made you think to keep side-curls? A shame your grandfather can't see you! Have you any money left? Go and get your photograph taken at once! Think of it! Who'd have guessed I had such a handsome son!' Sashka's mother had one indisputable virtue; in her presence you could at least be silent. She did all the talking.

I poked Vitka, but he seemed to have forgotten his cigarette. Cocked jauntily, it jutted out from the corner of his mouth. Sashka's mother looked at Vitka, then at Sashka. Her bulging eyes grew even bigger.

'What's that I see? You've started smoking?'

'Why "us"? You can see it's only Vitka who has a cigarette. The fellow's got toothache.'

'And what about his eye? Has he got eye-ache as well?'

'Oh that's nothing. Just a small sty.'

'Just think of it! Just think of it! My head feels as if it's going to burst. That people should actually become soldiers of their own free will!' Sashka's mother looked at me. 'I suppose your mother's pleased.'

'That's just where you're wrong!'

'There you see then! A mother's still a mother whether she has a Party Card or not.'

One of Sashka's mother's friends called to her out of the chemist's open window. While they were chattering we slipped away unnoticed.

'I must call in and see my mother,' I said firmly. 'What'll you be doing till six?'

'We'll wait for you,' said Sashka.

'No use waiting for me, I might be held up.'

'What d'you want to stay with her so long for?'

'Various things. She'll want to know how I got on with the exam.'

'Will she really?'

'A mother's still a mother. . . .'

'Let's go and have a swim meanwhile,' said Vitka.

'You're crazy! To spend all that money on face-cream and eau-de-cologne just to wash it off again straight away! I'm not going to wash for three days!' Sashka answered. He looked hard at me, and I felt like a traitor, but I was ready to put up with anything, so long as I could see Inka soon.

We stopped opposite the Centre for Education in Hygiene. My mother had transferred her office there when it opened.

'And have you thought about tickets for John Danker? Where are we going to get the money for the tickets from?' asked Sashka.

'What am I to do about it?'

'Go to the beach and earn some!'

'O.K. I'll be down on the beach in an hour'

'But my father promised us fifteen roubles,' said Vitka.

'But seats in the front row cost eighteen. And we promised the girls front row seats. And if they want a drink, to say nothing of ice-creams, if they want a drink, are you going to take them to the water tap? Are you?'

'O.K. I'll come to the beach.'

'So you will, will you! And who's going to wait for you on the beach till three o'clock?'

'Well, it's no good going now. It's two o'clock already.'

'So you're going to your mother?'

'Yes, I am.'

'Fine. And you'll do the explaining to the girls.'

'O.K.'

'So you're really going to your mother?'

'Oh get on with you! But where'll you both be? Where are we to meet?' Sashka was already going off along the street, but Vitka still stood, not knowing what to do next.

'Come round to me at six. My father'll be home by then,' he said.

I started across the roadway. The street narrowed so much at this point, that the tops of the trees on both sides intertwined overhead. All along the middle of the road, patches of sun came through. I went in at the front entrance, stood for a minute or two, then looked cautiously through the glass panel of the door. Sashka was hiding behind a tree on the other side of the road.

There was nothing for it, I had to go and see my mother. The head of the Health Department was with her, and I realised at once that they were having an unpleasant conversation. My mother was smiling, but her eyes were glittering. The head of the Health Department was delighted when I came in.

'Congratulations! Congratulations on your son, Nadezhda Alexandrovna,' he said. 'And to you too, Volodya, on making a good start on life. Well, I'll be going, Nadezhda Alexandrovna, I don't want to disturb you.'

'What do you mean, you're going? We haven't settled anything yet.'

'What is there to settle? The Ministry of Health Central Committee have refused to back our application. I can't go over their heads'

'But you agreed. The position of the nurses is quite abnormal. They are paid too little for the work they do.'

'I agree. And we both signed letters to all the proper authorities. But the Ministry of Health Central Committee's answer was clear—now was not the moment to bring up the question of higher pay. And then, Nadezhda Alexandrovna, do you know how the rate for a given amount of work is reckoned? I don't. And without that, we can't prove our case.

'All I know is that on 275 roubles at today's prices, a working man is living on the edge of starvation, that's what we ought to be writing to the Central Committee and to Comrade Stalin about.'

'No, Nadezhda Alexandrovna, I'm not writing to anybody else. I don't feel I have the right to bother Comrade Stalin.'

'All right,' said my mother, 'I'll send the letter through the Party Executive. Then it's you who'll be blushing.'

'I'm always ready to admit my mistakes. Goodbye. I wish you every success, Volodya.'

The head of the Health Department went out, but my mother still sat looking at the door, and her lips smiled and her eyes flashed. And I suddenly realised, somehow, how alone she was, and that she couldn't by any means achieve everything. Until now I'd always thought she was very strong, and could get whatever she wanted. And again, as I had this morning, I felt sorry for her, and I loved her very much.

'I got a Grade A for History.'

My mother turned her head towards me, and now her face looked quite different.

'I'm very grateful to you. I'm very glad that I have you.'

I'd never expected such an admission, I'd never heard anything like it from my mother before. I'd always felt it was I who ought to be happy and proud to have a mother like her.

'Don't exaggerate!' I said, and smiled. I can't forgive myself for that self-satisfied smile. I went up to the table and put my hands on it, at the same time turning away to the window so that my mother shouldn't catch the smell of wine and tobacco. She put her hands over mine and looked at me.

'I'm saying this absolutely seriously,' she said. 'I've given you very little attention. And now it's too late. You don't need it any more.' She opened the drawer of the desk and took out a parcel. 'You can put this on now. Leave your old shirt here, I'll take it home.'

In the parcel was a cowboy shirt in the same colours as the one I was wearing. When she was buying the shirt, it had probably been difficult for her to imagine what other colours would suit me, so she'd chosen what her eye was already used to. I hugged my mother, and kissed her on the forehead. Then remembering that she might catch the smell of wine and cigarettes, I moved away and started putting on the shirt. My mother looked hard at me, and for a split second I thought she'd noticed something. Perhaps she did sense something new about me, without knowing what it was. She didn't even notice I'd had a shave. My mother was always absorbed in herself, her work and her problems.

'I wanted to have dinner with you today,' she said. 'But it's not working out. I've got a meeting in the office at three.' She spoke as though apologising to me, but I answered with a light heart, 'Never mind. We'll eat together another time,' and thought to myself: 'dinner would really have been the last straw!' I was looking at myself in the new shirt, and imagining how I'd look in the flannel trousers and new shoes Seryozha had sent. And I was also thinking that in ten minutes I'd be seeing Inka.

Now I'm over forty. I have grey hair and a bad heart. People with my illness don't live much more than ten years. They're concealing this from me, but I know. At night I hear my heart stumbling. One day it will stumble and stop for good. No one can say when—tomorrow, or in one year, or in ten. It's no use thinking about the inevitable. But when you are coming to the edge of the abyss and the black emptiness, you can't help looking back. What was I? An egoist? A youngster incapable of thinking or feeling deeply? Very likely a bit of both. I lived in a town where there was always sun over the ever-changing sea. Inka and my friends lived near by. I was sure that all life's joys were in store for me. For my happiness' sake my mother served her term of exile, and Seryozha had killed, and had been himself twice wounded in the Civil War.

I loved and often repeated those words of Lenin's, that you can only be a Communist when you have enriched your mind with all the wealth of human knowledge. At school, and wherever I studied afterwards, I was always at the top. And it seemed to me that this was enough, that everything else would follow of its own accord—the main thing was to come top. But now, when I'm alone with myself in the long, sleepless nights, I realise that I knew very little then. I knew all Hegel's and Kant's mistakes by heart, without having read either.

The world of reason, the only world worthy of man, was for me that country where I was born and lived. All the rest of the planet was waiting to be liberated from its suffering. I believed that this liberating mission would fall to me, and to my contemporaries. I was getting myself ready, and waiting till my hour struck. I could think only within the framework of this vision of the world. I reduced the most complicated manifestations of life to this simplified notion of good and evil. I lived accepting these over-simplifications as the absolute truth. I have had many different duties to perform in life —great and small—but I never felt their burden. Everything I did was as natural to me as breathing.

All these, of course, are only facts from my private life. Nothing more. No two men's lives, taken individually, are ever alike.

3

—◦∈ ✣ Э◦—

It was unlikely that Sashka was still watching out for me, but just in case, I went out through the yard and climbed over the wall to the side street. It led to the tramstop at the corner. There were many short, quiet streets like these in our town.

I waited for the tram round the corner and jumped onto it as it passed. I had a look back at the turning, but neither Sashka nor Vitka were visible. The conductor told me to get on properly, but I pretended I hadn't heard him, and jumped off opposite the square. I could have gone by tram to the wastelands where the Promenade begins, but I was afraid Sashka might be lying in wait for me there, so I went across the square.

I ran all the way to Inka's, and took the stairs at a run, I usually went up five at a time anyway. I was dashing up now, my trousers creaking ominously at every step yet it seemed to me that I was going very slowly. I tried seven steps at one go, without reducing speed, but the toe of my shoe unexpectedly slipped and I almost hit my chin on the edge of a step, and only just saved myself with my hands. When I got to Inka's floor my knees were shaking.

I knew that Katya and Zhenya were there with Inka's mother, altering their frocks for the evening. When I rang, I thought to myself, Zhenya will open the door! I made myself think this in the hope that if it wasn't Inka, at least it would not be Zhenya. Zhenya opened the door.

'We did ask you not to disturb us till six!' she said.

I was so angry I nearly shouted: 'John Danker's been cancelled for today'; I don't know how I stopped myself.

'Don't get worked up. Nobody's going to disturb you.'

'Then everything's fine,' said Zhenya, and was just shutting the door, but I managed to force my way through, sideways, with my back to her, into the corridor.

'Watch it!' I said. 'Don't get above yourself. I'm no Vitka!'

Inka's mother came out into the corridor pushing aside the heavy curtain over the door, and the first thing she did was switch on the light.

'Ah! Congratulations!' she said. I'd heard that word about fifty times that day, but just what Inka's mother meant by it, it was difficult to know.

Anyway, I said: 'Thank you.'

Inka's mother's eyes were red-brown too. I could always guess from Inka's eyes what she was thinking about, but not from her mother's. When Inka's mother looked at me, I felt as if she were seeing right through me. True this hadn't bothered me till Inka's and my conversation on the Promenade.

'Is Inka in?'

I wasn't looking at Inka's mother, but all the same I knew she was smiling.

'Can you believe it? She's been sitting at her books since morning!'

'We won't be ready by this evening if we don't get on with it,' said Zhenya.

'I'll go in to Inka, shall I?' I said, and it sounded as if I was asking permission.

'Lord! What fools!' said Inka's mother, and went into the kitchen.

Inka was kneeling on a chair, her elbows propped on the table. She turned her head, glancing sideways at the door. The moment I opened it she bent over the table. It was silly pretending not to see me, but she did.

I stood behind her. The fingers of her left hand were hidden in her hair, and in her right she held a pen, she was even writing down some figures.

'Stop pretending!' I said.

'I'm not pretending. I'm working. I've worked out all the answers. You check them! It's true, it's true!'

I could see Inka was speaking the truth this time without checking. She'd worked out the problems, and the theorems on separate pieces of paper, and laid each one against the question. In any case, the last thing I'd run all this way for was to scold her. And what had made me think she was pretending? Probably it was just that neither she nor I could for a moment forget yesterday evening at the entrance, even if she wasn't actually thinking about it. And that she too, as well as I, was expecting some kind of sequel. But once I'd started talking, I couldn't stop, and found myself doing and saying the opposite of what I had meant to.

'Lying again!' I said. 'Here's one you haven't done!'

'What d'you mean? I'm doing it now! I got muddled trying to find the root.'

I put my elbows on the table, took Inka's pen from her and started working out the cube root. Of course it was pointless even trying. I couldn't even have answered right off what two and two made! I sat blind and deaf, just feeling her breath on my cheek.

'Volodya, you've been drinking!'

I would never have thought that this could have made her so happy!

'All right, I had a drink. So what!' I was pleased with the casual way I said it. I painstakingly wrote down a few figures and formulae, realising I'd got them hopelessly mixed up.

'And you've been smoking!'

Inka said this as if she'd caught me out, but each new discovery made her still more happy. Me too. I'd come running to show off my new self to her, but I hadn't expected to give her that much pleasure.

'Volodya! You've had a shave!' said Inka, and her voice fairly rang with joy. 'You've had a shave, and they've sprayed you with Red Mask toilet water. How did you know Red Mask was a man's eau-de-cologne?'

Actually I didn't. I didn't even know that the eau-de-cologne Tartakovsky had sprayed us with was called Red Mask.

'And how do you know, anyway?'

Finally I thought, to hell with the cube root, and looked at Inka. She was leaning back in her chair, hands clasped behind her head, and the light from her red-brown eyes streamed over me.

'I know *all* about it. There's a pilot in my father's squadron who has a brandy every morning, and uses Red Mask after shaving. He always smells of wine, tobacco and Red Mask!'

'D'you like that?'

'How could I like him? He's thirty. He's almost the same age as my mother.'

It'd never entered my head that Inka might like anyone except me.

'You've got a one-track mind. I was asking about the smell.'

'You know, Volodya, when we get married . . .'

Inka didn't finish saying what would happen when we got married. We were looking too hard into each other's eyes. She got down from the chair and came round the table. Next door the sewing-machine stopped. Zhenya asked:

'Is it all right now?'

'Yes, now it'll do,' Inka's mother answered. 'But remember, here the stitches must be very neat.' Inka, leaning sideways against the table, turned her head and looked out of the window.

'How will it be when we're married?'

'It won't be like anything. You've told me yourself I'm scatter-brained! D'you want me to wash your shirt? You

155

should always wash a new shirt before you put it on. Look how stiff it is. D'you want me to?'

'No,' I said. 'How'll it be when we're married?'

Inka was already beside me, taking off my shirt, and I was helping her, lifting one arm, then the other, and still asking like a prize idiot:

'*How* will it be when we're married?'

Inka was already by the door when she said:

'I'll give you cognac in the morning, and the cigarettes I'll buy you will smell nice—not that muck!'

She went out of the room, and I shouted:

'Shows how much you know! Those were Northern Palmyras.'

Where are you now, Inka? Who are you with? Three years later I was drinking not cognac, but neat vodka. I began drinking it on the Finnish Front. Our ration was one hundred grammes, but it wasn't stated how often we were to get it. Quantities were indented for the previous night, but the next day, many of those who'd been alive were dead, and we drank their hundred grammes. I couldn't shave every day either. The skin on my face endured blistering heat and 50 degrees of frost; scorching winds, and snow as sharp as needles. But it couldn't have borne the touch of a razor every day. I used Red Mask daily for as long as it was on the market, it seemed to vanish just before World War II. All my life I've wanted to be like that pilot whom I never even saw. That's in memory of you, Inka. But I never did become one of those men who send women crazy. One of my women acquaintances says I only look like a man women fall for. It's annoying, but I never could do anything about it, Inka.

I stood in front of the wardrobe mirror. The water was running in the bathroom. The sewing-machine chittered next door. At first I only listened. Then I began to look at myself in the mirror. Not bad! A chap like any other. With a hardly perceptible movement I flexed and unflexed my muscles,

156

making them quiver slightly. I was engrossed, and didn't notice Inka coming back into the room. Then I saw her in the mirror. She came up to me, and stood between me and it.

'Come on! Do it again!' she said, prodding my chest with her first finger.

I flexed my muscles again, and she prodded them with each finger in turn, with great concentration.

'Volodya, would you like me to buy you a new shirt?' Inka looked up into my face. 'Would you? I've saved some money. It's true, it's true! D'you want me to?'

When Inka looked at me like that I always knew she'd made a mess of something. But now I couldn't have cared less. I was thinking that whatever happened, I must kiss her. All I had to do was bend down. But like a fool, I went on looking into her eyes, so I couldn't bend down. And all the time it seemed to me that she knew what I wanted to do.

'D'you know what kind of a shirt I'll buy you? A pale blue one. I spotted this one a long time ago. Let's go now, and I'll buy it. It's a shame you don't have one silk shirt. And you'll wear it this evening to the Spa Hall.'

It was very nice that Inka should be bothering herself about me, and I had nothing whatever against a blue silk shirt . . . but all this talk about shirts was preventing my kissing her.

'What do I want two new shirts for?' I said. 'In a month's time I'll be in Army uniform anyway.'

Inka's mother came along the corridor: 'Inka!'

Even before she'd called her, Inka had darted out. From her mother's voice I realised that something had happened, and I really started listening.

'What on earth have you done?' Inka's mother asked.

'Nothing in particular—I just washed a shirt!'

'For crying out loud! Who on earth washes things like that in hot water? It should've been washed in cold water and salt!'

I could clearly picture Inka and her mother, facing each other, talking. When Inka's mother came with her to enter her at school, I thought they were sisters. And not only I— everyone thought the same. Inka's mother was thirty-five. Most of all I was afraid of the time when Inka's beauty would begin to be dimmed with age, so I loved looking at her mother, and thinking that at any rate Inka would still be beautiful for another nineteen years. This reconciled me to life. Of course, nineteen years isn't eternity, but it was longer than I'd lived. Besides I reckoned that Inka's mother, and that meant Inka as well, would stay beautiful till they were forty. Why till forty? For me this age was a limit—till you reached it, there was no need to be ashamed of thinking or talking about love.

'For crying out loud, you don't know how to do anything properly!' Inka's mother was saying from the bathroom.

'I'm learning!' answered Inka. 'After all I'll have to learn sometime how to wash shirts. And please talk more softly. Volodya will hear.'

'It'd be a good thing if he did!'

'I'm going to buy him a new shirt.'

What had Inka done with my new shirt? This was by no means a matter of indifference to me. I'd seen myself so distinctly in my new shoes and my new shirt that I simply couldn't imagine myself without it. But when Inka came back into the room, I put on a look of complete indifference. At least, so it seemed to me.

'Did you hear?'

'Of course.'

I sat on the chair and smiled. Inka looked at me suspiciously.

'You're not really mad at me?' she asked.

'No.'

'You're truly not upset?'

'No.'

Inka stood leaning against the table, looking at me.

'Tell me what you want me to do, so that you won't be mad at me. Tell me!'

'I'm not mad at you.'

I took Inka's hand. She came up to me of herself, I didn't pull her. And it was she who bent towards me. I kissed her. But because it was light in the room and someone might have come in at any moment, I didn't feel what I'd felt yesterday. Or rather, I felt it, but not so strongly. Inka laughed. And straight away, my desire to kiss her vanished.

'What are you laughing at?'

'Nothing. I've known for ages that you wanted to kiss me. I could have kissed you first, but I wanted it to be you. When you want to kiss me again, you don't need to look at me or say anything. Just kiss me, that's all!'

'You don't have to teach me! I know all about it,' I said. 'And tell the girls, we're not going anywhere this evening. There's no money, see? No money!' I'd let go of Inka's hand, but she hadn't moved away. She put her hands on my bare shoulders.

'Volodya! You've drunk it all away!' Again she seemed delighted. Any violation of conventionality made her happy. It was difficult to imagine how Zhenya would react to this.

'You're a good guesser,' I said. 'Tell the girls: we'll go to the Spa Hall tomorrow.'

'And where are we going to get the money from tomorrow? I'm not giving mine! I'm buying you a shirt with mine.'

'Nobody's asking for your money. And in any case . . .'

What I meant by 'and in any case . . .' I didn't know. It just came out and I hadn't even thought of what I'd say next. I kissed Inka on the lips. She wasn't laughing any more, and I wasn't angry with her any more. I couldn't even imagine I'd been angry with her a moment ago. And I wasn't afraid any more that someone might come into the room. I even wanted Inka's mother to come in, then I'd have said to her: 'I love

Inka, and it's unimportant that I'm only eighteen, because I shall love her all my life, to my dying day. . . .'

I stayed to dinner at Inka's. At table, Zhenya teased me about my shirt. Pink had run into the white stripes, and indefinite patches of colour had been added to the variegated checks.

'In Brazil that'd be very fashionable,' Zhenya joked.

'To hell with it! It's still a new shirt,' I answered. I could have been a lot ruder of course, but I didn't really want to. I didn't want to lose the feeling of grown-upness, and spoil my mood. I just kept glancing at Inka, and for answer met the look in her shining eyes.

Inka's mother said:

'Lord, what fools!'

I gave a smile, which I felt was casual enough, yet full of meaning. Before going out I said:

'By the way; you can take your time over your frocks. Inka knows all about it!'

Zhenya's long face got longer, but I was already out of the room. I was pleased with myself, first because I'd kept my word and told the girls we weren't going to the Spa Hall, and secondly, because I was avoiding the hysterics.

Inka fluttered her fingers at me through the crack in the door as she shut it behind me. She needn't have done this. I never could stand flippant gestures. I ran downstairs to the next landing, jumped onto the banister and slid to where it curved. There I jumped off, and walked the last flight like a normal human being.

4

Sashka was waiting for me at the tram roundabout in Old Town. He was sitting on the lines, playing a game of 'penknife' with himself.

'Were you at your mother's?' He wiped the penknife blade with his fingers.

'Yes.'

'Well, well, so you really did go!' Sashka was examining my shirt with great interest and, feeling the material. 'Don't understand it. Is that it's natural colour, or is it a reject?'

We walked along the wide street whose smallest details we knew so well. Sashka went on looking hard at me.

'You were at Inka's too, of course,' he said.

'Yes.'

'And you told the girls we wouldn't be going to the Spa Hall?'

'What d'you suppose? Of course I did.'

'Just one intimate question. Are you and Inka by now on kissing terms?'

We had no secrets from each other, but now I felt instinctively that I shouldn't tell Sashka the truth.

'And what about you?'

'*Men* don't answer questions like that. They just smile non-committally.' Sashka smiled. But I didn't. I suddenly realised: Sashka and Katya had been on kissing terms for a long time and so had Vitka and Zhenya. And then I began

to remember how they'd unexpectedly disappear, and then
pretend they hadn't understood where we were to meet. And
to think that I'd never guessed: while Inka must have understood everything. What a clot I must have looked in her eyes.
I thought about it as I walked along the street with Sashka.
He was saying something, but I wasn't really listening. On the
other side of the low walls they were watering the kitchen
gardens. A queue was forming at the Siltings' only water
fountain, we pushed our way through it.

> 'Many eyes are more beautiful than yours,
> Grey ones, black ones, green ones,
> But I have never seen
> Such grey-green, black ones . . .'

Sashka recited. I knew the poem was his by the way he spoke
it.

'Like it?' he asked.

'Is it Blok?'

'Are you feeling quite all right?' asked Sashka, tapping his
forehead with his finger.

'It's yours? Then go on!'

'I've still got to make up the next bit. I composed that verse
sitting on the tramlines.'

The best way of praising Sashka's poems was not to believe
they were his.

> 'On the su-unny bea-each in June,
> In their pale blue pyjamas . . .'

sang Sashka, in a sort of whine, then said: 'How's that? Not
bad, what?' He'd heard Vertinsky's latest song somewhere;
Sashka could take off Vertinsky marvellously. He talked a bit
nasally anyway, but to make it even more like, he'd hold his
nose. We all pretended not to take Vertinsky seriously, but as
soon as we heard any of his songs, we pricked up our ears.
Only Zhenya would have no truck with him, and stopped
up her ears when she heard him. But I think she did this
on principle. She had a coloratura soprano, and only believed

in classical music. When we were all together, Sashka would do a take-off of Vertinsky as a joke, the way people used to sing 'Oh, my poor Karapet, why are you so pale?'

Vertinsky's records made their way into our town via Odessa, where they'd been smuggled in by sailors from the big liners. They caught on, and you could hear them all over town. We even had to have a special Komsomol campaign about it. Alyosha made a speech calling for protection of the young against the baneful influence of bourgeois decadence. We didn't really know what 'decadence' meant, but the word 'bourgeois' decided Vertinsky's fate. His songs were declared ideologically tainted. True, this didn't mean they were sung any the less, but listening to Vertinsky was reckoned an Anti-Komsomol-Act. After this we forbade Sashka to imitate him even for a joke. We neither sang these songs ourselves, nor allowed others to. It wouldn't have entered our heads that one could pass a resolution and then go against it. So we couldn't believe our ears when, last year, we'd heard Vertinsky's voice as we were passing Alyosha Pereverzev's house. Of course, we could have called up to Alyosha straight away, but we didn't; we heard the song through to the end first. Though we'd heard it before, we finished listening to it all the same.

'There where sorrow melts away and vanishes,
There where the almonds blossom . . .'
the final words came over sadly and huskily. The gramophone hissed a moment longer and was silent. We looked at each other.

'Alyosha!' Sashka shouted loudly.

Someone's hand pulled the curtain to.

'*Al-yo-sha!*' we called out in chorus.

The gramophone started hissing again, but stopped at once. Alyosha came out on the veranda, remains of lather still on his cheeks. He must have been shaving.

'Hullo!' he said.

'Alyosha, you know what we've called you out for, don't you?' I said.

Alyosha pushed the hair back from his forehead with both hands, and went inside. After a minute he came out with records in his hands, Nyura ran out after him, in a short frock she had long outgrown, paper curlers sticking out of her hair. Aloysha raised the records above his head and flung them down hard on the steps. Nyura let out a screech and ran back into the room, Alyosha sat down on the steps and lit a cigarette, his hands trembling.

'They stick to you like something contagious,' he said. 'Where on earth she collected them all from. . . . Well, that's how it is, Professors,' Alyosha spoke as though trying to justify himself. But I was thinking: 'Nyura got those records with his consent.' But something stopped me from saying this to Alyosha. I don't myself know what. . . .

> 'Then the verandas were deserted,
> The cabins were taken away from the beaches,
> Even the fishermen's boats
> Sailed far out to sea . . .'

Sashka intoned, glancing at me every now and then. I smiled ironically, yet at the same time a fleeting sadness caught at my heart.

'Why did we decide Vertinsky was a corrupting influence?' asked Sashka. 'It certainly doesn't affect me.'

'You may think it doesn't, but in fact it does,' I said. I had a whole collection of such stock phrases stored up. I used them without attaching any particular significance to them.

We came out into Vitka's street. The sea looked surprisingly deserted and calm. Uncle Peter was loosening the earth round the tomato plants. When he saw us he went along between the beds to the other end of the kitchen garden.

'Nastya! Fetch fifteen roubles,' he said loudly. Aunt Nastya was tying up the tomato plants. She straightened herself, and saw us.

'A-ha. Right away!' she said, and went into the house. Vitka was lugging buckets of water from the water-butt, and watering the weeded beds. Of course he noticed us, but gave no sign of it. Aunt Nastya came to the gate and pushed the money into my pocket.

'Go down to the shore,' she said quickly. 'Vitka'll be coming down too.'

We sat on the still warm sand and watched the fishermen getting ready to put out to sea. They took up their dry nets off the stakes, and carried them on their shoulders to the boats. Two of the boats had already run up sails, and heeling over to starboard, were making for the horizon.

'We shouldn't have taken the money,' I said.

'Why not? The two things have no bearing on each other.'

'It might have had some effect on Uncle Peter!'

'So far it's we who are feeling all the effect!'

Vitka came up and sat down silently beside us. Sashka took out a pack of Kazbeks. He'd bought them on the way to the Siltings. Personally I didn't feel like smoking, my mouth tasted bitter enough without, Vitka didn't want to either, but Sashka said:

'Softies! If you want to learn to smoke you have to force yourself. Later on you'll get used to it.'

We lit up.

'My father's not speaking. My mother's crying secretly. Maybe I shouldn't go to the Training School after all,' said Vitka.

'That's brilliant! So what did you need to get yourself a black eye for?'

'*I* understand you, Vitka. Uncle Peter's different from Sashka's mother. . . .'

'I like that! What's my mother got to do with it?'

'Shut up a moment, Sashka! Look, Vitka, I don't feel too happy about it either. But just think—it's our start in life. Think how lucky we've been. Think of it, Vitka!'

'You think I'm not? I've been thinking about it till my head's splitting.'

'Ignore it! Your head's splitting from the cigarettes. So is mine,' said Sashka.

Mishka Shkura came climbing up the sand dune towards us. He'd grown up a lot during the last four years, but he was still as dim as before.

'Give us a smoke,' he said, panting. Sashka opened the packet.

'Look at that, Kazbeks. Where does the lolly come from?' Shkura quickly grabbed five cigarettes at once. He lit one and kept the other four clutched in his fist. 'To treat the fishermen with,' he explained.

We waited silently for him to go, but he didn't. He stood beside us, his feet up to the ankles in sand.

'Yesterday, on the Mainaki, we got hold of a bird. Not a bad one either,' he said smiling, and blowing the ash from his cigarette carefully.

'You got your smoke, now clear off!' I kicked sand at Mishka with the toe of my shoe. He skidded down, raising the dust. At the bottom of the slope he stopped.

'Vitka, tell your buddies: we'll be there for the next punch-up,' Shkura roared with laughter and went down to the edge of the water. 'Have you heard? Styopik's back! Just you mind that!'

Vitka stood up. I caught his hand and pulled him down again.

'Don't have anything to do with that shit.'

'Interesting though. Has that halfwit really got in with the gang?' asked Sashka.

'He's trying to raise his value,' answered Vitka. 'You shouldn't have stopped me. Someone ought to bash him one on the snout just in case.'

'Funny Styopik should be back so soon. Must've escaped,' said Sashka.

'No, I don't think so. Shkura may be a fool, but he wouldn't blab if it was that way.'

Vague rumours were going around town, that at night in the Spa area, some gang was waylaying and raping unaccompanied women. Mishka Shkura, when he met us, would say: 'Got hold of a blonde yesterday . . .' Shkura classified women by their colouring. Occasionally, by way of a change, he'd call them birds. We didn't believe him. For a long time he'd been trying to make us think he was in with the 'underworld'. But Styopik was another matter. He'd come into our life absolutely by chance. This twenty-five year old, green-eyed Greek, as slight as an adolescent, was surrounded by a fascinating mystery. We'd met him occasionally in the street, or at the Spa Hall. He dressed smartly in wide trousers, and short 'Charleston' jacket. Small, almost puny, he appeared everywhere with two hop-poles of companions. And wherever he appeared, there were people who recognised him, and murmured behind his back: 'That Styopik! . . .'

Once we saw him having a brush with the Chief of the Town Police.

'Ah, Stepan,' said the Chief, 'Still outside?' He had stopped Styopik at the corner not far from Popandopoulo's cellar.

'My name's not Stepan, but Styopik. If I were you and you me, you'd have been inside long ago!' Styopik's voice had a boyish ring.

'Whistling in the dark, are we? Don't worry, we'll soon catch up with you!' said the Chief of Police, clapping Styopik on the shoulder. Styopik took a snow-white handkerchief out of his breast pocket and dusted himself off.

'No need for familiarity, Citizen Superintendent,' said Styopik, and went on down the street, bored and blasé, his two hop-poles on either side of him.

We'd just been reading Babel's *Odessa Stories* at the time, and of course we knew Styopik was no 'King'. So we were very upset to see the arm of the law so openly flouted by him.

One day that winter, we were at the cinema; I don't remember what the film was. After the show we were going single-file towards the exit. In front of us was a merchant-seaman.

Suddenly, there was a movement in the crowd, and we were pushed back against the wall. Styopik passed me, and for a split second jostled the sailor, who screamed, clutched his stomach, and was then swept out into the street by the crowd. The sailor fell down on the pavement, and lay writhing, his hands pressed to his stomach. Everything had happened so quickly that no one noticed or realised anything. Neither did I straight away. Then a woman in a warm scarf said in a surprised and frightened way:

'They've knifed him!'

A chap leant over towards me, his peaked cap pulled down over his eyebrows, the collar of his light overcoat turned up.

'By the way, they fixed that smart guy because he'd too long a tongue,' he said, and went off along the pavement. I saw Styopik at the corner, under the lamp. He was walking away unhurriedly as usual, his inevitable bodyguards on either side.

'What did he say to you?' Sashka kept asking me. But I just stood and didn't know what to do. The sailor was lying still now, his clenched teeth bared in a grin, groaning. People were bending over him, speaking to him, then they picked him up and carried him to the hospital.

'Let's go to the police,' I said.

'Did you see anything? Did you?' Sashka kept pestering me.

On the way to the police, I told them everything I'd seen and Vitka and Sashka insisted on coming with me.

'You're not going anywhere with me. It was I that saw it, not you.'

'Then you're not going either,' said Vitka, and barred the door.

'Idiot! Hearsay evidence doesn't count anyway.'

Sashka and Vitka decided finally that we'd all go to the police together, but that only I'd do the talking. The girls, particularly Inka, backed them up. The policeman on duty with a moustache à la Chapayev, already knew what had happened. He questioned me at length and in great detail.

'So you mean, you didn't see the knife, you only saw Styopik pressed right up against the sailor?' he asked. 'And who was keeping the crowd back? You didn't notice? Well, that's that. Let's get it all down properly on paper.'

It took him a long time, and he occasionally asked me about some point again. Then he said.

'Is there somewhere you could go away for a couple of weeks?'

'Well, I wouldn't go, even if there were.'

'You mean, you're not afraid?'

'No.'

'Being brave doesn't mean you have to stick your head in a noose. So for the time being be careful going around alone at night. And in general, keep a bit of a look out in the streets.'

That very night the police raided the Siltings, Old Town and the port. Styopik was arrested too. Vitka, Sashka and I got ourselves Finnish knives. What we really wanted them for, I don't know. I'm sure we wouldn't have used them in any circumstances. But we wore them, and probably because of this we wandered off to the loneliest parts of the town, intensely enjoying the feeling of possible danger. Of course, we didn't take the girls with us on these walks.

The trial took place a month later. The examining magistrate didn't let me give evidence. Both the Police Chief and Alyosha, with whom I'd registered my strongest protest, answered that they could manage without me. But I went to the trial just the same. Three of the accused said they had struck the knife-blow. Styopik admitted walking past the sailor, but said that he'd never set eyes on him till then, and hadn't the slightest need to settle any scores with him. All the accused declared they didn't know each other at all. The sailor died. The medical report gave the cause as one knife wound in the liver. For two weeks the court sat trying to find out which of the accused had done it, but they didn't succeed. The three who insisted they'd struck the blow, each got five years for complicity in the murder. Styopik was acquitted for lack of evidence, but on the basis of numerous previous arrests, the court made a special ruling, sentencing him to three years' exile. Amongst the accused was the fellow who'd warned me not to blab. He recognised me, and when our eyes met, he gave the shadow of a smile.

Only four months had gone by since the trial.

'We'll have to check up. Maybe Shkura is lying,' said Vitka.

'To hell with Styopik. You'd better start thinking what you're going to do. And it had better be a good think! We've got to think of this as the start of our *whole lives.*' I don't know how I hit on that one, it was simply that I didn't want to part from Vitka.

'Three friends once lived in a Spa,' Sashka said unexpectedly.

'Why lived? We're living, and we'll go on living, though it's not very important where,' I said briskly. But all the same I felt sad. Probably because Sashka had used the past tense, 'lived' and it had reminded me that there are inescapable unpleasantnesses in life such as goodbyes.

I got up, shaking the sand from my trousers. The day that had begun so cheerfully, was ending sadly. From that evening, and for the rest of the time we lived in our town, joy and sadness walked side by side.

5

The dark shadow of the trees ended at the pavement's granite kerb. But a torrid white heat lay on the road, the beaches and the sea. It was only ten in the morning, but a hum like the distant noise of an agitated crowd, came from the beach. People were coming out onto the street, in bathing costumes, and drinking mineral water under big umbrellas.

Though I didn't hurry, I was first at the 'Dulber'. By the restaurant's open doors stood two chairs with their backs to the street.

'What did I say! He's here already,' said Sashka.

'Where's Inka? Has she finished her exam?' asked Zhenya as she joined us.

Surprisingly stupid questions. If Inka had finished her exam, where would she be if not here with me? I didn't bother to answer Zhenya. She had on a new straw hat with a wide brim, and she thought it made her look extremely elegant. I turned my back on her and said to Vitka:

'Any news?'

'None.'

'So you're going?'

'Yes, if it's Leningrad.'

'We put it clearly in our application: Naval Training School, City of Leningrad,' said Sashka.

'Well, I don't know what you put, but I'm sending my entrance form to the Leningrad College of Music tomorrow! This was Zhenya trying to impress us with her determination. As if we didn't know Vitka was under her thumb.

Sashka said:

'O.K., then. Goodness! Have you ever seen so many people on the beach so early. Come on! Or we'll have to climb on the top of the awning.'

'I have to call for Inka at school.'

'Here it comes!' said Sashka. 'Well, so long as you're on the beach in an hour's time. We'll be under the third awning. Remember, there'll be a chess partner waiting for you.'

They moved out onto the roadway and were lit up by the sunlight. Everything looks brighter in the sun. They crossed the road and the opposite pavement, Katya and Zhenya sat down on the low, wide stone wall dividing the beach from the street, and started taking off their shoes. Vitka bent down and undid Zhenya's laces. Sashka stood and watched while Katya, her foot propped on her knee, was unbuttoning the straps of her shoes. I watched too. Since my yesterday's talk with Sashka, I was seizing on every trifling detail that might confirm my guesses. I could no longer think of Katya and Zhenya as just friends. In my eyes Katya was now surrounded by a disturbing mystery. And because I didn't like Zhenya much as a girl, it was an unpleasant thought that she and Vitka might be on the same terms as Inka and myself.

Katya put her legs over the wall, jumped down onto the sand, and walked towards the sea. Sashka was saying something to her as he put his hand on her shoulder. She lifted her face to his and laughed. She was stumbling, because it was difficult to walk in the shifting sand without looking.

I took out the cigarettes. Even before I lit one I could feel the rough, bitter smoke, but I lit one just the same, walking unhurriedly along the street. Then I sat in a cool corner of the school yard, waiting for Inka. I didn't have to wait long. Of course I should have started smoking right away, but the mere thought of it made me feel sick.

'Inka!' I shouted, when she came out into the yard.

She didn't come over to me, but waited for me to go to her, and I guessed at once that something had happened.

'Have you failed?'

'I haven't failed anything!'

Several of the boys and girls from Inka's class came out into the yard. Inka said loudly:

'Let's get out of here!'

I thought she must have got a Grade C, and that as usual she'd decided she'd been unfairly treated. We went out into the street, to the right and along the harbour wall. It was quicker this way to the beach.

'They can do what they like, but I'm not going!' said Inka.

'Where aren't you going?'

'You don't know where? You don't know? To weed vegetables, that's where!'

'When d'you have to go?'

'It's all on the notice board. In a week's time.'

'Have you talked to the other kids?'

'I've talked to everybody, explained to everyone. *No*body wants to listen to anything. They all say anyone can find a valid excuse. What excuse? What kind of an excuse?'

What was I hoping for? What was the use of asking? As soon as Inka said where she had to go and what for, I understood: there was nothing to be done—Inka would *have* to go. But I myself had to get used to the idea that in another seven days, she wouldn't be there. But it was impossible to get used to it. Till yesterday, the inevitability of parting had still been vague; at sometime or other, I would have to go. But I simply couldn't imagine being in our town without Inka.

'*You* talk to Yurka.'

We crossed the square. The young trees gave no shade at all, and the dusty benches were baking in the sun. I walked in silence. What could I say? I knew that I couldn't ask Yurka to let Inka stay behind. I couldn't, because I myself wouldn't have allowed anyone to stay behind if the whole class had been going to the collective farm our school was linked to. But I couldn't bring myself to say this to her straight out.

'*Will* you talk to Yurka?' Inka raised her face to mine; her eyes, full of tears, still glimmered with sparks of hope. It was better not to look into them.

'I can't,' I said, and I didn't recognise my own voice, because my mouth was dry and my voice hoarse. I repeated, 'I can't,' to myself. I'd heard the word before somewhere, quite recently, and I tried to remember where. But of course, it was when I'd asked my mother not to speak to Aloysha Pereverzev, and I think she'd answered, 'I ought to, but I can't.' But why 'ought'? Perhaps I too 'ought' to talk to Yurka. My head was in a whirl. While Inka walked on in silence, looking intently at her feet.

'Inka, let's consult the others. Perhaps Sashka'll be able to think of something.'

'O.K., let's,' said Inka. It seemed to me she was blaming me somehow, and this I couldn't bear.

'Actually, I don't think it's such a tragedy. If we're held up here in town, I'll come over to see you. D'you hear?'

Inka said nothing.

'D'you hear?'

'I'm not deaf.'

Then I didn't know what I know now. It was Inka who was right, not I. She could not reconcile herself to this premature goodbye. But I couldn't go to Yurka Gorodyetsky and explain that Inka had a right not to agree. Was I perhaps frightened for my reputation as a Komsomol leader? It must have been partly that. But deep down inside me I could not allow myself to think that Inka might be right. I was angry. Not with myself, but with her, for making me feel how powerless I was. . . .

If only I'd been able to look at it all then with more human eyes . . .

We turned the corner, and crossed the road before coming to the 'Dulber'. Inka sat down on the stone wall, kicked off her shoes, and began taking off her socks. She left her socks on the wall, and jumped down onto the sand. She went down to the sea without looking round. I bent down and picked up her shoes, still faintly damp and warm from her feet, put the socks into them and followed. I didn't even think of catching her up, I walked behind her, carrying her shoes. How could she know I was going to? I'd never done it before! She'd barely glanced at me before jumping down onto the sand, and was now walking ahead without looking to see whether I'd taken her shoes.

'Why do I have to carry your shoes?'

'Don't!' Inka didn't even turn her head.

'Watch it! I'm going to throw them down in the sand now!'

'Fire ahead!'

Of course I wasn't dreaming of it. I liked carrying her shoes. I was just amazed by her cocksureness. We found Katya sitting alone, not far from the water's edge.

'How did you get on?' asked Katya.

'Just imagine! I got an "A".'

'Where's everybody?' I asked.

'Vitka and Zhenya are bathing. Sashka's dashed off somewhere. He came running up twice asking for you.'

Katya was facing the sea, her legs stretched out and covered with sand. She looked up at us, her head tilted. Katya's eyes, like Alyosha's sister Nyura's, were changeable as the colour of the sea. Girls who live by the sea often have eyes like that. Their blue deepens sometimes, to navy, sometimes pales almost to transparency. The sea and Katya's eyes were the same colour.

'A heat like this and you're not swimming!' Inka undid the hooks on her skirt and it slipped to her feet.

She stepped out of it, sat down, and began pulling her blouse over her head.

'Sashka wouldn't let me. He told me to wait for you.'

Inka bent towards Katya, said something quickly in her ear, and laughed, her teeth just catching her lower lip. Zhenya was walking in the water, avoiding the swimmers but not coming out onto the beach. Up to her knees in water, she was wringing it out of the baggy pants of her bathing costume. Zhenya's legs were very thin above the knee, and she wore baggy pants to hide them. She was wringing them out because they were wet and clinging to her. I think Inka had been saying something about Zhenya's legs. My sisters were right. Zhenya did turn out a beauty, but now she looked like a wet hen. Sashka came charging along the shore, and in his wake the sunbathers he'd sprinkled with sand lifted their heads.

'You couldn't have made it later still, could you?' shouted Sashka, only then stopping in front of me. Anyone not in the know might have thought he was going to attack me.

'I came when I could. Don't go on at me.' I was standing over Inka, trying not to look at her, but looking at her just the same. This was the first time we'd been on the beach together since our talk on the Promenade. I looked at her, and everything about her seemed different. Of course there wasn't really anything different about her. It was just that my attitude to her was different, and hers to me.

'Have you turned into a statue?' asked Sashka.

Inka laughed. She just looked at me and laughed.

'Let's go!' I said.

As I followed Sashka, Inka called out:

'Volodya, Volodya, come here a minute!' I came back to her. She was sitting, her knees drawn up. 'Bend down!' I squatted on my heels, and bent my head. Inka whispered: 'If you win, let's go and have an ice-cream? Shall we?'

'I'll think about it,' I said, and pressing a hand on her knee, I got up.

'Wait, bend down again!' said Inka. I bent down. 'Don't forget, you promised to consult the others.'

'Stop whispering!' said Sashka. 'Katya, you're not to swim without me.'

'Can't I have just one dip. Look how hot it is.'

'All right, just one little dip, then.'

'Dictator Ali Pasha speaks!' I said.

'Don't you come meddling in this!' answered Sashka.

He walked on ahead of me, keeping to the right, so as to avoid a second encounter with the sunbathers he'd just scattered with sand. This was pure self-preservation instinct! I couldn't think how he'd managed to run at all. We had great difficulty in stepping between all the spread-out arms and legs. People were all talking, shouting and laughing at the same time, and this tangle of sounds seemed to exist on its own, side by side with the ringing, echoing silence of the beach. It's always like this by big open spaces of water. Every time Sashka wanted to say something to me, he stopped and waited for me to catch up with him.

'You've never had a chess-opponent like this one!' said Sashka.

'O.K., O.K. Come on!' I said, giving him a shove.

After a few steps he stopped again.

'I had to run all over the place till I found this one. Firstly, he always wins. Secondly he doesn't know how to play. And thirdly he's quite unaware of this! Even I could've beaten him if I hadn't thrown away my castle.'

'Rook, Sashka, Rook. When will you learn to call the pieces by their proper name.'

'D'you want an opponent, or a terminology?' asked Sashka.

Sashka was very good at finding opponents for me. He would sit himself down by the players, and study the set-up for a while. Then he himself would play a game with the stronger of the two players, quickly lose to him, and then say, casually, 'You must be First Category. I've a friend who's in that class too, he plays almost as well as you, perhaps even a bit better.' Usually, my future opponent was not in any particular category, but it's always easier to persuade an amateur that he has an expert's skill, than prove to him that he doesn't know how to play. More often than not, Sashka's words at once roused the desire to pit his strength against mine. Then I would make my appearance. The most ticklish part of these contests was deciding on the stakes. Sashka and I would settle this between us.

We went into the shadow of the awning. This was the domain of the mothers and children, the card players, and the chess enthusiasts. We went up to the players. All the self-styled experts were sitting and standing around my future victim. They always knew or could foresee everything. They alone knew the best move, and if the players did something different, the know-alls would declare the game lost. My future opponent was sitting cross-legged, Turkish style, his huge stomach resting on his knees. He looked down on the board, and when he had to move a piece, it was very difficult for him to get his hand to it, his stomach was in the way.

'Just a little check!' he said, picking up a knight with two fingers.

Someone said: 'Check isn't the end of everything!'

'True. Check isn't the end. But who's talking about an end?'

My future opponent's eyes had a glazed look. I realised straight away: he could only see one or two moves ahead. His opponent unhurriedly brushed the sand off his hands before moving his King.

'Another little check-let! And another!' The pace of the game quickened. Black could have been mated long ago if there hadn't been so many senseless checks.

Not far away some mother was cooing:

'Who's going to eat her din-din? Lenochka's going to have some din-dins. We're not giving it to anyone else!'

'That's the way to ruin children, right from the start!' said Sashka loudly, so as to draw attention to us, as he fixed my future antagonist with his eye.

'You're back? Where's your friend?' he said. 'Ah! Maestro,' he said to me, guessing I must be the one Sashka had mentioned. 'Come on! Let's play!'

'He's only come to watch your game. He doesn't want to play himself,' said Sashka.

'Is he scared?'

'What of? It's simply that in a month's time I have to play in an important tournament. Beach games spoil one's form,' I said.

The experts observed a reverent silence. Sashka's description of me as a First Category player acted on them like magic. Actually, I was only Second Category, but it didn't really have much significance.

'I did warn you he didn't usually play on the beach before tournaments,' said Sashka.

'Nonsense! Just let's fix the stakes as a matter of interest. How about fifteen roubles a game?' He roared with laughter, pretty sure that this would scare me. The blood rushed to my head at the mere mention of such a sum, and I only just stopped myself from saying 'yes'. Instead, I said:

'Oh come off it! I haven't got that much money!' modestly implying by this, that I wasn't at all sure of the outcome of the game.

'What about ten?'

Sashka was right. It was almost boring to see the chosen victim so easily hooked. We nearly always had to suggest the prize money ourselves, and I usually played for five roubles a game.

'What! Still scared?' My future opponent laughed again.

'A First Category player, and so stingy!' said Sashka. 'People are asking you to play with them. They'll think I was lying. I'll go shares with you, and give you five roubles!'

I stood as though reflecting, and still undecided. One of the experts said:

'We know your kind of champion!'

But as usual in such circumstances, others came to my defence.

'He's just explained, he's got to play in a tournament soon.'

Meanwhile the man with the stomach was slaughtering his opponent. He seemed almost to have lost interest in me. Or perhaps reason was stirring in him and he was already regretting the suggestion he'd made. Sashka grasped this before I did.

'Haven't you ever heard about form? You haven't? Well, a real chess player must always keep himself in form. Volodya, I beg of you . . . prove to these specialists what kind of a player you are. You won't lose your form in a couple of games.'

'O.K. Let's play,' I said.

They made room for me. The previous antagonist of the man with the stomach had resigned. We drew for colours, and I got white. The experts obligingly helped set up the pieces. They were thirsting for blood; the more so, since whatever the outcome, none of them stood to lose anything. My opponent looking very sure of himself, loomed over the board like a monument.

'Shall we begin? Have you got ten roubles on you?' he asked.

I took two fives from my pocket and handed them to Sashka.

'Mind! In the event of my losing, you'll give me back five!'

'What d'you suppose! You, I take it, have ten roubles?'

My opponent laughed, and when he laughed his stomach shook like a jelly. He took his wallet out of his hip pocket. The financial transactions were now entirely in Sashka's hands. My job was to play. I moved: e2 to e4 (P to K4). My opponent replied e7 to e5 (P to K4), and started taking out his money. I wasn't worried about the outcome of the game, the difficulty lay elsewhere. I had to play in such a way as to make my opponent and the spectators believe all the time in his chance of a rapid victory. After my third move, my knight on f3 (my

KB3) was pinned by his bishop, and the chance of one of the classical traps cropped up. I castled. My opponent played knight to f6 (KB3) threatening my central pawn. I made a stalling move: a3 (P to QR3) and roused the experts' animation. One of them said, 'The little pawn smiled,' after which trust in me was somewhat shaken. My opponent looked thoughtful, the ease with which I'd sacrificed my pawn put him on his guard. You could see at once he was not a person who took things in life for granted. Finally he said, as if to cheer himself up:

'Well, if you're giving it away . . . I'll take it. . . .'

One of the experts backed him up:

'Even pawns aren't to be sneezed at.'

After which, without a hesitation, he took my pawn with his knight. I moved my knight to c3 (B3). This time the man with the stomach didn't think for long, he was quite sure he'd heard somewhere, that doubled pawns lead to a weakening in the position, so he took my knight with his. He was now at my mercy. I was sure that if he himself didn't see that by moving his pawn e5 to e4 (to K5) he could win my knight, one of the know-alls would point it out to him. Several of them were already looking at me maliciously. I took the black knight with my pawn. My opponent, it seemed, had only been waiting for this, and immediately moved his King's pawn. Everyone waited tensely for my answering move. As soon as I picked up my knight one of the experts said:

'If you've touched it . . . you must move.'

It was extraordinary how well everyone knew tournament rules!

I moved my knight to e5 (K5). The black bishop could take my Queen. . . . I saw big beads of sweat appearing on my opponent's forehead. He looked at my Queen, and raised his hand several times over the board and put it down again. Some instinct prompted him it would be fatal to take the Queen, but at the same time he couldn't resist such a magnificent catch. I heard some unflattering remarks about me from the experts:

'Ostap Bender in Vassyook.'

'Don't worry. These kids won't get away with it!'

Sashka was looking at me anxiously, trying to judge from my face whether I hadn't gone too far. My opponent too, looked at me fixedly, hoping my expression would tell him what he couldn't see in the pieces on the board. I was sprawling, my legs stretched out, propped on my left elbow, and dribbling sand from my right to my left hand. I wasn't looking at the board. One of the know-alls, tentatively, advised taking the knight. I doubted if he realised just how crafty my plan was. More likely he was guided by the well-tried principle—'easy does it'! He was set on by the ones thirsting for a quick kill.

'You must take the Queen . . . the Queen. . . .'

'Let her be for the moment,' said my opponent, and moved his pawn to h5 (KR4). Finally he overcame all his doubts and looked round, triumphantly, first at me, then at the experts, as if inviting them to bear witness to his chess-playing genius. His plan was not devoid of commonsense; having protected his bishop, he left my knight and Queen *en prise*; assuming that if I'd left the Queen unguarded by mistake, I'd move her at once and he'd be content with the knight, but if my sacrifice were premeditated, he could upset my plans by not taking either piece. He explained this tersely, to the disappointed experts—'to hell with the Queen!'—to which one of them replied:

'But he'll take your bishop with his knight!'

My opponent hadn't noticed even this simplest of moves. He glued his eyes to the board again covering himself with:

'Let him try!'

I didn't even begin to. I took his pawn on f7 (KB2) with my bishop, putting him in check. His eyes slowly shifted from the knight to the bishop. The know-alls were the first to sense the impending tragedy in my unexpectedly confident moves. Things are always more obvious to those on the sidelines. It was only my opponent who didn't realise the game was over. He moved his King onto the only free square e7 (K2) looking furtively at my Queen. He seemed already to be regretting not having taken her. I moved my black bishop to g5 (KKt5) and said:

'Mate!'

Even those who had foreseen the outcome had not expected it to be so quick.

'So it is!' said my opponent, 'and there was I, thinking it was only check.'

I'd given him and the experts every chance of looking for a non-existent way out. The trap was not my own invention. It was already well known in the last century, and since then, every variant had been analysed through and through, by hundreds of chess players.

'Mate! Nothing to be done!' said my opponent.

He resolutely scooped up his pieces and pushed them over to my side of the board. Opinions about the game were divided. Some reckoned it would have been better to take the knight, other went on insisting it should have been the Queen. The man with the stomach said nothing; thirsting for revenge, he was already setting up the pieces.

'Maybe you've had enough?' I asked.

'What the hell . . . enough!' he said, determinedly. 'You won that one, now let me retrieve my losses.'

I couldn't have wished for anything better. I'd won this game whilst giving the impression that I'd won by luck—almost, you might say, by bluffing.

'Well, let's have another then,' I said, setting up the black.

The game began with the bold move of the King's pawn. I was in no hurry to reply. I waited. My opponent showed increasing impatience. Finally he said:

'Your move, maestro.'

'I beg your pardon,' Sashka said politely. 'I don't want to seem impertinent, but it was I who talked my friend into playing, and I'm responsible for his tournament form. . . .'

'In short . . . money down first?'

'If you'd be so good.'

My opponent's quickness was quite disarming. He reached into his hip pocket and, while he was getting out his money, I made my answering move, sacrificing my pawn. It was taken at once; he had to put his wallet down to do it. I moved my King. This move threw the experts into confusion. One of them decided that I must have mixed up the pieces.

'That's the *King*!' he remarked.

I was half-lying on my side, trickling sand from one hand to the other, anticipating the rising storm. The know-alls could already see the check with the Queen, which was too good to miss.

'Don't flap!' said the man with the stomach, although no one besides himself and the experts was dreaming of it. With unexpected swiftness he bent over and moved his Queen with a bang.

'Check!' he said, as though the mate was already in his pocket. I interposed with the King's pawn, and had hardly let go of it, when it was seized.

'Check again!' My opponent supposed he'd lost the first game through unnecessary caution, so now he was grabbing pawns and muttering: 'Pawns don't grow on trees either!'

He felt he was already the victor, and was again tossing off bits of chess-amateur jargon.

'Another little checklet . . . and again another checklet!' he said, pursuing my King. His chatter got on my nerves.

'You said yourself, check isn't the end of everything,' I said.

'You get on with it, move!'

184

I moved, and with each move threw the experts into ever greater confusion. How could they know that I'd spent hours on this gambit, analysing all the variations. But chess is chess, and in chess it's impossible to foresee everything. There was a moment when the outcome of the game hung by a thread. I managed to avoid mate by exchanging white bishops. Finally my King, protected by the rook and the black bishop, reached his destined square. The white Queen loomed, solitary in the middle of the board, bereft of support. This is the point of gambit. Repulsing the white Queen's attack, and sacrificing pawns, black brought all his pieces into action. From being the hunter the white Queen became the prey and quickly fell into the trap. The game ended before my opponent could taste the raptures of an anticipated victory. He took the Mate as an unexpected and malicious blow of fate, and without asking if I agreed, announced:

'We'll play a third one, to decide.'

'That's enough. Chess isn't cards,' I said.

'All right, all right, but let's have another,' he said, reaching into his pocket.

If it hadn't been for Shashka I'd never have played that third game. Sashka was looking at me threateningly, and I didn't want trouble. I played, but I was furious. Instead of bathing with Inka and lying on the sand, I had to be deafened by the screams of the children, and the wailing of the mothers, and watch this great stomach quivering before my eyes. My opponent considered for a long time which tactics to use, and decided that the least dangerous would be to repeat my moves. There was no point in making matters worse by sacrificing pieces. Now he didn't take any of mine even if I'd missed something. If I'd wanted to lose the game to him, I doubt if I could have, he'd been so scared by the two previous ones. He studied each move for ages, but this didn't make him play any more intelligently. The game dragged boringly on. Fortunately, everything comes to an end sooner or later. When I got up it was as if a mountain had been lifted from my shoulders.

Sashka was consoling my opponent and giving him change from a thirty note.

'I think you were just tired,' he said. 'You played several games before, whereas he was as fresh as a cucumber!'

6

·•◄ ►(3·•·

A man in glasses came up to me. He was a head taller than me, and every bit as thin as Sashka.

'Let's have a game,' he said, adding quickly, as if embarrassed, 'on the same terms, of course.'

'It's hot, I want to swim.'

He stood in front of me, thin and tall, and I could see his piercing, light-blue eyes behind his glasses.

'That's very natural on the beach,' he answered.

I don't know if he'd been amongst the know-alls whilst I was playing, but I was sure he hadn't said a word. I would have known his voice, muffled and thin. We were talking quietly, but Sashka heard us all the same. The rustle of the notes had roused his money-grubbing instincts.

'Why shouldn't you have another game?' he asked. 'You were playing with someone who was tired. Have a game with a fresh opponent. Why don't you do what you're asked!' I gave Sashka a long look, but it was useless, he deliberately avoided my eyes. 'Wait, don't put the set away yet,' said Sashka, gently shoving me towards the board.

'Why force him?' said the man in glasses.

'No, no, it's all right . . . it's just his modesty,' answered Sashka.

I sat down by the board, deciding to make mincemeat of Sashka afterwards. Why did I agree to play? I suppose out of vanity. I enjoyed the deference of the know-alls, and the interest in my play shown by the man in glasses. He sat down,

187

his wide, bony shoulders poised over the board between his long, doubled up legs. When we drew for colours, I got white again. I didn't really want to play, and I made my first few moves without any definite plan. When I forced myself to analyse the state of play, I discovered that my position was turning out to be very much like that of my previous opponent in the first game. Only instead of the King's knight, black was pinning the Queen's knight. To suggest sacrificing the Queen at this moment was risky or as chess players say 'incorrect'. Instead of my Queen, my opponent could take my knight, and leave me without pieces. I looked at him, as my previous opponent, when in the same position, had looked at me. The man in glasses was sitting, his head bent over the board, his big hands hanging between his knees. I'd still not decided whether to sacrifice the piece, but my hand was already taking the King's pawn from the board and putting the knight in its place. The man in glasses raised his head. For a second I saw the penetrating look in the light-blue eyes with their black pupils, and knew at once that he had seen and understood everything, as I had.

He raised his hand, and of course, took the knight. How was it I hadn't guessed at once, if only from his handling of the pieces, and the concentrated and intelligent way he looked at the board, that I was faced by an experienced and accomplished player. I had to save the game somehow. I began to play with all my might, as I hadn't played in years. I managed to castle on the Queen's side, to open a file on the King's side, and make a strong attack on the black King. But just at that moment I saw that I hadn't enough pieces left for a decisive blow. I made a few more moves, almost mechanically, but even the experts knew; the battle was over. A few still kept their belief in me, but the majority mercilessly went over to my opponent's side. Someone said:

'Now's the time to pocket the King.'

I wasn't thinking of the lost wager. I somehow, suddenly

felt indifferent as to whether I lost or, by some miracle, won. I didn't even know what I was playing for. What did I need more money for if Inka was going away before we could spend even what we had? How could I waste so much time when there was so little left? Instead of moving again, I knocked the King over, a sign that I acknowledged defeat. Beside me, Sashka was rustling the notes, selecting the more tattered ones. The man in the glasses pushed his hand aside and said:

'D'you want a return game?'

'No!' I got up and went out from under the awning. After the shade, the sunlight and the glare of the water were blinding. I looked back. Sashka and the man in glasses came up to me. They looked to me like two skeletons—Sashka waving his hands about and saying maliciously:

'Does your father own the Azov-Black Sea Bank?'

'I haven't got a father. He died ten years ago.'

'Too late for condolences!' said Sashka. 'How d'you like that! He doesn't want to take the money!'

'Why not?'

'Let's introduce ourselves—it's easier—my name's Igor.'

'Alexander, Sashka to my friends.'

'Let's choose something in between . . . Shura. And you're Volodya, so now we know each other.'

'You yourself said the game was to be on the same terms as before. So—you take the money,' I said.

'Let's forget about it. True, chess does bring me in some income, but by rather different means.'

'You don't approve?'

'Well . . . not particularly. I expect you have your reasons.'

'What reasons d'you suppose? We just need pocket-money!' I said.

'That's a reason too. But you play pretty well for a First Category player.'

189

'I'm Second Category.' Sashka gave me a dig in the ribs. 'Oh stow it!' I said.

Igor laughed.

'It's only a formality. You were pressing me quite hard even without pieces; did you guess I was playing a special variant of that opening?'

'I did, but too late. I simply didn't reckon who I was playing with, and I wanted to win the game as quickly as possible.'

We walked slowly, stopping from time to time; Igor and I in front, Sashka behind.

'Did you find that trap for yourself?'

'No. In Razin's *Openings and Traps*.'

'Well, well! It's a small world!' said Igor, and laughed. 'If that's how it is, let's go over to my wife, and I'll give you a present.'

Under a blue umbrella, a woman was lying on a Turkish towel, reading. Igor led us up to her.

'What ages you've been!' she said. 'It must be time for us to go.'

'We'll go in a minute. But first, Zoya, I'd like to introduce you to some nice youngsters.'

I shook her hand, it was frail with long and astonishingly supple fingers. I was struck by the look of suffering in her big, grey eyes. She laid the book down on the towel as she shook hands with us and I read the title: '*Stories* by I. Babel.'

'What's that old boy really after? All he thinks about is his horse, and bashing someone on the snout, and having a vodka,' said Sashka. He was hinting he knew all about the writer of the book the woman was reading. Zoya smiled, but the look in her eyes was unchanged.

'A marvellous writer,' she said. 'When you read him, your own sorrows don't seem so big. D'you remember *Tale of my Dovecote*?'

'Of course I do! And Guy de Maupassant! D'you remember . . . "and I looked at life, as at a meadow in May where women and horses wander about . . ." It's absolutely fantastic!'

Igor turned and handed me a book. It was *Openings and Traps* by I. Razin. I looked at him, then at the book again, and blushed. I opened it, and written obliquely across the title page were the words:

'You're right, Volodya! Chess is not cards. If you always remember this, you may turn into a good player—Teacher of Mathematics, Leningrad University, and Unsuccessful chessplayer, I. Razin.'

As I read the dedication, Igor said:

'I had a copy with me by chance. I was thinking of bringing it up to date for the new edition in my spare time, so forgive my marginal notes.'

I never did become a good chess player. Nor were you, Igor, a great figure in the chess world. That's not what mattered. You turned out to be a real human being. And at the time we met again in Leningrad, to go on being a real human being was not so easy.

Vitka came up to us.

'Where on earth have you been? Shall we go and have some ice-cream? Inka's asking.' Vitka kept looking at us, and then at Igor, not quite gathering what terms we were on.

'Igor . . .' I hesitated using his first name, 'come and join us, and Zoya too. We'll introduce you to the rest of our lot. We've got a yacht. We can go to the islands.'

'Thanks, Volodya, but our little boy's in the sanatorium; there's a nasty thing called tuberculosis of the bone. Another time. We come to the beach every morning.'

'We'll come and find you tomorrow then.'

'Goodbye boys!'

As we left them I looked back. Igor, squatting down, was helping Zoya gather up the beach things. Sashka snatched the book from me and read the inscription, Vitka looking over his shoulder.

'I'm telling you . . . to be beaten by a chap like that is no disgrace at all.'

'You lost?' asked Vitka.

'Who's lost? Him? Just look at this!' Sashka took the crumpled notes from his pocket. 'I wish to goodness we could lose like this every day! In fact it's a good thing you did lose one game, or everybody'd be afraid of playing with you tomorrow.'

'I'm not going to play tomorrow, nor the day after! In fact, I'm not playing for money again!'

'What are you shouting at me for? Do I force you to play? Do I? D'you think I *like* running up and down the beach finding you opponents? You think I *like* squeezing money out of them?'

It wasn't I who was shouting, it was Sashka. He, too, was probably fed up with our gambling racket. But he manfully carried his cross in the name of the financial good of all. And I'd imagined he'd enjoyed extorting money from my opponents.

When we joined the girls Sashka gave Inka the book, held open, with the money scattered on it.

'Tell this smart guy that Belov and Co's Gambling Firm has gone into liquidation.'

Everyone took this as one of Sashka's usual jokes. The girls were dressed and sitting in the shade of the awning. Inka pushed the money off onto her lap and read the inscription, Katya and Zhenya moved over to her to read it too.

'Volodya, where is this Razin? I want to look at him. Come on, show us, where is he?' said Inka.

'It's Inka's lucky day for celebrities!' said Zhenya.

'It's true, it's true, I got to know John Danker! Don't you believe me? You ask *them*!'

I could believe it only too easily. I could just see Inka getting to know the King of the Hawaian Guitar, and Vitka looking on, as he was now, with a silly, satisfied grin on his face! There's a real friend for you, I *don't* think! And all that while Sashka and I extracting money from people by the sweat of our brow! Vitka intercepted my look and the smile was wiped from his face.

'You needn't boast about it,' he said. 'He's got friends like you all over the beach!' At least Vitka's conscience was beginning to prick him. But Katya and Zhenya were looking at me and laughing.

I sat down on the sand and started undressing.

'And the ice-creams?' asked Inka.

'Go and get them yourselves, you've got the money.'

Sashka was undressing, too. I heard him say to Katya:

'And you don't need to look at me so pathetically. I'll talk to you later!'

I went into the water at the same time as Sashka, but a bit away from him. I didn't look back once at Inka.

'We'll wait for you at the exit,' shouted Vitka.

Avoiding the bathers, I waded till the water was up to my chest and I reached the first 'reef' (as they call these sandbanks about forty feet from the beach). Beyond it, there were fewer people, and I started swimming. When I passed the second one, where no one other than the locals ever went, I looked back. Sashka was nowhere to be seen; I was alone. The water was warm, and the sun burnt my shoulders, and all I could see in front of me was the water, and the sky, whitish above it. I dived, my eyes open. Deep down below me, shifting shadows closed in on me. With every stroke of my arms and legs I was going away from the warmth and light, down into the cold depths. I don't know how many metres of water were pressing in on me from above, but my arms felt the resilient power of those depths trying to force me back, while I was battling with it, with short, rapid strokes. There mightn't be enough air in my lungs to get back up to the surface. I considered this absolutely calmly; but I did get a fright when I was finally forced back, and saw the dim transparency of the light far above me. I was being thrust violently up to meet it, but still, it seemed to me, so slowly, that my heart must burst before I reached the surface.

I shot up, head and shoulders out of the water, gulping air with my open mouth, and at once began to sink again. Then I turned and lay on my back, and was rocked gently by the barely visible swell, the hot sun warming my shivering body.

Even today I don't really know what happened to me. But only when I turned back and saw the flat beach and the tiny figures on it, did I experience the utter loneliness, and my terror of it.

I don't suppose I'd been in the sea very long in fact, because when I reached the shore, Sashka still wasn't dressed. He was pulling on his trousers, while Katya stood by him, holding his shirt. I came up to him and, my back to him, said:

'I say . . . I was wrong.'

Sashka understood, though Katya of course didn't.

I just stood, my teeth chattering with cold, while I tried with all my might to stop them. Sashka gave me a quick look.

'What happened?' he asked.

'I don't know. I dived down, and I very nearly stayed there. It's pretty cold down there.'

For some reason Sashka looked at me very hard then said, 'You idiot!' then, as if he'd had another thought, added: 'you bloody great fool! By the way, here's a rare sight! A King without trousers! Have a look!'

A stocky man in black swimming trunks and a white belt was standing by the water's edge, talking to a woman and laughing. He had very white teeth, harsh lines at the corners of his mouth, and glossy, jet black hair. He seemed to me to be very young. Younger than on the posters.

'Oh to hell with him!' I said, and sat down on the sand.

'Get dressed, they're waiting for us,' said Katya.

Vitka waved to us from the Promenade wall.

'Wait for me in the pavilion. I'll get warm first, then I'll come.'

'Let's go. Leave him to get warm,' said Sashka.

I stretched out on the hot sand, and as I stopped shivering, felt the bitter chill of the depths gradually leaving my body. Then I sat up and looked at the woman John Danker had been talking to. She was standing quite close to me now. I had never seen such beautiful women before, probably because I just hadn't noticed them. Now I was discovering that looking at beautiful women was very interesting. I watched her, while she stood facing the sea, where, beyond the first 'reef', bobbed the head of the King of the Hawaian Guitar.

A handful of sand stung me in the face.

'That'll teach you to look!'

I turned my head. Inka was trickling sand from one hand to the other.

'She's not bathing because she's all made up,' she said.

Then Inka told me to wash the sand off and get dressed, but I said I couldn't even look at water, and began brushing it off with my hands, while she helped. As I was dressing, John Danker passed close by us. He was walking towards the woman, but looking at Inka and smiling. He didn't look so young near to. He had bags under his eyes, and the whites were yellowish, like an old man's. Inka hid behind me, but I noticed she was smiling too, only now I didn't care a damn! We went off, Inka put her hand on my shoulder, trying to keep in step.

'I know why you're mad at me,' she said. 'Because I didn't wait for you. I did it on purpose. D'you realise now how awful it'll be when I'm gone? Do you?'

This time Inka had got it wrong. But I didn't say anything.

What I needed from Inka was very little and very much. I constantly needed to feel that she loved me; so long as I did, I couldn't be mad at her.

We went into the pavilion. Almost all the little tables were free. Only fools like us could want to eat ice-cream before dinner. Our lot had already nearly finished theirs. I think they'd been talking about us, because when we arrived, they stopped. Inka sat down at the little marble-topped table, and pulled the metal cup of ice-cream on its long thin stem towards her.

'How much does this hold?' she asked. Sashka answered: 'Two hundred grammes.'

'Is that all?'

'Listen Inka. Vitka's got a soft heart. That's his bad luck. Whether you go or not doesn't depend on us.'

Inka pricked up her ears, she was licking the ice-cream off her spoon with the tip of her tongue.

'And supposing I just don't go? . . . Just supposing. . . ! Well, what can they do to me? I'm an irresponsible person, let them re-educate me! But meanwhile I don't go, and that's that!'

'What are you looking at me like that for?' Sashka asked Vitka, who was sitting looking at him, red-faced and angry. 'So much for your handiwork! Inka! You're a sensible girl. You're the most intelligent girl I know. You're as intelligent as Vitka. Work it out for yourself; what does "they" mean? "They" are simply *us*. We'll be gone, but you've got to live with the kids for another two years. They'd never forgive you, and *we'd* never have forgiven you either.'

'Vitka, *you* say something! Why don't you open your mouth?' Vitka was Inka's last hope. I suppose, while Sashka and I weren't there, she'd been trying to convince him that she needn't go.

'As a rule, Sashka talks a lot of rubbish. But he's right that you'll have to go,' said Vitka.

'Inka, you know the kids don't like you as it is. It's no use looking for an ally in Vitka,' said Zhenya. No one had asked her, but Zhenya was speaking the truth. I could never understand why they didn't like Inka at school, when I liked her so much.

'What've I done to them? What've I done to them? Why don't they like me?' Inka was rubbing her eyes with her fists. 'Don't I have the right to wear pretty clothes? Come on, tell me! Am I a clothes maniac? Am I?'

Inka did love new clothes, but she certainly wasn't a clothes maniac. She would calmly help us tar the yacht in her most expensive frock, not caring what happened to it, and then wear an old one patiently until a new one was made for her. She felt no different whether she was in an old frock or a new one.

Now after many years, I can understand; it had nothing to do with frocks. Inka was unpopular because she was different from the rest of us. What mattered to her were her own desires, and these didn't very often coincide with what life was demanding from us. Put bluntly, Inka was unpopular because she was what she was.

'I agree with what Sashka says. I told Inka so before. But I don't understand Zhenya. If Inka can't rely on all of us as friends and allies, then neither can I!' I said.

'You didn't get me right,' said Zhenya.

'Volodya, stop making mountains out of molehills!' said Vitka.

'Sh!' Sashka raised his hand. 'Inka's got to go. It was a unanimous vote. Now let's see what we lose by it. This evening we're going to the Spa Hall, Inka's departure won't prevent that. In three days time we'll be celebrating leaving school at the Floating Restaurant. Inka will be there with us too. That leaves only the Islands. Well I ask you, what difference does it make if we go to the Islands, or to the Point? We'll help Inka during the day, get her stint done in two days, and take her into town. We can't allow you not to go, but who's to prevent us from helping you?'

'Just let 'em try!' said Vitka.

I envied Sashka. It wasn't as if he'd suggested anything extraordinary, but Inka seemed to have calmed down. I pushed my ice-cream cup towards hers, and scooped some from mine into it.

'You honestly don't want it?' she asked. Her eyelashes were still wet with tears, but she was smiling already. What I think she liked best about Sashka's suggestion was that, this time too, she was going to be different from everyone else.

We went out into the street, and all saw Inka to her door. We stood about discussing where we should meet in the evening. Then Inka asked me in to have dinner. It wasn't ready, so I sat down on the divan and went to sleep. I don't myself know how it happened. When I woke up, Inka said she'd been to sleep too. It turned out we'd been sleeping in the same room, and for some reason this gave me a strange feeling. Inka and I had our dinner together in the kitchen, her father had already eaten and gone to the aerodrome. Her mother sat with us and watched us eat.

'After dinner we'll go and buy you a shirt. And don't argue! I've a right to give you a shirt for your birthday, if I want to. As you won't be here on your birthday. I'll give it you now, it makes no odds!' said Inka.

I wasn't arguing! Particularly as Inka's mother said:

'Quite right! You'll just have to do without that extra pair of shoes. You'll know another time how not to spoil a shirt!'

Inka's mother didn't trust her, and came with us to buy the shirt. It seemed unnecessary; buying a shirt alone with Inka would have been more interesting.

7

———•◦⟨⟩◦•———

The name Spa Hall is self-explanatory, and as our town was a Spa, we had a Spa Hall. An ordinary hall has walls, floor and ceiling, but instead of walls our Spa Hall had a man-high wooden paling, its floor was the sea sand, and above our heads arched the milky sky with its pale stars. Of course the sky wasn't always milky, nor the stars pale. When the earthly day-light faded, the sky turned velvety-black and the stars twinkled. I can't say anything about the stage, it was like that of any ordinary hall. This structure stood near the sea, in a park full of flowers, poplars, and acacias, where decorative palms grew almost as tall as they did in their own country. And the sea on those warm, summer evenings was like the sea in the lands where palm trees grow. You might say—but that's an ordinary, outdoor summer stage! It may be to some people, but in our town it was the Spa Hall.

The light from the stage fell onto the front rows. I could feel the darkness at my back. You can't of course actually feel half-darkness at your back—not if you're in a normal state, which I wasn't. In front of me was the lighted stage, and behind me, the half-dark. And I not only felt it, I heard it! It was full of breathing, faint noises and movement. There was the gritty sound of sand under our feet, and the air rustled. (It has long ago been found that the air consists of particles of matter, so why shouldn't it rustle?) I felt wonder-ful! I was wearing a blue silk shirt, and Inka was sitting beside me. Those who have never worn silk shirts next to their skin can have no idea what it means. It felt as though a cool gentle hand was stroking my bare shoulders.

On the stage, a short plump man was singing. Everything about him shone, his patent leather shoes, his cheeks and his bald patch. He rose on tiptoe trying to persuade us all that he was like a weathercock, changing his women as often as he changed his gloves. He sang the duke's final aria with special abandon. . . .

'. . . bu-u-t I am the first to decei-i-ive them . . .' he sang with a soft honeyed *ralentando*.

It took a bit of believing! He got some applause, not very loud, but applause all the same. I clapped too, it would have been embarrassing not to. Whenever the clapping began to die down he came bouncing out onto the stage, as though the sight of him must make everyone happy. It's not nice offending someone, so we had to start clapping again.

We were sitting in the second row. We had never sat so near the front before. We usually bought standing-room tickets, and stood in the gangway, crowded up against the paling. It was easier for us in the gangway, there at least, nobody paid any attention to us. But here, we were noticed as soon as we came in. We took our seats about a quarter of an hour before the concert began, and this was our mistake. I think it was Vitka's black eye that aroused our neighbours' darkest suspicions. The concert was late starting, and we had to kill time somehow.

In front of me sat a woman, her back bare to the waist. She must have wanted everyone to see what an even shade of suntan she had. She could fool anyone except us. We knew it was simply a matter of suntan-lotion. A man sat pressed close against her shoulder. His hair was smarmed down and shone glossily. He brilliantined it to stop it being blown about by the wind. That meant he had a bald patch underneath. Not a big one, but a bald patch all the same.

'You're divine today! I'm crazy about your back,' he said.

'Only today?' said the woman, turning her head away a little.

'Don't twist my words!'

Personally I think that kind of conversation's enough to make any normal person feel sick. Certainly I did. And when Vitka artlessly let out: 'My right shoe's too tight, I can't stand it!' the man looked round and said: 'Disgraceful!' Then Sashka advised:

'Take your shoe off then! Your socks are clean, I hope!'

Sashka said it on purpose. Now the man stared at him. But Sashka wasn't Vitka. People could look at him as much as they liked. He could stare anyone out, so he and the man stared at each other in silence for a long time. The man gave up first, probably his neck hurt.

'Disgraceful!' he repeated.

'Frightfully rich vocabulary!' said Sashka, and I added:

'There's logic for you! It's all right to talk about a naked back, but if a chap's shoe hurts, he has got to keep quiet!'

'Let that be a lesson to you!' said the woman with the bare back. 'You shouldn't make vulgar remarks!'

That was fair enough anyway! And there the whole matter might have ended. We hadn't started it in any case! But someone in the third row had a mean idea.

'We'll have to call the usherette and have them thrown out!'

A modest enough wish, you might say! I turned round to see who this great mind was. It was a man of the most nondescript appearance, so nondescript that I can't even remember him. I only remember a straw hat; it was the only hat in the whole Spa Hall, and it was pulled down onto his ears like a trilby.

I hadn't even opened my mouth, I only glanced at him. But even this infuriated him, and he stood up.

'Miss!' he called out loudly (how naïve of him to think he could get hold of an usherette so easily!)

Zhenya said: 'I'm going!'

Vitka tried to persuade her not to. He looked at us beseechingly.

'What's the fuss about?' asked Sashka. 'We're sitting in our lawful places!'

Someone said:

'It's our own fault. We spoil them too much!'

'Here comes the Self-Criticism,' I said, 'now everything's O.K.!'

'Leave the youngsters alone!'

I recognised the voice at once, thin and muffled. Igor was sitting in the third row, near the gangway. When I looked round, he waved to me and said:

'Good evening! Volodya.' Zoya waved too. She looked very beautiful, and seemed less sad.

'How's your little boy?'

'Thanks, Volodya, he's better today,' Igor answered.

'They've promised to take the support off in two weeks time.' I didn't know if taking off the support was a good or a bad thing, but Zoya was smiling, so I reckoned it must be good.

'Congratulations!' I said.

We were no longer taking any notice of our neighbours. In my opinion the whole fuss was because we had sat ourselves in the wrong seats. There's nothing worse than people being out of place.

'Is that your Igor?' asked Inka. 'But he's very young!' Inka was sitting, legs crossed, her elbow propped on her knee, her chin on her hand. The toe of her shoe was almost touching the vast behind of the man in front. Once it did touch it, and the man turned and stared.

'I beg your pardon,' said Inka.

The man smiled and nodded. Not of course because Inka

had politely apologised. She wasn't looking at all polite at the time. I had made a study of her expressions, what her eyes were saying was: 'I could spit in your face, not just poke you with my shoe, you'd smile just the same!' Inka simply knew her worth. Now the man began glancing round more often, pretending it was not at her. I took hold of her foot and put it down on the ground. Her ankle was warm, I could feel its warmth through the sock.

'But I was more comfortable that way!' said Inka.

'But I wasn't!'

During the concert the man looked round several more times. We paid no attention to him. We watched the conjuror Jack doing his tricks. He produced a ping-pong ball from the air, put it in one ear, and took it out of the other; he put the lighted end of a cigarette into his mouth and made the smoke come out of his ears. He did many different tricks, but somehow it was always his ears that seemed to work hardest. I liked him. When he came onto the stage he warned us right away that he was going to take us all in, it was up to us to guess how. But nobody tried much. Most of the spectators had come to the concert for John Danker.

The Compère brought out a chair from the wings. He put it down, came up stage, and stood for a long time looking at the audience, he must have been trying to think up a joke.

'John Danker!' he announced, loudly and solemnly and stepped back into the wings.

This is how you should herald the entrance of Kings. My feet began to tingle. The solitary chair stood on the stage, sharply lit by the footlights. It seemed as though stage and chair were suspended in mid-air. The warm night encircled the stage. You could hear the night-sound of the sea, not loud, but it was there if you listened carefully. The palm leaves tapped, they were hard, and as though cut out of tin. The sharp smell of stocks and gilly-flowers came in waves. The flowers in the park must have been watered not long ago. I could not remember such a velvety night in our town for a long time past. Behind me, people were clearing their throats impatiently, the sand crunching under their feet, from the back rows came an occasional clap. Their nerves were giving way! It'd better be good. I deliberately pictured this King, as I had seen him on the beach—in nothing but bathing trunks, the black ones with the white belt, true, but all the same only in trunks. And what about his smiling at Inka? I felt like spitting in his face for that alone.

Actually, I missed the entrance of the King. The air quivered with applause. In the black depths of the stage a rectangle of light was blotted out, and there was the King standing beside the chair, in black tails and a snow-white stiff shirt. In his right hand he held the black guitar inlaid with mother of pearl, the left rested on the back of the chair. He gave a hardly perceptible bow which emphasised his sternness. On stage he looked very young and handsome but I knew the man on the beach and the man on the stage were one and the same. Yet I couldn't help it, I clapped too, louder with every second. I call it herd instinct. I was in ecstasies. John Danker sat down, and the Compère immediately came up to him; he must have been waiting in the wings for just this solemn moment.

'Inka, it's him! I didn't recognise him at first!' Katya had to lean across Sashka's knees to say this.

'Who's that?' I asked Inka.

'The Compère. He had a row with John Danker on the beach. Well, not a row exactly; John Danker said something to him, and the Compère said something back, and he walked off towards the sea.'

Sashka started to get interested in what had happened on the beach too, but for other reasons. He asked what John Danker'd said and what the Compère'd answered.

'But what phrases . . . what expressions did he use? Can't you tell me?'

On the stage, the Compère was bending towards John Danker and they were whispering together. Then the Compère straightened himself, and turned to the audience.

'A Hawaian Waltz!' he announced and retired deferentially.

Again the night shook with the applause. What was there to clap about? So far, John Danker had only put his guitar on his knees. He laid it flat on them, which was interesting anyway. How can you play a guitar when it's flat on your knees? He put his left hand into his trouser pocket, brought it out again, waved it for a second in the air. He was showing everyone that he was holding a little white metal disc like the one the doctors use to get down your throat with. He grasped the neck of the guitar, his four fingers and the little disc above the strings, his thumb under the neck. Right hand poised, John Danker raised his head and looked straight in front of him, and under his long gaze the applause died out. The sound of the sea was heard again, and the gentle tapping of the palm leaves. He quickly lifted his right hand, and let it fall onto the strings.

A strangely pure and plaintive sound filled the night. I thought it was a kitten mewing somewhere. Then his right hand took on an unexpected lightness, energy and strength of movement. It rose and fell as if pecking the strings. Now it wasn't a kitten but a lusty full grown tom-cat whose highest feline notes warned his rival of the cruel laws of love. I'd never thought of cats as having such marvellous vocal potential! They simply don't know how to make the most of their possibilities. Under John Danker's hand a cat's ordinary top notes formed an exotic melody, it took shape out of the separate sounds somewhere in the air above our heads.

'How does he do it? Just tell me, how does he do it?' Inka pestered me.

How should I know. I was amazed myself. I do know now. Anyone can imitate a Hawaian Guitar. All you have to do is hold your nose and miaow any old tune. But I only found that out later. Sashka taught me.

'It's an ordinary guitar,' the man with the camouflaged bald patch said, turning round to do so. Very gallant of him—so he hadn't lost hope yet. 'The strings are raised,' he said, look-at Inka.

Inka barely glanced at him, and forgot him at once. Technicalities were the last things to interest her. The man finished his explanation looking at me. I heard him out magnanimously. It cost me nothing to be magnanimous, since Inka wasn't taking any notice of him. I was even ready to give him a little pleasure by discussing the weather in the Hawaian islands. But for some reason he turned away hurriedly. I think my eyes gave me away, they must have told him what I thought of him.

I don't remember the exact moment when my mood began to change. Everybody was having a good time. Only Vitka was truly bored. He kept wriggling his foot. He still hadn't made up his mind to take off his shoe; innate delicacy prevented it. I kept making signs to him to take it off, but his only answer was a martyr's smile and a shake of the head.

Every time the last chords of a number died away the Compère came onto the stage. He stood and waited till the applause stopped. Notes were thrown onto the stage and names of songs called out. The woman with the bare back knew the words of all the song-hits John Danker played. She called out the names of several songs, not very loudly, as she didn't have to shout from the front row. But only once did a title correspond with what the Compère announced.

'Oriental Tango!' he called, and the woman was the first to clap.

I recognised the tune—admittedly not straight away. It was the one Sashka had been humming to me yesterday on the way to Vitka's. But now the melody seemed made up of

206

a variety of unusual sounds, and I liked it better. It somehow seemed to fit in with the image of our town.

> The people there are shy and wise
> And the sky there's like blue glass . . .

Probably, to an outsider, smiling ironically while listening with rapt attention looks pretty silly. But I wasn't looking at myself from outside.

Inka had been on her best behaviour all through the concert. She was still sitting with her legs crossed; I just kept an eye on the toe of her shoe, to make sure it didn't touch the wide behind of the man in front.

During the Oriental Tango I wasn't watching her. The sad, long-drawn out sound died on the air like a distant moan. Inka leapt up and started clapping. She clapped, and shouted 'Over the Pink Sea'. She leaned over the back of the bench in front, her breast almost touching the man's shoulder, and went on shouting: 'Over the Pink Sea'.

Maybe the man liked feeling Inka's breast on his shoulder, but this I could not allow. I half got up.

'Excuse me!' I said to the man, as I bent over him, and taking Inka's arm, made her sit down. Everything that happened afterwards may have been pure coincidence; masses of people were asking for the same song.

The Compère announced:

'Over the Pink Sea!' And as he said it, John Danker looked in our direction. Whoever he was looking at, it wasn't me!

By then I was in a bad mood, though just when it had started I don't remember. I no longer heard anything. I just looked at Inka. She was sitting absolutely still, her chin cupped in her hand, the toe of her shoe moving in time to the melody. It made no odds to me now whether it touched the man's big behind or not. I didn't care about this thickly-brilliantined smart-alec. He simply didn't exist for me.

John Danker appeared again, played, went off, and was

again called back. Looking a little tired and very handsome, he spread his hands in a weary gesture and shook his head. The Compère was already standing at the front of the stage waiting to announce the end.

'The Grove. . . !' screamed Inka, her voice ringing with excitement.

There could not be the slightest doubt: John Danker must have heard Inka's voice above all the others. He looked our way and smiled. He didn't even nod to the Compère. He just sat down and started playing. The woman in front looked round, stared hard at Inka, then gave me a glance, and I noticed a faint smile at the corners of her mouth. Inka didn't notice anything. She was singing softly:

'Timorously sensitive to every sound
Is the Grove in its July slumber.
Quietly joking, you then stretched out
Your tender hand to me.

But that hot night's intoxication
And your slender childish grace,
I know I can never forget. . . .'

I doubt if Inka attached any real significance to the words of this trivial song, even I paid no attention to them. As to what John Danker was thinking as he played the melody, I had no means of knowing. Once again he was applauded, and again he bowed and made the weary gesture with his hands, and a lock of his black hair fell across his dusky forehead.

I didn't know what sort of a person I really was—good or bad. People told me I was good, and I believed them. It was only when I met brilliant or specially gifted people, that I began to suspect everyone was wrong about me, and that I alone knew how ordinary I was. What on earth could Inka love me for when she could see brilliant people around, such as John Danker, for instance. Without going into details: his success merely confirmed his genuine talent.

From the back rows people came running down the gangways towards the stage, we too had done this on other occasions, but now we had nowhere to run to. In the front rows, you clapped sitting down. The smartly dressed and well-washed men and women in front knew what they were worth. Katya and Sashka were saying something—I didn't hear what it was. They were standing up, clapping and shouting, and everyone was looking at them. Zhenya and Vitka were standing up too, although Zhenya said she didn't care for such frivolous shows. Only Inka sat. She sat clapping and looking at the stage. Then she got up. I put my hand on her shoulder. She looked round. She seemed not to see me, then suddenly, she did. Her eyes were like a guilty dog's, and I couldn't bear to look at them. I was sweating, my silk shirt sticking to my shoulder blades. There must have been damp patches showing on it already. I didn't know what to do or how to behave. When Sashka said, 'Say what you like, but he really is a King!' I shouted: 'And you're an idiot!' And when the man in the third row, the one who had kept on his straw hat said, 'Pure caterwauling!' I began clapping frenziedly.

8

When we came out into the park, Katya and Zhenya ran to the back of the stage to see the artists leaving. They called Inka, but she didn't go. She stood beside me. We stood together in the half-dark, not far from where the two avenues crossed. I leant back against an old acacia and lit a cigarette. When I struck the match Inka said:

'Give them to me for a minute.' She lit two matches together, and when they'd burned half-way, she licked her fingers and took hold of the burnt ends. Now the other halves were burning. Inka watched them burn out, and their light was reflected in her eyes.

'See? We'll always be together. See?' she said.

She held the matches up to my face. They were charred and interlaced. She threw them away and laughed.

'Let's go and see the artists, shall we?' she said.

In the avenue Sashka and Vitka were talking to Pavel Baulin. People were coming out of the auditorium and walking past us to the intersection of the avenues. A woman was saying:

'He's just terribly good-looking. He's got a classical profile.'

Inka turned her head slightly. Then she looked at me.

'Does smoking make you feel awful?' she asked. 'Let me have a try on the way home.'

Katya and Zhenya came up to where the avenues crossed.

'Vitka, where's Inka?' shouted Zhenya.

Vitka looked round, but from where he was standing under the light, he couldn't see us in the darkness.

'She was here somewhere with Volodya,' he said.

'I must go to them. . . . It's awkward . . .' I said, and crossed the avenue.

'Where's Inka? Zhenya's looking for her,' said Vitka.

'She's coming now.' As she came up, Inka looked hard at Pavel.

'Now I'm all mixed up! Let's get it straight, Professors. Those two are Sashka's and Vitka's . . . so this one's yours?'

'Anything more you'd like to know?'

'Not bad little dames! Hasn't anyone been after them yet? You ought to get cracking with the redhead anyway . . . it's in her eyes! And the little blonde too. Blondes are always easy. But the dark one's a bit of an acquired taste . . . flat as a board!'

'Pasha, would you talk about your sister that way?' asked Sashka, and his nose began to grow.

'Now he's all upset! I was just giving you a bit of advice —as I would my very best pals!'

'Take your words back!' said Vitka.

'Look at that! Now you're getting shirty too! Let's get it quite straight—which words am I to take back! I used quite a lot of words! If you mean "best pal" . . . I'll take that back!'

'I'm counting three! One . . .' said Vitka.

Pavel stepped back to the clipped pomegranate bushes. He slowly doubled up his fists, and his head went down between his shoulders.

'Out of my bloody way, you Professors! . . .' he said.

Those who were coming out of the Spa Hall, or sauntering through the park stopped talking as they walked past, and looked at us. Pavel had his back to the bushes, while we stood in a semi-circle round him.

'Two . . .' said Vitka.

Pavel took a half step nearer the bushes, watching us narrowly, his eyes sharp and clear. I looked at his fists, and everything went dark before my eyes. Somehow or other what Pavel had said hadn't seemed offensive to me, and I didn't in the least want to fight him. But a fight was unavoidable, and the best thing was not to look at his fists. I knew from experience before a fight, that, you should never think of the consequences.

'I don't really feel like fighting you. I'll take back the words. You can choose which ones!' said Pavel.

Vitka was still looking at him hard. I think what'd hurt him most was Pavel's describing Zhenya as 'flat as a board'. And then there was his shoe. When your shoes hurt, it doesn't take much to touch things off.

To be on the safe side, I put my arm round Vitka's shoulder, and made a sign to Sashka that it was time we were getting along.

'Pasha, when you talk about women you ought to keep it pure. Those aren't my words, they're Gorky's,' said Sashka.

We were walking away down the avenue, when two fellows we didn't know came up to Pavel. One asked:

'Where on earth did you get to?'

'I've met some chaps I know. We were having a few words. . . .'

'What? *That* lot? Sling 'em out by the neck!'

Vitka looked round.

'We can give you some of your own back!' he shouted.

'Look at that! Trying to tell us where we get off,' said Sashka.

We found the girls at the park gates, they were talking with Igor and Zoya. Zhenya saw us and said:

'Finished nattering at last, have you?'

Vitka bent to flick an imaginary speck of dust from his spotless trousers. He was always shy with people he didn't know well.

Igor said to me:

'Seems it's a happy coincidence! We've met in your town, and you're going to live in mine. You will think Leningrad gloomy at first, whereas I get tired of your sun!'

So that was it. Inka must have been chattering to them about Leningrad. How nice it would have been to know, all the same, where we really were going!

'And there's not enough sun for me,' said Zoya. 'I miss it awfully. It's always raining in Leningrad. . . . White nights and rain!'

Igor and Zoya were staying a block away from the Spa Hall, and we saw them to their door. We knew this small house at the back of the courtyard very well. Vitka had discovered it three years ago, and Zhenya's father had kept the address in his notebook ever since. Of course, none of us mentioned this in front of Igor. Zhenya didn't like strangers being told about her father's profession; as though the worst thing about him was his job! Zhenya and Vitka weren't with us, they'd dropped behind somewhere, but all the same, we didn't tell Igor how we came to know his house. We went back to the corner and Zhenya and Vitka joined us. Vitka was walking barefoot, his shoes sticking out of his trouser pockets. Pavel and his friends were standing by the Spa Hall palings; presumably waiting to see who they could pick up. People were still coming out of the park, walking across the lighted asphalt, and disappearing into the darkness under the trees. We turned into Third Longitude Street, only the first half was lit by the Spa Hall lights. The girls were in front. We walked fast, and when someone said 'Where are we rushing to like this?' we slowed down, but gradually we speeded up again. I think it was Sashka who first said: 'Where are we rushing to?' After that we all kept repeating it, the girls as well. I can't have been the only one to want to be alone with his girl as soon as possible.

Walls lined the road on either side. We didn't see them, we

only saw the occasional lights of the sanatoria between the trees. In places where the trees stood back from the walls, the road was a little lighter. Sashka was telling some story of how, as a small boy, he'd made himself sick on sugared almonds.

'For five years I couldn't even look at a sugared almond!' he said.

'And I'm supposed to believe that?' I said.

'I can hardly believe it myself, now.'

'Shut up!' said Zhenya.

Inka bobbed up in front of me, as though she'd sprouted out of the ground. I didn't actually see her, I just felt her beside me. Katya and Zhenya were there too.

'Didn't you hear anything?' asked Katya.

'What should we have heard?'

'A woman screamed,' said Zhenya.

'Sure you didn't imagine it?'

'It was Zhenya heard it first, we were listening to Sashka. And then we all heard it. Out on the wastelands—a woman screaming,' said Inka.

All we could see of one another was our eyes, gleaming in the darkness.

'Cheerful business!' said Sashka.

'Girls, you go back to the Spa Hall and wait for us,' I said.

'We can wait for you here, or go as far as the corner, it's light there,' said Inka.

The road ended where it dropped away suddenly into the darkness of the wastelands. At the end an electric bulb burned on either side. The white leaves of the trees cast black shadows on the asphalt. A tram passed us, coming from the station and a narrow strip of light showed up the bushes. Some chap or other came round the corner, stood for a moment looking about him, and went back, as if someone had called him. Then Styopik came from the same corner with others behind him. He had a cigarette in his mouth, and Mishka Shkura gave him a light. Styopik was coming in our direction. In the dark, someone—Katya, I think—gave a sob:

'I'll give you a leg up. Come on! Why are you trembling like that?' said Sashka.

On the other side of the fence, there was a crash in the bushes as she landed.

'Run to the sanatorium!' said Vitka.

'Inka!' I called softly, my hand groping in the darkness, then suddenly heard her shoes on the asphalt. Inka was running. Someone else ran out from the corner, but stopped. Now we couldn't see anyone. All we heard was the sound of feet, and a whistle. Then everything went quiet. It was about a couple of hundred yards to the corner. We stood, our backs pressed to the wall, its stones cold and rough. How long does it take to run two hundred yards?

'Say what you like, but John Danker really is a King!' said Sashka.

'Sashka, you've said that already,' I answered.

'Have I?' asked Sashka, and said no more.

None of us spoke, we were listening, then all of a sudden we heard the sound of many feet. They came nearer quickly, then stopped in the road in front of us. A torch-beam fell on the wall, then onto Vitka's face.

'Hi! Vitka, boy,' said Mishka Shkura.

'Who's that?' I recognised Styopik's boyish voice.

'One of ours, from the Siltings,' answered Mishka Shkura. The torch's beam moved on to Sashka.

'The Yid?' asked Styopik.

Sashka said nothing, and all the time I was thinking, 'If only I'd seen Styopik's knife that time at the cinema, he wouldn't be here now.'

'Inka! Styopik has a knife!' I yelled. The light blinded me.

'What knife? Who are you shouting to?' asked Styopik. Then snapped at someone else, his voice rising: 'Stick up your shiv! you bastard!'

I shielded my eyes with my hands. The light went out. I dodged and the air whistled past my face, Sashka gave a muffled scream on my left. I hit someone. Sashka came hurtling backwards at me, lurched forward again, and was again thrown back, hitting the wall beside me. Several of them set on him at once. I grabbed someone's hair in the darkness and pulled. Then I was dragging and twisting someone's arm, and close beside me I could hear Sashka's choking breaths. Then stars splashed across my face. I don't remember what came first—the blow or the stars. Nor do I remember falling, only the sharp, nauseous smell of sweat and someone's fancy shoe. I caught hold of it, and tried to push it away from my face . . .

Then I saw stars again. I seemed to be lying at the bottom of somewhere, and there were stars and voices on the surface, and water surging in my ears and rocking me. Someone was asking in a tearful voice:

'Why did you hit him?'

'Don't come from behind, you fucking bastard!'

Where could Pavel have sprung from? But it was Pavel who'd said 'bastard'. I heard a blow, then another, and another, and the crash of bodies falling. I was lying in the road, and the asphalt was very cold. My hand felt the curb of the pavement, and I tried to get up, but I fell back again. But I did get up and, reeling across the pavement, propped my elbows on the wall.

It was getting lighter. The moon must have been rising, because I could see the edge of the wall, and below it the darkness. I remembered the fancy shoe near my face; I wanted to push it away, but my hand was very heavy; I could hardly lift it and as I dropped it I hit someone.

'Volodya! It's me!'

Where had Inka come from? But I couldn't be bothered about her now, nor anyone else. I felt sick from the stench of sweating feet. Inka held me round the shoulders, and my feet scrabbled against the wall. I felt like pitching over it, I was vomiting so much.

People were talking in the road. I wasn't retching any more now, but I still couldn't think straight.

'Pasha! They're trying to fix me! I can't talk to you about it now, but we'll meet,' said Styopik.

'Fine!' answered Pavel. 'And I'll get even with you about Nyura Pereverzev at the same time. I only tumbled to it too late, or you wouldn't have got away from me then!'

Styopik laughed.

'Pasha! You're on my scent like a blood-hound! Don't do it, Pasha! I've been very jumpy recently!'

'Oh, just you bugger off! Wait till I get your whole gang sewn up!'

'So long, Pasha!'

I was standing, propped against the fence, swaying, my eyelids closing of themselves.

Then we were sitting in the square; Inka, Zhenya, and I. Vitka and Katya had taken Sashka to the Sacco and Vanzetti sanatorium; his head was gashed open. Pavel had seen us to the square. On the way, as we were skirting the wastelands, Pavel said:

'You should all have run together!'

'Why should we have to run?' I asked.

'It's the best thing to do at a moment like that. I'd have beat it for certain. Who are you to take on Styopik?'

'We couldn't all have run off. They'd have caught up with the girls!'

'You're right there! I'll say you've got guts, you Profs!'

As he said goodbye, Pavel turned to Inka.

'Let's make a pact, Redhead. If ever you think of changing boy-friends, don't forget Pavel Baulin!'

I wasn't annoyed with him. I had an awful pain in my jaw, and a front tooth was broken. Someone must have butted me on the chin. Sashka had been hit with knuckle-dusters, and I by someone's head. If I'd been hit with knuckle-dusters, my chin would have been smashed up. As it was, only my lips were cut, they were swollen and painful. It might have been a foot that hit my mouth.

Katya and Vitka came back with Sashka. He was trying to joke.

'Well, we've got our first wounds!' he said, sitting down beside me on the bench.

We sat in the square waiting for the streets to empty. We didn't want anyone to set eyes on us.

'Calling me Vitka, boy! . . . making out I'm a friend . . . the reptile!' said Vitka.

No one had even tried to have a crack at him. Mishka Shkura and some other fellow had laid him out, and talked him into staying put. Vitka couldn't bear to look at either me or Sashka, and kept on repeating:

'Reptile! Just you wait, you reptile!' He kept trying to get up and go somewhere. Presumably to find Shkura.

Zhenya said:

'It's not your fault! Would it be any better if you'd been bashed up too?'

Zhenya was right, but all the same I didn't agree with her, I understood how Vitka felt.

We took Sashka home and waited in the street for Katya. Not that we were all that much afraid of Sashka's mother, it was just that it was better for us not to meet her. We decided that Sashka should say he'd fallen out of a tree. Stupid idea of course. But we'd learned from experience, the sillier the tale the more likely it is to be believed. You just have to stick to it. And it would be easier for Sashka to stick to it on his own.

Then we took Inka home. I didn't feel sick any more, but I was still giddy at times. Zhenya took me aside and said I shouldn't leave Vitka alone. He and I took Katya and Zhenya home, then I went to Vitka's for the night.

The two of us slept in the shed—Vitka's family had lived there while the house was being built—now they kept a cow in it and hay in the bunks. I lay in the dark beside Vitka and was afraid to go to sleep. Underneath the bunk the cow was chewing its cud, and that made me even sleepier. Then it heaved a sigh, and damp cowpats slapped onto the wooden floor. I shut my eyes, fell asleep instantly, but woke up very soon. Vitka had gone.

'Vitka!' I called.

He was standing in the lighted rectangle of the doorway.

'I can't bear it,' he said. 'I'm going to meet Shkura. He always comes at sunrise.'

I climbed down the creaking ladder and went out with Vitka into the yard. It was already dawn. The sky was green and starless, but the sun had not yet risen, so there were no shadows on the streets. We went to the tram roundabout, calling in at Shkura's yard on the way. He too, like Vitka, slept in the hayloft, but he wasn't there.

We sat on the damp, cold tramlines. In our town, the sun rose over the steppes and, before that, the sea softened to pink along the horizon. Shkura appeared from the street and walked, swaying, across the wastelands. He saw us and stopped. We got up and went towards him. There was nowhere to escape to. Shkura came to meet us, swaying even more. He fell before Vitka hit him, the blow glancing off his face as he went down. He lay on his back.

'Are you going to hit a man when he's down? Are you?' he asked.

Vitka grabbed him by the arms, trying to get him up. I helped. I realised, Vitka had to have his fight.

'Get up!' I said to Shkura. '*I* won't touch you! It won't be two against one.'

But Shkura wouldn't get up; we hardly got him onto his feet before he flopped down again.

'You can't hit a man when he's down. You can't . . .' he kept on saying.

And of course Vitka couldn't, and burst into tears. He just stood over Shkura, crying. I led him away. We went down to the sea, had a swim, then, warmed by the sun, fell asleep on the sand, and only woke up when the fishing-boats came back with the night catch.

At home, I found a note from my mother. It said the school watchman had come to say the Headmaster wanted to see me. The Head wasn't in school, he'd gone to the Local Education Office. I wandered through the echoing corridors looking into the empty classrooms. They'd already taken the chairs and desks from some of them in readiness for redecorating. Silence in school is a contradiction in terms, like noise in a cemetery. I sat for a little in my own classroom, at my own desk. I thought about myself, and about Inka, and about how when I'd gone she'd still be coming here for another two years. I opened the desk. On the inside of it, 'A+R' had been carved with a penknife. In the past year, I'd got to know this formula of a stranger's love only too well. Who were 'A and R'? Where were they now? Strange that I hadn't tried to find out about it. Desks and classrooms at school are handed down, so it wouldn't 've been so complicated to find out who the previous owner of my desk had been. I pulled a nail out of the wall, and scratched on the inside bottom: 'three years, not five.' If Inka should get my desk in a year's time, she wouldn't have to rack her brains about whose inscription it was. I wondered what she'd think when she read it; and where I'd be at the time.

Yurka Gorodyetsky looked into the classroom.

'I've been looking for you all over the school. Come quickly,' he said.

'Where to?'

'The Regional Executive Committee. A car's waiting for us there.'

'In two words: what's it about?' I asked.

'We're to go to the Red Front Collective Farm. I'd have gone by myself, but the Head said you were to go with me.'

Fair enough! The new secretary was impatient to show off his organisational genius. Personally I'd have given him the chance. The last thing I wanted was to go to the collective farm. But unfortunately, it wasn't up to me. The German collective farm 'Red Front' was considered the richest in the district. But the collective's chairman, Franz Karlovich, a stern and thrifty man, laboured under an out-dated idea; he suspected everyone, especially schoolboys, of laziness. I looked at Yurka, and thought: You'll find out. You'll be going round in circles when the youngsters working in the fields don't get their drinking water brought to them on time, and their tongues stick to the roofs of their mouths with thirst, or they get stomach ache from unboiled milk, and a lot of them can't work, and Franz Karlovich goes on demanding the daily norm. He had a favourite saying: 'He who gets his bread for free, doesn't know what a good life is.' Not a bad saying when you came to think of it. The thing turns on what you mean by 'for free'! I could see the director was right sending me with Yurka, but that didn't make it any the easier for me.

'When'll we be back?' I asked.

'Soon. In time for dinner tomorrow.'

Call that soon! Maybe 'dinner tomorrow' was soon for Yurka, but it didn't suit me. Anyway, I caught hold of Seryozha, the school watchman's boy, in the courtyard.

'Will you do me a favour?'

Seryozha didn't like doing people favours, especially for nothing.

'Haven't got time,' he said.

'Well, try and find a minute.'

'What for?'

'No, you tell me first if you're going to.'

'Haven't got time. I'm going swimming.'

'That's fine. It's right on your way. You know Sea Street? You know the Pilot's house? You know Inka Ilyina? Right! First entrance, top floor, flat 15. Tell Inka: Volodya's gone to the Collective, he'll be back tomorrow for dinner.'

'I haven't got *time*. And I don't go to the beach. I swim in the harbour.'

'That's a pity. You can get very good ice-cream wafers on the beach, and fizzy fruit juice.'

'Haven't any money.'

'What are you talking about? I'm asking you to do something for me, so it's on me. Here, take it!'

Seryozha took my fifteen kopeks. This seven-year-old knew what he was worth all right! It gives me the shivers to think what he will have grown up into! Yurka was standing by the gates looking at me disapprovingly. Never mind! He could wait.

At the Collective, to Yurka's great disappointment everything was settled, as I expected, that same day. And not just with anyone either, but with Franz Karlovich himself. As a rule he avoided direct negotiations. We toured the beet field in his wagonette. The beet was so overgrown with weeds that the tops were invisible. I'd never seen anything like it at the Red Front Collective. Franz Karlovich kept taking off his peaked straw cap and wiping his sweating forehead. He was clearly not at all happy about the field himself.

'New strain. Foreign seed . . . no good' he said.

We started discussing how long weeding would take.

'A week and a half' said Franz Karlovich.

I took a good look at the field. It began at the road to the railway station and ended by the estuary shore. To weed a field like that you'd need not less than two and a half weeks.

'Three weeks!' I said.

222

'Three *weeks*! In three weeks everything'll be dead!' said Franz Karlovich.

'No it won't. We'll be weeding every day.'

'Two weeks' said Franz Karlovich.

'Agreed' said Yurka, as if someone had prodded him. I didn't say any more. We went to the farm office. Franz Karlovich hitched the stallion to a post instead of taking him back to the stable. That meant he was going on somewhere else. In the office he suggested that the School Brigade should sleep on the threshing floor, by the beet field. He mentioned it, while signing some papers the accountant had brought him. Yurka again said:

'Agreed.'

I waited till Franz Karlovich had finished signing, then said:

'Won't do.'

'Why not?' asked Yurka. 'Very handy, the Labour Front-Line is right there—no need to waste time going to and fro. And sleeping in the open air's very pleasant.' Yurka badly wanted to look very responsible. Fancy thinking up a phrase like Labour Front-Line.

Franz Karlovich was smoking his pipe and nodding his head. I never would've thought Yurka could be such a fool.

'You see, Yurka, there's a bog by the threshing floor. And for some reason frogs like living in that bog. And as you know from your zoology, grass-snakes live on frogs. . . .'

Franz Karlovich began to look a bit uneasy. He took his pipe out of his mouth and said:

'Grass-snakes are peaceful creatures.'

'True. But for some reason girls are scared of snakes.'

'Oh come now!' said Yurka. 'You'll never get anywhere if you give in to moods. They'll get used to it. And it's a fact it's handy for the Labour Front-Line.'

'Theoretically, it's fine. But the girls will screech when the

223

snakes come creeping under the blankets, and in the morning you'll never get them to wake up. And if you do get them to wake, they'll be sure to fall asleep again on the field, and they'll get sunstroke for certain. Say what you like, Franz Karlovich, the kids must be put in the school or the granary.'

'No, no, that's an hour's walk to work.'

'It's a ten-minutes run in the truck,' I answered. 'And another thing, Franz Karlovich, you must allot us a horse. We'll fetch and carry our own food and drink. Last year we'd an awful time with it.'

'No, no, that's pandering . . . not work. "He who gets his bread for free, doesn't know what a good life is." You want a horse, you want a truck—it'll be a dead loss!'

'Franz Karlovich. What did the Collective give us a bonus for last year?'

'That was politics!'

'You yourself said the School Brigade made you a profit. And a profit—that's economics!'

'O.K. The work'll be the same as last year, and there'll be a horse and a truck.' Franz Karlovich gave in unexpectedly soon. He seemed to be in a hurry. We said goodbye on the porch. Franz Karlovich went off, but Yurka announced he had to inspect the school and the granary. And yet he'd agreed to the threshing floor without having looked at it. There's logic for you! I didn't go with him. I sat down on the bench in the little garden in front of the farm office. In the middle of a flower bed stood a bust of Friedrich Engels. It was odd seeing him without Karl Marx. I'd seen him three years running, and I still couldn't get used to it. Yurka came back.

'Shall we spend the night here?' he asked.

'What for?'

'It's not done, somehow, to come back the same day.'

I said nothing. I just started walking along the road towards the station. We had to run the last mile and a half along the seashore to be in time for the evening train from Simferopol. In the carriage Yurka pestered me with conversation. At first I pretended to be asleep, then I really dropped off.

9

—••❩❨❩❨❩❨❩••—

We went by tram from the station. Crossing the wastelands, the wind came blowing through the open second carriage, and the long running board kept almost brushing against the bushes. I was getting off when Yurka asked:

'I don't know, d'you think I should go to the Head now?'

'No, wait till he goes to bed!' I answered, and jumped off at the end of the wastelands, opposite Sea street, while the tram was still moving. Who'd have thought Yurka was such a nit! And it was I who'd put him up for secretary.

Summer-visitors in smart clothes were already out, following their usual evening route: Promenade; Spa Hall; Floating Restaurant; 'Dulber'. I was hurrying to Inka's, sweating and dusty, my lips all cut. I ought, of course, to have run home and changed, but I didn't want to waste so much time. I caught sight of Inka unexpectedly. I happened to glance over to the other side of the street, and saw her. Inka never walked that side. To do so she had to cross the road in front of her house. She was walking past the railings of the square. I was so surprised that I didn't call to her right away. It'd never occurred to me that Inka could be going anywhere, let alone hurrying, when I wasn't around.

'Inka!'

Inka stopped, and then ran across the road to me.

'Oh how marvellous that you're back! You can't imagine how marvellous it is that you're back!' she said. I was looking

226

at her and smiling. Her face looked odd somehow, I just couldn't make out what it was she'd done to it. And her eyes looked a little scared.

'Where were you off to?'

'Oh, I'm so glad you're back. I did think you'd come back. Only I wasn't sure.'

I went on looking at her face, and still couldn't think what she'd done with it.

'Don't you like it?' Inka asked. 'I put on a tiny bit of powder, and tiny bit of lipstick. After all you have to try it out sometime!'

Now I realised why it was she looked so beautiful. You could see the freckles much less under the powder. As for the lipstick, you couldn't see that at all; her lips were always very red anyway.

'Haven't you anything else to do?' I said. 'Let's call in at my place. I must change.'

'Yes, let's,' said Inka.

I stepped off the pavement opposite the entrance to the square, then stopped because Inka said:

'Let's go along the street, shall we?'

We always went through the square. I couldn't understand why she should want to go round it instead, and I looked at her.

'When we go that way, my shoes get all dusty. Let's go by the street,' she said, glancing at the square as she spoke. I looked round too. Near the entrance, sitting on one of the benches, his profile to us, was John Danker. I came back onto the pavement and we walked along the street. I thought it was simply that Inka didn't want to pass in front of the King of the Hawaian Guitar. I myself didn't want to see him much, either. But then another thought struck me, and I stopped dead.

'All right then, hit me. Hit me! In front of everyone!' said Inka.

I walked along the street and Inka followed me. She was only a little behind, and kept on saying:

'All right, so hit me! Why don't you want to hit me? Hit me—you'll feel better right away!'

I walked on, as though stunned. Everything stood still inside me, and I didn't understand anything. I only thought that my mother probably wouldn't be home yet, and walked very fast, and paid no attention at all to Inka, though knowing all the time she was walking beside me. My mother wasn't in. Inka had often been to our place before, and more often than not, when my mother was out. I'd never given it a thought before. But now I did. I washed and changed in my mother's room, remembering all the time that we were alone together in the flat. I could see Inka through the open door. She was standing by the window, her elbows propped on the sill, looking out into the street. The room was dark, only the windows showed light. I went up to her. I took her by the shoulders, turned her round to me, and kissed her, and my lips began to bleed. Inka was frightened. She took a handkerchief from the low neck of her frock, and dabbed my lips with it, and her fingers pressing the handkerchief, she kissed the corner of my mouth. Then I said something I hadn't in the least meant to say.

'My mother'll be back soon.'

I thought Inka had either not understood or not heard what I said. Then I realised she had.

'Let's go. I called by at Sashka's this morning, and promised to come again in the evening. Let's go, shall we?' she said again. And a moment later asked: 'Where's your blue shirt?' she asked.

'I got blood all over it.'

'Give it me to wash. Don't worry, I won't spoil it.'

I got the shirt out from under the mattress, and quickly bundled it up in a newspaper. I wanted to get out as fast as I could.

We used the front door. Lights were on in the houses and in the streets, and it was quiet, but it was an evening, not a night-time quiet. There were a lot of people about.

'How's Sashka feeling?'

'I think he's all right. Nothing was broken. His mother says he's got concussion, but his father says there's no question of it. I think he's guessed what happened. Sashka's mother said to his father: you're as much of a doctor as I'm a Dutch queen. Then Sashka said if he hadn't got concussion already, he soon would have if his mother went on screaming!'

'Were you there for long?'

'Not very. I felt awkward, so I went away. Katya was there too. Then Vitka and Zhenya came, but by then I was just going. . . .'

I waited for Inka to say where to, but she didn't say any more.

'It was a good thing you thought of getting hold of Pavel,' I said.

'I suddenly thought of him, and ran. I was only scared he might already have gone. But he hadn't. The two that were with him didn't want to come at first, but Pavel came running with me, and then they came after us. We could hear you fighting. Pavel shouted: "Out of my bloody way!" He told me not to come near, but I did. They shone their torches on him. He swore at someone, then knocked him down. He hit somebody several times.'

'Why did you come so close? He told you not to, didn't he?'

'I didn't *really* come close! I waited till I saw you. I saw you when you were trying to get up.'

'You're jolly plucky! If it hadn't been for you we'd have been in a mess for sure!'

'I'm not brave at all. You just don't know me. I'm only brave if I don't think. If I'd thought first, I'd never have come close!'

Inka went in to Sashka's by herself. It was out of the question letting Sashka's mother even catch a glimpse of my lips in the state they were. As Inka went in I shouted to her:

'Don't sit there ages!'

The light from the chemist's fell on the pavement. I waited for Inka behind the advertisement hoarding, so that Sashka's mother shouldn't see me out of the window. For lack of anything better to do, I lit a match and burnt out John Danker's eyes and nose, first on one poster, then on the other. Inka came out with Vitka.

'We were summoned to the Commissar's office today,' said Vitka.

'What for?'

'They've got the posting instructions.'

'Where are we going?'

'That's the point. They didn't say. They wouldn't talk to me alone. We've all three got to go there in the morning.'

'Will Sashka be coming?'

'He says he will. But Aunt Sonia goes on screaming that she won't let him.'

I looked up at the top windows. They were open, and the light shone white on the leaves of the trees. I could hear voices in the room that faced the court.

'I don't like these mysterious goings on.'

'Sashka doesn't either,' answered Vitka.

Inka looked at me, the light reflected in her anxious eyes.

'Tell Sashka I'll come and call for him in the morning.'

Vitka went back into the house while Inka and I crossed the road opposite the square. The Komsomol had laid the square out three years ago. By now I expect the trees will be big, and the square a pleasant place to sit in. But in those days people only used it as a short cut, or for brief rendez-vous. We passed the bench John Danker had been sitting on a couple of hours ago.

'Did you go to the beach?' I asked.

'Yes, before dinner. Igor and Zoya were there too. I was

with them. It's true, it's true, I was. You can ask them tomorrow.'

'Why should I?'

'Well *I* know what you want to ask about, I know!' Inka slipped her arm into mine. 'There was nothing like that,' she said. 'He said that you and I'd be separated anyway, and I said it wasn't true. I told our fortunes three times with matches, and three *times* they got all twined up! The second time not quite so much, but more or less. Three times can't be coincidence!'

'How does he know about me?'

'But he saw you on the beach! And afterwards I told him. He asked me to meet him, but I said you were out of town, and that when you were away I didn't go anywhere.'

'Did Igor and Zoya talk to him too?'

'Oh *no*! They didn't *see* him. We were talking together in the water. I was swimming beyond the second reef, and he was by the first one. He swims awfully badly. I told him that if he didn't swim closer to me I wouldn't talk to him. I said it on purpose, I thought he'd be afraid, but he did swim out to me. Then, when we were coming back, he almost drowned! It's true, it's true! You can't think how frightened I was!'

We stopped at the gate of Inka's house. I thought to myself: where would Inka be now if I hadn't come back when I did? My heart turned over, and now I really could have hit her, but I didn't because there were people in the street.

'Come with me to the entrance,' said Inka.

'I must get some sleep. I've hardly slept at all.'

'No, come with me!'

In the entrance Inka pressed her fingers to the scab on my lower lip, and kissed the side of my mouth. I knew she was going to, and I leant back against the wall, waiting.

'*Say* something! Don't just go on saying nothing!' she said. 'I told you before I was wicked. I don't know myself what comes over me. I just wanted to know what he'd talk to

231

me about. You saw yourself how glad I was to see you! You did see, didn't you?'

I kissed her, and my lips began to bleed again. Inka couldn't see the blood, she must have felt it on her lips.

'Don't kiss me again, or it won't heal for ages,' she said.

We stood in the entrance hall, behind the staircase, not saying anything. Inka's hands were on my shoulders, and I was pressing her close. We were both very tired, but we only realised it now.

'I told you, my mother's sister lives in Leningrad, didn't I?'

I couldn't remember if she'd told me or not. Maybe.

'She'll be coming to us for the summer. I can go to her in the holidays. It'll be grand if they send you to Leningrad.'

Where were they sending us? I would only know tomorrow. I wanted the night to be over soon, and the morning come. But for that I had to go to bed, and to go to bed, I had to go home. It looked as if Inka were right. It would be nice not to have to go anywhere!

10

—••E⟩E⟩••—

There can never have been any sun in the Commissar's office. This thought struck me as soon as I opened the door.

I went in first, followed by Sashka and Vitka. Vitka turned and carefully shut the door. Then we stood in a row with our backs to it; me with my cut lips, Sashka with his bandaged head, and Vitka with the remains of his black eye.

I don't know what impression we made on the Commissar. He was a reserved man. He only looked at his watch and said:

'You're a quarter of an hour late!'

He was sitting sideways to us, and kept glancing at Alyosha across the desk.

'Congratulations, Professors, we're going to Leningrad,' said Alyosha.

Vitka smiled broadly, and rubbed his hands. Sashka and I looked at each other. Of course it was a good thing that at least we were going to Leningrad, but it was early days for rejoicing. Alyosha's voice was too cheerful.

'Well, aren't you pleased?' he asked.

'Which training school are we going to?' I asked.

'The Sklyansky Red Flag Training School, previously the Oranienbaum Machine-gunnery Course for Red Army Officers.'

'Comrade Pereverzev, let's talk straight to these youngsters,' said the Commissar. He turned to us, the chair squeaking under his weight. 'These are the posting instructions: There are three places in the Sklyansky Infantry Training School,

233

one in the Naval Medical School, and Baulin has been called up personally to Frunze Naval College.'

My heart was beating furiously. I could feel it thudding in my ears. Probably it was this that prevented me from hearing properly. Even today I don't hear well when I get agitated. I strained my ears, but there was only one thought in my mind. Neither in Vladivostock, nor in Sebastopol would I be meeting Inka with flowers. I could think of nothing else. Through the window I could see the sun-lit courtyard, spread with sand, and the soldiers marching. A lieutenant was standing with his back to the window, shouting:

'One . . . two . . . three. One . . . two . . . three.' He said the word 'One' loudly and distinctly. The soldiers, there were eight of them—were marching round and round. On the command 'One!' each put down his foot, and on the words 'two . . . three . . .' slowly raised it. I looked out of the window and thought: I shan't be meeting Inka with flowers, either in Vladivostok or in Sebastopol.

'It only remains for us to decide which of you is to go to the Medical School,' said the Commissar.

'Kriger, wasn't it you who wanted to go to Medical School? It's as if this vacancy was ready-made for you!' said Alyosha.

Sashka said nothing.

'Isn't it possible to change anything?' I asked.

'For what reasons?' asked the Commissar.

'We've grown up by the sea,' said Vitka.

'We can navigate in any weather, day or night. We know our way round the gulf as if we were at home,' I said.

'That's a point,' said the Commissar. 'We've discussed this too. But there are plenty of such sea-faring lads, and only two Naval Training Colleges, one for ordinary seamen, the other for engineers. Their quota is always full. And any other reasons? The snowy tunic? The cap with the crabs on it? The gold anchors? Did I guess right?' the searching eyes of the Commissar twinkled under his heavy brows. 'Did I?

Belov?' I could only endure his gaze for a second, and then looked away.

'I want to go to the Infantry Training School too,' said Sashka, 'there have always been the three of us, since we were kids.'

'You can't go right through life as a trio,' said the Commissar. 'The reorganisation of the Army is a serious business, and it must be treated seriously. I can tell you from personal experience, you'll never get on in the service if you put your own wishes first.'

Alyosha pushed his hair back from his forehead.

'The posting instructions were received long ago,' he said. 'I persuaded the Commissar to send a letter asking for them to be changed. Kolesnikov signed it too. But it didn't help. Yesterday the Regional Command confirmed the previous postings by telegram, so that's that, I'm afraid, Professors. I was hoping to go to the Political Training School myself, but no luck!'

'Tomorrow, medical board at eleven hundred hours. Then call in at my office with your new application forms. And get into the habit of being on time!'

After the cool and rather gloomy room, the day seemed particularly bright and warm. Actually nothing unexpected had happened. No one had *promised* to send us to the Naval Training School. It was we who had imagined sea-faring youngsters like us could not be sent anywhere else! But all the same, we felt as though we had been cheated. The soldiers were no longer marching up and down in their boots, now they were 'scissor-jumping' without their tunics over the horse. They took their run from the porch, and they gave off a sour smell of sweat and boot-polish. The lieutenant was standing beside the horse, as catcher. I looked him over: the disproportionately wide-topped boots, the legs sticking out of them like sticks, the crumpled tunic, and the sweaty, ageing face—none of it impressed me—better not look at him. I had three years of training to go through myself before being a Lieutenant!

Once outside, Sashka said:

'I felt all along that Alyosha was hedging.'

'He tried. You heard: he did send a letter,' said Vitka.

'That's not the point. Alyosha was afraid we'd refuse to go to infantry school, so he didn't tell us anything about it. That's a lack of political trust,' I said.

'I wanted to say right out what I thought of him,' said Sashka.

'A good job you didn't. No use washing our dirty linen in public. We'll have it out when we're alone with him,' I answered.

We went down to the harbour. The girls were supposed to pick us up at the Commissar's office, to go with us to the beach, but we didn't want to meet them. We were afraid of having to tell them we were going to the Infantry School. We had somehow first to get used to the idea ourselves.

The yacht was standing on its trestles. We took the tarpaulin off, got the tool-kit out of the hatch, then turned her keel-uppermost. We got ready to work, so that the girls should see what we'd come there for.

'The Commissar turned out to be a shrewd old boy,' I said.

'Does that make you feel any better?' asked Sashka.

'Of course. He's an infantry major too.'

We were cleaning the old paint off the sides with scrapers. To start with we scraped because we had to be getting on with something—then we got carried away.

'The Commissar's shrewd all right. He's got it all taped,' said Vitka.

'Such as what?' asked Sashka.

'Zhenya was already picturing me in my white tunic meeting her after a concert. All the same it's not true. It wasn't *only* the tunic . . .'

I was scraping the left side of the hull, and kept quiet. I'd

236

never have believed Zhenya had such a fertile imagination!

'What are we going to say to the girls?' I asked.

'For the time being all we need say is that we're going to Leningrad. Alyosha was right up to a point,' said Sashka.

Vitka looked at me. He didn't trust Sashka.

'O.K. we'll tell them that, then,' I said. 'And if they ask which training school, we'll say the "Sklyansky". I don't think they'll cross-examine us on what kind of a training school it is.'

'The red lead lasts well. Let's just caulk the sides and we can paint her over right away,' said Vitka.

'We'll caulk her and paint her, but who's going to sail in her?' asked Sashka. He slapped the side of the boat, and its well-seasoned spruce gave a hollow ring.

'Get ready for it,' I said.

Katya and Zhenya were coming along the sand between the upturned boats.

'Why didn't you wait for us?' asked Zhenya.

'We had to get on with fixing the yacht. May need it any day now,' said Vitka.

'D'you know where you're going?'

Zhenya's public-prosecutor-voice was getting on my nerves.

'Everything's O.K.,' answered Vitka. 'We're all three going to Leningrad.'

'I knew it!' said Zhenya. 'All you have to do is stick up for your rights!'

Vitka looked at Zhenya, grinning stupidly. I could swear our secret wouldn't last out the day.

'How smashing!' said Katya. 'We'll all be together again. That calls for a celebration!'

'We'll celebrate tomorrow,' said Sashka. 'Tomorrow we'll go to the "Floating Restaurant" and have a quiet little celebration.'

'Where's Inka?' I asked.

'She and her mother went to Simferopol. Her father was

summoned somewhere urgently, and they went to see him off. Zhenya and I were at the station,' said Katya. 'Inka said to tell you not to be miserable!'

I not only didn't intend to be miserable, it was actually a weight off my mind. For the first time ever, I had no objection to not seeing Inka in the evening! I'd work for another hour or two, and then go home, I said. I wouldn't go anywhere that evening. And I really didn't go anywhere; just went to bed early. If you sleep soundly all night, all your troubles will have lost their edge by morning. For the first time in my life I felt duty weighing on me, and to do my duty would mean putting my own feelings aside.

I woke in the morning worrying about the change in my future. Everything was working out, but not as I'd wanted it. Later, in the Army, I often had to sacrifice my personal wishes to the demands of the service. Gradually it became a habit. In time I came to like subordinating my life to duty and to my oath of allegiance. Every time I had a sharper sense of being needed and of value. When, many years later, I was released from the Army, I asked the Colonel whose orders I would now come under, and when he replied, 'Your own', they were the most frightening words I've ever heard.

We arrived for the Medical Board on the dot of eleven hundred hours. To be dead on time, we'd stood for about fifteen minutes round the corner from the Commissar's office. All those on ordinary call-up were at the Medical Board too, but we went in to the doctors first. After that we sat in the Commissar's office while he went through the medical reports. The biggest discrepancy, if it could be called such, was between our weight and our height. Even Vitka was nearly a stone less than the average.

'Where there are bones, there will be flesh,' said the Commissar. We smiled politely. The Commissar pulled our applications towards him, but didn't start reading them. 'Is there anything you want to say, Belov?' he asked.

'What is there to say? Nothing.'

'But there is. There's something we should get straight. You're tough youngsters, you don't need any consoling. And you're wrong to look down on the Infantry. People have an out of date idea of it. An infantry officer is an all-round army officer. In battle, all take their orders from him. So he has to know about all the other branches of the service so as to organise combined operations. And the uniform is no worse than the naval one either. You've only got to get used to it. What's wrong with my uniform?'

'But you're a Major,' I said.

'Majors' and lieutenants' uniforms are the same.'

'Especially the one who was drilling the soldiers yesterday!' I said.

'The joke's on me! Real professorial types!' said the Commissar. He got up, went to the door, opened it and called:

'Lieutenant Miroshnichenko!'

He returned to his desk, leaving the door open. A lieutenant came into the room, certainly not the one we'd seen yesterday—for some reason I'd thought it would be that one.

'Comrade Major?'

The Lieutenant stood at the door looking now at us, now at the Major, whose face crinkled into a smile.

'Are these young fellows' papers ready?' he asked.

'We only have to make copies of their applications.'

'It's been done. You may go. We'll discuss it later.'

We realised at once why the Major had summoned the Lieutenant. But the Lieutenant didn't. He only knew it hadn't been to ask about the documents. He went out.

'You saw that? You must know how to wear a uniform!' said the Commissar.

'Pure propaganda!' said Sashka.

The Major was amused. He looked at us and laughed.

'What, me a propagandist? Pereverzev is the propagandist. I'm a soldier. Any questions? Right. Then you're free. But

239

don't go anywhere out of town. Go and read today's copy of *The Star* in the yard. You'll find it interesting.'

As we went out Lieutenant Miroshnichenko went in to the Major, and we heard them laughing together as we walked along the corridor.

We found the article at once. 'They are the Red Army of the Future.' We stood in front of the notice board and read it through. There was no doubt about it: this future of the Red Army was us! The article was about military training schools being ready and waiting to take boys who had completed their secondary school education, who would rejuvenate the officer 'cadres' and complete the mechanisation of the Army.

We went to the beach.

'We've had luck, all the same,' I said. 'This campaign might have started a year earlier or a year later, and we wouldn't have been in on it.'

'I was thinking about it all night. Actually I'm the only lucky one,' said Sashka. 'It makes me feel an absolute heel when I think of you.'

'You don't have to. In no conceivable circumstances would either Vitka or I want to be doctors. Would you ever want to?' I asked Vitka.

'What sort of a doctor would I make! When I tried to chop up a frog in the biology class, I vomited for two days,' said Vitka.

'You only have to see a frog to feel sick,' I said.

'A bit less, now,' answered Vitka.

Inka was on the beach. She'd come back from Simferopol by the morning train, and was sitting with the girls, near Zoya. Igor was playing chess under the awning. Inka and I hadn't seen each other since the evening before last, and it seemed a whole eternity to me.

'Greetings to all and sundry!' said Sashka.

'Volodya!' Inka called out. She wrote 'Leningrad?' with

her finger in the sand. 'Yes?' she asked. I nodded, and started to undress.

Then I went over to Igor under the awning, so as not to stay too close to Inka, or she'd have had it all out of me in a trice. She didn't understand. At first she tried not to take any notice of me, but she couldn't hold out and came over and sat down beside me.

'I'm going to swim,' she said. 'Are you coming?'

Igor was finishing a game.

'Shall we have a swim?' I asked.

'Of course,' answered Igor.

By the very edge of the water, John Danker was walking with the woman he'd been on the beach with, two days ago. I recognised her at once. Sashka had to go home for something. Katya went with him. As he went off he shouted:

'We'll meet at the Floating Restaurant at nineteen hundred hours!'

Inka looked at me and smiled.

11

—◆◆€)€3◆◆—

A man in white trousers and a dark-blue jacket went past us. Supporting his companion lightly by the elbow, he stepped on to the little bridge like a ship's gangway. People were queuing on the narrow terrace in front of the entrance to the Floating Restaurant. So were we, only we weren't on the terrace, we were still on the beach at the foot of the little bridge.

'What are we standing here for? Let's get on to the terrace! Well what *are* we standing here for?' Inka kept saying.

'Drinking itself is unpleasant. But it's nice afterwards . . .' Vitka was saying.

'Another couple of big occasions and Vitka'll be an alcoholic!' I said.

'So what if I am? I still say it's unpleasant while you're drinking!'

'Stop it! It's disgusting listening to you!' said Zhenya. Of course she was wearing her new straw hat.

'We're standing around outside like poor relations! Do let's get onto the terrace,' said Inka.

'Try anything once!'

'It's about time your father thought up a new saying.'

We were saying whatever came into our heads, because we didn't want to go up onto the terrace. We remembered the concert, and were afraid of finding ourselves in the wrong place again. Then Katya came out onto the little balcony above the terrace, and beckoned to us. Inka was first onto the bridge. I wanted to support her by the elbow, but I didn't quite make it. We squeezed one by one between those waiting to get into the queue. Katya's sister Maroosya was waiting for us at the entrance. She said to the doorman—who looked like a sailing-ship's bo'sun:

'Let them through, Mironich.'

'Let them pass, please. They've a table reserved!' said the doorman.

The man in the dark-blue jacket moved a fraction to one side.

'Youths and maidens hurrying to the initiation!' he said.

I came last, and the doorman lowered a brown, wooden board after me. Inside, on the steep stairway like a ship's ladder, it smelled of fried onions, meat patties and wine. We reached the veranda and made our way between the little tables. Ours was over in the corner, right by the balustrade. I hardly remember how I got to it. It's not so easy walking between little tables with everyone watching you. The great thing is not to hurry. I kept my mind on this. But Vitka got in my way, and I had to keep pushing him in the back. Katya was sitting at the table already, and Sashka sat down beside her and started scrutinising the bottles. My eyes were popping out too. I'd never seen such an array of hors d'oeuvres before. Now of course I understand. Maroosya herself must have added something to our thirty roubles. We sat ourselves down at our table, and at once forgot that we weren't the only people on the veranda.

'First toast to Maroosya!' said Sashka.

'Toast whom you like, only do pour the wine into the wine-glasses! Those tall ones are for water,' said Maroosya.

'So what, we can drink out of the wine-glasses,' said Sashka.

He'd already poured the wine into the tumblers, so now he emptied them into the wine-glasses. There was a burst of laughter behind me. I looked round. At the next table sat 'Mr Tinsmith' and his party. But it wasn't 'Mr Tinsmith' laughing, it was the others. He wasn't even looking in our direction.

'Ssst! Volodya! First we'll drink to Maroosya, then settle with him!' said Sashka.

But after that we forgot all about 'Mr Tinsmith' and his crowd, and we drank to the girls, to ourselves, to our history teacher Vera Vassilyevna, and to her eventual marriage; Zhenya said:

'To all who sail the seas!'

Zhenya of course meant no harm. But it was just like her to wreck our mood, without even realising it. The sun was setting over the sea, and the glasses on our table were aflame.

'You have to breathe out first, and then drink,' I said to Inka.

But she wasn't listening to me. She was sipping hers and not screwing up her face at all. The wine was cold and sour-sweet, quite different from what we'd had at Popando-poulo's. That evening I began to suspect that there were many different wines in the world. Until then I'd simply never thought about wine. Maroosya came up to us—she often came over to our table.

'Don't hurry,' she said. 'You have as much hors d'oeuvres as you like.'

'Why should we hurry? You could sit at a table like this till morning!' said Sashka.

'Boys! In a restaurant, it's up to the men to look after the ladies. I'm banking on you, Sashka,' said Maroosya, and went away again, called to another table.

'Sure!' said Sashka, helping himself to salad.

'That's what Sashka calls looking after the ladies!' I said.

'What's that? . . . Ah, yes . . .' Sashka handed on the salad to Katya, and looked round to see what else he could have. I'm sure he wasn't pretending, it was just that we were beginning to get tipsy, and forgot what we were saying and doing. The waves swelled gently under the Floating Restaurant, and it seemed to me that the veranda was floating towards the pink horizon. Then I would look at the beach, and things came back to normal. At 'Mr Tinsmith's' table everyone was laughing. A woman sitting facing us, kept looking at us. She was a little drunk, and she propped her cheek on her hand, and smiled.

'Now's the time to rub them all out,' said Vitka.

'Who's "they"?' asked Katya.

'Volodya, you explain!'

'Well there's plenty of shit in the world, isn't there? There's always someone putting spokes in your wheel. So to stop them, you rub them all out.'

'But who d'you mean?' asked Katya. 'I don't want to . . . without knowing!'

'I know who. Come on, let's drink!' said Zhenya.

'Would Styopik do?' asked Sashka.

'O.K. Let's rub Styopik out! I'm not sorry for him,' said Katya.

Inka said:

'Volodya! Let's rub her out! Shall we?'

'Who's she?'

'Well, that one,' Inka stopped, and looked out at the sea. '*You* know, the one you were watching on the beach.' Inka laughed, and looked me straight in the eyes.

'O.K. Let's,' I answered, but as I drank, it never struck me that the woman Inka meant was the one who'd been on the beach with John Danker.

Inka drank, then suddenly held out her glass across the table. I looked round. The woman at the next-door table was smiling at Inka and holding out her glass too. Then she got up and came towards us.

'May I join you?'

'Mr Tinsmith' brought a chair for her, and went back to his own seat.

'You've just left school, haven't you?' asked the woman.

245

'Who told you?'

She shrugged.

'It's not hard to guess. My little sister's been right through secondary school, too.'

'Very touching!' said Sashka. 'So you've a little sister who's been right through secondary school.'

'And what about you?' I asked.

'I'm a geologist.'

'Very touching! You're a geologist, and your neighbour there is Captain of an ocean-going liner,' said Sashka.

'So what?' asked the woman. She was still smiling, but I think she was already sorry she'd come over to us—you could see it in her eyes.

Zhenya said:

'Let's drink to everyone who's left school this year. May all their dreams come true!'

The woman held out her glass, she'd brought it with her, and the girls clinked with her, but we only looked at each other without drinking ours.

'You look a nice lot, but in fact, you're spiteful . . .'

The woman went back to her own table. We couldn't tell her that our dreams were already not coming true. And even if we could have told anyone, it wouldn't have been her. 'Mr Tinsmith' came for the chair. He hesitated, and I saw his knuckles go white as he clutched the chair-back. He went, and Inka said:

'What did you have to hurt her for? Why did you hurt her?'

'She probably doesn't know anything about him. She ought to be told,' said Katya.

'We've tried already. We're fed up with it,' I said.

'I shall tell her all the same. I'll see her on the beach, and I'll tell her,' said Zhenya.

'You don't need to tell her anything! What d'you want to tell her for,' asked Inka.

246

We weren't angry with the woman; it was merely incomprehensible to us that a geologist could be in 'Mr Tinsmith's' party. Records were coming over the amplifier, and on the veranda they were dancing. Sashka was brazen enough to get up and dance with Katya. I don't know how they managed it, but they did. I had a go too, but it wasn't too successful. Inka could dance, but I couldn't. I'd just never bothered with it. Then we started spitting into the sea. We stood by the balustrade and spat. It was Inka began it. A bottle was bobbing about on the waves, neck upwards, and Inka tried to see if she could spit that far. A bad example is always catching especially if there are a lot of drunks around. They stood by the railings and spat. One bottle wasn't enough for all, and each new group threw in its own bottle. Then the manager of the restaurant came out and told them they ought to be ashamed of themselves; but by that time, we were back in our places.

Inka and Katya went off somewhere. Maroosya was standing by the wall between the open windows of the inner room, and I watched her for a long time. Her shoulder leaning against the wall, she was looking into nowhere; just standing with her eyes open. Her eyes had the transparency all girls' eyes have, who live by the sea. Her full lips were pale, in spite of some lipstick, and instead of dimples, the first wrinkles were beginning to show on her cheeks. When people called her, she went over to them and listened, looking away somewhere over their heads. Maroosya called all customers 'guests', but I think she was fed up with them, and hadn't a high opinion of them. She looked round, and came over to me.

'Well, Volodya. How's things?' she asked.

'Not bad! You're very beautiful.'

'I used to be,' said Maroosya, running her large, white hand with brightly painted fingernails through my hair. 'I'm just going to bring you the meat patties,' she said.

We ate the patties, and Inka gave me half hers.

'In return for the ice-cream!' she said.

Now, though I kept glancing behind me, the veranda was floating all the time. It was a good thing there was no more wine left, there'd only been two bottles of it, but there was plenty of cream-soda. It tickled your nose, and cleared your head. Why drink wine when you can have cream-soda! True, you can't get the sort of cream-soda nowadays, that we had then. Or maybe it only seems that way to me. Inka pointed with her finger and shouted suddenly:

'Look!'

The sun had set long ago, and the flat shapes of the mountains were blue against the faintly pink sky. They stood on the water like vertical shadows. Sitting at his table, 'Mr Tinsmith' was explaining to his friends with the air of an experienced captain:

'It's a marine mirage. Columbus's sailors saw them like that.'

A lot he knew! Mirage my foot! It was simply that on such calm, transparent evenings you could always see the mountains of the southern shore. I don't know why he had to invent things when the evening, and the sea, and the mountains were so beautiful anyway. I'd have been feeling fine if I hadn't kept remembering that I'd never be going to sea on board a warship. The mountains got bluer, and gradually merged into the sea and the sky.

Maroosya came up to us.

'That's the lot!' she said. 'Satisfied?'

We didn't at all want to go, but Maroosya said that a lot more 'guests' were waiting downstairs. On the veranda the lights had long been lit, and as we left we saw them reflected in the oily-black water. Maroosya saw us to the stairs.

'Remember—my house is your house!' said Sashka.

'I will,' said Maroosya. 'The sooner you have one, the better!'

248

Vitka, the first to come down, was trying to convince Zhenya that it was a completely different staircase.

'Don't make things up! It's you that's different!' said Zhenya, and her voice was very tender.

Then we went for a swim. The water was warm; so was the sand, you only had to scrape away the top layer. Many people were bathing, but you couldn't see them in the darkness. Suddenly somewhere a woman would laugh, or a man would say something. I lay beside Inka. Lights appeared on the sea and we could hear the distant clanking of anchor chains.

'Inka, I'm not going to a Naval Training School. D'you realise? Vitka and I have to go into the Infantry. We're more needed there. An Infantry officer is an all-round army commander. Only that's rubbish. He's just an Infantryman. . . .' I hid my face against Inka's knees, and she put her hand on the back of my head.

'Don't. . . .' said Inka. 'It's not a bit important. It's still only three years, not five.'

Someone came out of the water and lay down not far from us.

'You didn't get your bandage wet, did you?' asked Katya.

'I wasn't even swimming,' said Sashka.

'Look how beautifully the squadron's coming in. There's no wind, you can hear the anchors,' said Katya. 'I wonder where our lot's got to?'

'Must be swimming. To think of putting sea-faring types into the Infantry! Volodya!' Sashka called loudly.

'Don't shout! I'm not deaf!'

Katya and Sashka said no more. That was the last evening we all spent together.

12

＊＊⊱⊰＊＊

Inka left the day after next.

Three lorries stood in the school yard. Inka sat in the first one with her back to the driver's cabin. She wore a white head-scarf tied under her chin, a faded blue T-shirt she'd grown out of, and a rayon skirt, and she sat and smiled. I was talking to Vitka and Sashka and some other people. Katya and Zhenya were there too. We were all reminiscing about last year's expedition, and roaring with laughter; I stood with my back to the truck. Last night hadn't smoothed anything out, or made it easier. What had happened to Inka and me yester-day, stood between us today.

Yesterday I'd said:

'Inka, we're quite grown up now. D'you know what I mean? That woman I looked at on the beach, and John Danker . . . it wasn't without meaning for us.'

'What are you telling me this for?' asked Inka.

I wasn't very clear about it myself, but once having started to talk, I couldn't stop. We were sitting in the remotest part of the wastelands, between the sea and the Mainaki salt-lake, and all around us were sand-dunes and woody-night-shade bushes. The others were waiting for us on the beach, but I said to Inka:

'Let's be on our own for a while.'

So we'd come here.

'I can't just leave you like this,' I said. 'D'you see? I can't. Think what you like of me, but I can't.'

'Let it happen then. I shan't think anything. Let it just happen. . . .' Inka went pale, and the freckles round her nose stood out.

There was the sun, hot on the nape of my neck, and Inka's auburn hair spread on the sand, and I remember thinking how difficult it would be to get all the sand out of that thick hair.

Then I was sitting up again, and no thought in my mind but fear: not for myself, but for Inka.

When I could bring myself to glance at her, she was sitting, hugging her knees.

'You've got blood on your lip.'

'It's nothing. I bit it.'

'It's all right, don't be afraid,' I said. 'It had to happen sometime.'

'I'm not afraid. I'm not afraid of anything! Don't be offended . . . but, we mustn't again. I don't think anything much happened . . . but, not again.'

Now it wasn't fear any more—only bewilderment and shame.

'Let's go down to the beach. Our lot's been waiting there for ages,' said Inka.

On the beach, she never left Katya and Zhenya. I knew why she stayed with them. I, too, was afraid of being alone with her—we'd have had to talk about something, and I couldn't talk.'

Then, Inka said unexpectedly:

'I'm going home, or I shan't have time to get myself organised.'

I watched her dress, thinking with fear that I'd have to see her home.

'Zhenya, you wanted that skirt pattern, didn't you? Are you coming?' said Inka. She didn't look at me, but I looked at her, and as I did, I felt my eyes fill with tears.

I wandered all that evening near Inka's house. The streets

had emptied, and in the windows the lights had gone out before I finally went away without having seen her.

Yurka Gorodyetsky went up to the Headmaster. He went in full view of everyone, and this must have been the most solemn moment of his life. He even had a catch in his voice as he repeated,

'The pupils of the Ninth Class, Postishov Secondary School, are ready to leave for the Collective Farm.'

'Right, they may go,' said Victor Pavlovich.

'Into the trucks!' shouted Yurka, and everyone laughed. Victor Pavlovich laughed too, because everyone who was going had been sitting in the trucks for ages. Yurka held up a small red flag. The class prefects—they were sitting at the back on the right—also held up small red flags. The red flags were an innovation of Yurka's, we'd got on very well without! Altogether, Yurka was turning out to be very active. He stepped onto the footboard of the first truck, and it moved slowly off, Yurka still standing holding the door open. I walked along close to the truck. Inka waved to our lot, then gave me a quick glance, smiling all the time. Her scarf had slipped forward and its shadow fell on her forehead and her eyes. To the right of the gates, the school orchestra was playing the march, 'Ever Higher and Higher . . .' The trucks passed me, and turned into the street. By the time I reached the gates they were already gaining speed. Dust spurted up from under their wheels, and three dustclouds rolled along the street.

'I'm so sorry for Inka,' said Katya. 'It's just her bad luck. No one's ever had to go to the Collective so soon after exams before.'

'I think she was crying,' said Zhenya.

'Did you actually see?'

'Well, I saw tears in her eyes anyway.'

'What's everyone going to do?' I asked.

'I propose we all go to the beach,' said Sashka.

252

'I'll go and finish caulking the yacht.'

'Let's all go. We promised Inka we'd come round the Point.'

I was afraid Sashka would change his mind about going to the beach. But he didn't.

'Oh come off it! We'll go to the harbour after dinner. We've got to pick up the paint anyway.'

'I'll be waiting for you at the harbour then.'

I crossed the roadway.

Down by the wharf Pavel was talking to a sailor from the *Poseidon* who was standing on the prow of his boat, choosing a cable. I got undressed, put my clothes together under a bush, and in only my bathing trunks, began mixing putty and red lead. Pavel came up to me.

'How's it you're alone? Doesn't seem right,' he said.

'No harm in being alone sometimes.'

'Quarrelled with the redhead?'

'I haven't quarrelled with anyone. She's gone to the Collective Farm.'

'Oh, I see. I thought there was something not quite so professorial about you. She's got guts, that girl! She comes running up to me, and says: "I saw you with Volodya, Styopik's there, beating them up!" "Wait right here" I say. So I come running. It's as black as inside a nigger's stomach after a black coffee. Even I've got shivers up my spine—scared of a knife, and there she is milling around, hunting for you!'

'I can't remember, did we ever say, Thank you?'

'What do I need your thanks for? Where'd I stick it? What's she see in you anyway? Maybe you've some kind of a secret?'

'You said something about Styopik and Nyura, what's he done to her?'

'Same as he'd do to your redhead if he could catch her. Nyura's husband walked out on her because of it.'

253

'How is it Alyosha's never said anything?'

'Didn't even know! I only got to hear of it at second-hand. Nyura, the fool, kept her trap shut. No proof. That is, all traces removed. You were born lucky. How did your mother have you?'

'I don't know what you mean.'

'Must've been borne in a caul. Thinking of marrying the redhead?'

'Yes.'

I had kneaded the putty with my left hand, and rubbed it with my right thumb into the seams and dents of the boat's left side. The most important thing was to get the prow well caulked. That's where the stress was greatest in heavy seas. Pavel lay on the sand, smoking and, from time to time, spitting through his teeth.

'You won't feel much like leaving town, will you?' he asked.

'Well, will *you*?'

'All one to me. I've been on the move since I was a kid. To start with, from one orphanage to another, and then on my lone. I've been up and down the whole coast. What are you messing about with the yacht for? Won't stop you going away!'

'We want to sail to the Point the day after tomorrow.'

'Paint won't be dry.'

'This heat's enough to dry up the sea!'

'Maybe it will, too. What are you going to do at the Point?'

'Our kids are working at the Red Front collective.'

'You mean, you're going to see the redhead? She's terrific! Give you some advice as a friend: you can't leave her like that, someone'll swipe her!'

'Oh shut up, Pavel! I can see you like Inka yourself. Don't keep on at me! If you keep on at me, we'll only have a row!'

'Sometimes I look at you and you're regular professors. And another time you're proper nits.'

'I could say a thing or two about you as well. I'd say it but I don't want to quarrel. We're in your debt.'

'There's nothing you could say about me I don't know already. And what I don't know, our Komsomol leader drums into me every day. I can see your lot, and Alyosha, are two different sorts of fish—but just what sort, I haven't worked it out yet.'

The sailors from the *Poseidon*—those we'd been with at Popandopoulo's—were sitting on the wharf. One of them shouted:

'Pavel! Finished your confession!'

'Just coming!' said Pavel. 'Tomorrow I'll be paid off, and in the evening I'll be going for a farewell blind. I can take one of you, or all three, to complete your education.'

'Thanks, Pavel, but I'm not in the mood. Vitka and I were unlucky you know.'

'I heard. But it's the same halter, whether it's Navy or Infantry! Will you come drinking with us?'

'No, we're going to the Point.'

'O.K. If that's what you want. . . .'

I took the rubber spatula, its end cut slantwise, and scraped off the surplus putty. The spatula bent resiliently in my hand. You had to take care that all the cracks and dents—traces of time, sand and water—were well smoothed over. Only my eyes and hands were working, my mind was free to think.

'Volodya! Come over here! Got something for you!'

Pavel was sitting with the sailors from the *Poseidon*. A plank lay on the coiled cable, and on it stood two bottles of vodka and a string of smoked fish.

'Was it you that put Styopik inside, last winter?' Pavel poured out quarter of a glass of vodka and handed it to me. I took it without thinking.

'Maybe. But I didn't see a knife on him.'

'So you didn't see a knife,' said the sailor. 'Killed him with his bare hands I suppose! You should've said you saw the knife and be done with it.'

'But I didn't see it!'

'Who else was in the fight the other night?' asked Pavel.

'There's a chap called Mishka Shkura. But we didn't actually fight with him. He wouldn't.'

'Which Mishka?'

'That nit from the Siltings. The one that dribbles.'

'Oh that one! So he's running with Styopik's rabble, is he?' said the sailor.

'O.K., we can muzzle Styopik. He's walking in the shadow of the noose now anyway. And you'll be off so no one will be any the wiser. Just don't let him set eyes on you. Drink up!' said Pavel.

I didn't feel like drinking, but it seemed churlish to hand back the glass undrunk.

'Let's rub them all out!' said the sailor, and winked at me.

My throat closed convulsively, and I choked. Blinded by the tears that had sprung into my eyes I held out the empty glass to Pavel, who put a smoked fish in my hand.

'Chew it!' he said. 'Fyodor, have a look if that onion's dropped behind the cable somewhere, will you?'

I went back to the yacht, still chewing. But the work went badly, I was seeing double, and my head felt unpleasantly heavy. I swore I'd never drink vodka again, and in general not to drink any more. I lay down in the short shadow of a bush and fell asleep.

Sashka and Vitka were caulking the stern. I was lying with my eyes open. The shade of the bush was on my feet, that meant I'd slept at least two hours!

'I wonder what Inka's doing now?' said Katya.

'Just what you used to do—stuffing mattresses with straw,' said Vitka.

'I bet she's expecting us tomorrow,' said Zhenya.

'She may even be expecting us today—that's up to her,' said Sashka.

Katya and Zhenya were sitting behind me, at the back of the bush—I could tell from their voices. Vitka said:

'We'll go to the Point the day after tomorrow, and that's that!'

'Look! He's woken up,' said Sashka. 'There's a smashing workman for you!'

'Stop badgering him,' said Vitka.

I stood up, and went down to the sea to wash.

13

—◦◦⟩(⟨◦◦—

But we didn't go to the Point the next day, nor the day after. For three days, every morning, and again after dinner, we had to report to Lieutenant Miroshnichenko at the Commissar's office, and we'd hardly get inside the door before he'd say:

'Nothing today. Don't go out of town though.'

I think he guessed we wanted to go somewhere. But I didn't know what on earth to do with myself in town. Vitka and Sashka had the girls, they were all right, but for me, being with them was still worse. They had the yacht, and from morning till evening they went skimming over the bay, and in the evening they'd go to a film at one of the sanatoria. All over town the posters of John Danker had been pasted over with new ones of Saul Lyubimov. Zhenya said we absolutely must go to the concert, and Igor and Zoya backed her up. They'd heard Lyubimov in Leningrad and said it would be worth going to. Igor and Zoya spent all their time with us. But on various pretexts I stayed on my own, and walked about the town alone. A town isn't only the streets and houses—it's people as well. Of those who were close to me only Inka was not there, yet straight away I felt an emptiness that no one and nothing could fill. And as if on purpose, the town seemed never to have been so gay as it was that summer. I went off to the remotest corners of Old Town, where I'd seldom been before. The quiet winding streets climbed steeply uphill, and grass grew between the cracks of the old paving stones. Behind high stone walls, Tartars and Greeks lived in houses with balconied façades. Huge dogs leapt up onto the walls when they heard the steps of passers by. They neither barked nor attacked, just walked along the tops of the walls, their hackles up, lifting their black-fringed lips in ferocious smiles. I would go to the far end of the Old Town, and come down again to the sea, the Promenade, the streets where so many lovely women were walking about. That summer, it seemed as if all the most beautiful women in the country had gathered in our town for a beauty contest no one had advertised.

Once, towards evening, I dropped in on the gardener at the Siltings who grew the blue roses. We hadn't seen him for two years. He was working on his rose beds, wearing a tall Panama hat, and faded navy trousers with cloth braces crossed over his back. I didn't think he'd changed at all, but he didn't seem to recognise me. I said:

'Hullo.'

'Hullo.'

I leaned my elbows on the fence and watched him raking compost into the beds.

'You haven't been for a long time,' he said.

So he had recognised me after all. I went through the gate and took the rake from him, while he sat down on an upturned barrow. We'd spent many an early evening hour like this in his rose garden. The blue roses didn't last long, and had no smell, for as long as we could remember, the gardener had been trying to find a way of prolonging their life, and of giving them a perfume. We couldn't understand why he bothered.

'Still trying?'

'No, I've chucked it. I developed three new strains, but not blue ones,' he said. 'You can't cheat nature. There are no blue roses. It must be that the colour blue has no smell. And you can't have a rose without a smell.'

'D'you still dye them like you used to?'

'Of course. What else can I do? I don't want to, but I do it. People demand it. All they care about is prettiness. Let it be dead so long as it's pretty.'

As before, I couldn't see why the gardener was dissatisfied. He and his blue roses had made our town famous, I wheeled him two barrels of water in the barrow, and went. Even here I was restless. Two years ago when I'd gone to Inka's birthday, I'd given her three blue roses. . . .

I walked right through the town to the Spa Hall. There were naval ratings walking everywhere on the Promenade. They patrolled it, sauntering up and down with measured, unhurried steps. They walked along the edge of the roadway, stressing their aloofness. Then I sat in the remotest part of the park on the balustrade of a half-ruined stone staircase. The lamplight barely reached here from the avenues. Lights were showing on the sea. A lot of jellyfish had been washed up on the beach—that meant there'd been a storm somewhere, but the sea was calm, and the ships' lights were reflected in the black water. There were lights all over the shore too; those that were farthest away and widest apart, were by the Saltworks. I could name all the streets running down to the sea, by the pattern of their lights. The concert was over—I could tell that from the voices in the avenues. I thought to myself, 'I ought to be meeting the others,' but I only thought about it, and went on sitting.

Someone was coming down the staircase.

'There's someone there,' said a woman.

'Be careful, the step's broken,' a man answered.

I loved our town. Its night air was heavy with the suffocating smell of flowers, but by day, cooling winds blew through its sultry streets. By day and by night, the town offered itself to the thousands who sought in it a brief and carefree refuge, it gave them its beaches and parks, its houses and worn paving stones, its sun, and the warmth and coolness of the sea.

I loved it, and I knew its soul because I myself was a part of that soul.

When you are young, all your impressions are sharper and brighter. But with the years, your feelings get blunted, and a blue rose is less a living flower than an exotic decoration. I'm pretty sure that's why I've never once been back to our town in all these years. It lives, and will always live in my heart and memory as it seemed in my youth, however much its face is changed. Any good that has been preserved in me, I owe to this town of my youth, the best of towns. I owe it something I understood once and for all: that you can't be human and remain indifferent to the fate of the country where you were born and live, any more than you can be indifferent to the woman you have loved, or the man whose heart stopped the bullet meant for you.

I've lost a lot in my lifetime, but there's nothing more terrible than the death of those dear to one. Vitka was killed near Novo Rghev on the eighth of July nineteen hundred and forty-one. The battalion he commanded withdrew leaderless from the counter-attack. Sashka was arrested in nineteen hundred and fifty-two, after the arrest of a number of prominent doctors in Moscow. Sashka, too, was a very good doctor and surgeon. He died in prison, his heart gave out. I've written out these dates in script so as to remember them better. Some friends have gone, others come, and I go on living, in accordance with some theory of probability. And I seem to be lucky in meeting people who become real friends, and in friendship I give more than I take. And why not? It's good to have something to give. But recently I seem to be more irritable and easily offended. I expect I'm tired. You always get tired towards the end—though it's a good fatigue. And that's all about our town.

At the bottom of the steps the woman laughed.

'Look how the water glistens! Pick it up in your hands! Go on! Pick it up!'

I don't know how long I sat there; in a state like that you stop noticing time. The man and the woman had long ago gone up the steps and away. Searchlights were hunting for something in the black sky. I was in my home town, and somewhere nearby my friends were strolling around; but Inka wasn't there, and I couldn't live without her.

On board the ships the watch was being struck, but I didn't count the chimes. I'd already started walking, and I knew that I was going to Inka. There was no one about in the avenues, and they seemed strange, so brightly lit and so empty. The padlock already hung on the iron wicket gate. At the back of the stage people were talking, presumably the night-watchmen. So as not to disturb them I climbed over the railings, and came out onto the wastelands by Inka's street. It was dark in the windows of their flat. All this time I'd very much wanted to go and see Inka's mother, but I knew that I couldn't have looked her in the eyes.

I crossed the wastelands, walking along the sleepers between the tramlines, and before reaching the station, turned onto the highway. Outside the town, a cool wind blew softly, full of worm-woody smells from the open spaces hidden by the dark, and I could feel the soft dust of the road under my feet. Beyond the Saltworks, which I left to one side, a lorry overtook me, showing up the road in front, with its wormwood bushes on either side. The lorry passed me, blinding me with its head-lamps, then stopped. An army driver got out of the cabin and said:

'Going far?'

'To the Red Front Collective Farm.'

'They're neighbours of ours! Get in, I'll give you a lift.'

From the other side of the cabin someone else got down, banging the door. A stream of water poured onto the ground. The driver asked:

'Have you got a fag to spare?'

I was already up in the back of the truck, but I leant over the side and reached him the packet of cigarettes.

'Take them.' He didn't find my hand straight away in the darkness. When he lit a match he held it up to have a look at me.

'German?' he asked.

'No, Russian.'

'Now I see you, you don't look like a German.'

The door slammed and the man who'd got into the cabin said:

'Let's be off.'

The truck started. There was someone else beside me up in the back. I settled myself in the corner, trying to shelter from the wind. The town lights flickered on the horizon, sinking lower and lower towards the earth. I dozed, woke, then dozed again. The black steppe showed clearly against the sky which was beginning to lighten. Behind me in the truck, the soldiers slept, their heads towards the driver's cabin. They were all covered up, and only their boots stuck out from under their greatcoats. I was woken by the silence. The lorry had stopped by the estuary shore, where the roads forked. Green reeds were bending in the wind, and the whole lake was covered with white wave-crests. The soldiers were sitting up, their backs against the cabin. Their faces looked crumpled and sullen. The driver was standing on the running board looking into the back.

'Getting out, or going farther?' he asked.

I jumped down onto the road, my numbed legs giving under me. I took out the cigarettes and handed them to the driver.

'Take the whole pack,' I said.

'What about you?'

'I don't smoke really . . . I've just been fooling around.'

'Oh, don't fool around!' the driver laughed, and lit a cigarette, screening it from the wind. Then he gave one to the other man in the cabin with him, and tossed the packet into the back of the truck. 'Here, you gunners! Have a smoke!'

The lorry went off along the lakeside. The sun rose. I walked on, getting warmer as I went, and by the time I reached the beetfield it was already hot. Boys and girls in shorts were working at the far end of the field. They were moving slowly, in a broken chain, from the side of the field bordering the road, to the other, and where they had passed, the earth lay bare in hot, grey furrows. I saw Inka straight away; she was lagging about thirty yards behind the chain. I turned off the road and started walking along the soft furrows. Inka looked round. She sat down on the ground and covered her eyes with her arm as though frightened I would hit her. But of course she wasn't frightened. She was simply crying, and on her thin dusty face, the tears left runnels. Some were dry, others still wet. I took her hand and pulled it away from her face.

'Inka, don't! What is it?'

She began to sob.

'Why didn't you come? You promised to come. And I believed you. Why ever didn't you come? Why didn't you?'

'But, darling, I *have* come. Do you know, I started out on foot. But I was lucky, I got a hitch.' Probably I shouldn't have said 'darling', because it only made Inka cry harder. I squatted on my heels in front of her, completely at a loss. Some of the kids were already looking in our direction. 'Inka, don't! Stop crying so! When you cry, it makes me want to go and hang myself.'

'I want to hang myself too!' said Inka. 'Every evening they go on at me for not fulfilling my norm. Do I do it on purpose? Do I?' Inka wiped her eyes with the corner of the scarf tied under her chin.

'Nobody's going to scold you today. I'll have to go back by

the evening train, but by then we'll have fulfilled a two days' norm. You'll see! I was already weeding, sitting on my heels. 'You go in front,' I said. 'Don't go too fast. When I catch you up, you just move forward.'

The wind blew warm and damp. It blew from the sea, and you could hear the noise of the waves.

'I'd better go facing you,' said Inka. I'd wanted it that way too, but hadn't liked to say so.

'Take hold of the weed nearer the root,' I said. 'Don't pull it sideways, jerk it out!'

'I *am* jerking it! But the top comes off, and the root stays behind! That can't be how it's done!'

'Stick your fingers in deeper down. Look . . . pull! and that's all. Again . . . pull! and again. . . .'

I weeded quickly and as the roots came out they turned up clumps of dampish soil. They showed up clearly against the fast drying furrows. If you looked back, you seemed to have done very little. Better not look! Better not look ahead either, because then it seemed that the far edge of the field was never getting any closer. You just had to go on weeding, and trying to think about something pleasant. I explained the artless secret of this exhausting and tedious work to Inka. Every now and then I looked at her and saw her bare feet, bruised and earth-covered, and her sweaty stomach. When I looked at her, she turned away, and when I caught her up, she got up and moved a bit further ahead.

'You weed two rows, and I'll do one,' she said, crossing over to the row on my left.

She kept lagging behind. To make it easier for her to keep up, I started weeding from the third row too, but even so she still fell behind. Then I realised she simply didn't want me to look at her.

'D'you want a drink?' she asked. 'We're allowed three mugs of water while we're on the field, and I haven't even had one yet. D'you want some?'

'Let's catch the others up first,' I said.

We caught up with them and Inka went for the water. Raya was weeding the furrow on Inka's left.

'That's just fine, encouraging slackers!' she said.

'Have you never heard of lending a comrade a hand? You haven't? Yurka's not done his homework!'

'No hints from you, thank you! Where does Yurka come into it, anyway?'

'Well, how shall I put it! He's supposed to be the secretary.'

'She's just spoilt! Thinks she's some kind of a princess!'

I didn't answer, I went on weeding. Raya said all she wanted to, and finally stopped. Inka came back. Her face was covered with fine beads of sweat. She handed me the bottle of water.

'I forgot to warn you. It's not a good idea, drinking in the heat. It won't quench your thirst anyway.' I rinsed my mouth out and handed the bottle back to Inka.

'Are you sure you don't want any more? Then I'll drink it,' said Inka.

'Don't!'

'But I want to.'

While Inka was away fetching the water, I'd got far beyond Raya. We were about twenty paces ahead of the chain. Raya came up behind us, to our furrow.

'What does she want?' asked Inka.

'Public inspection. Pay no attention!'

The sky was shrouded with a whitish haze, and the day not particularly bright. But it was hot all the same. My head was throbbing. Most likely from lack of sleep. Even Inka's closeness to me didn't disturb me much.

'Why didn't you come to the Point as you promised?' asked Inka.

'We were forbidden to leave town. I didn't tell anyone I was coming to you now. I ought to have come straight away.

But I thought after they told us when we're actually going, there would still be a few days left.'

'And now you think there won't be?' asked Inka.

'I don't know. They haven't told us anything yet. You're not angry with me any more, are you?'

'I wasn't before.'

'When d'you mean—before?' I asked, and at once realised that my question had sounded ambiguous.

Inka didn't answer. Yurka came up to us.

'Sashka rang,' he said. 'You must be at the Point by one o'clock. They're coming for you in the yacht.'

'What's happened?'

'You're leaving tomorrow.'

'Yurka. Inka's coming to see me off at the Point.'

'She never completes her norm.'

'Today she will. Understand? I'm asking you as a favour.'

'I don't know what to say. The kids won't like it.'

'They won't even notice. So long as you don't egg them on.'

Inka looked at Yurka, her eyes full of tears, but they were angry too. I asked Yurka what the time was.

'About twelve. There'll be a dinner-signal at twelve-thirty.'

'Does he work too?' I asked when Yurka had said goodbye to me, and gone.

'He did the first day,' answered Inka.

'Sashka would say: "A fine secretary I've saddled you with!"'

Inka didn't say anything. I went on weeding though my hands were shaking. By this time tomorrow I'd have left our town, and from where I was going to, it wouldn't be so easy to get to Inka. Near the threshing floor, the bugler sounded the dinner signal. There were still about six yards left to the edge of the field.

'It's time I went. You can finish this bit when you come back,' I said.

267

'Yes,' said Inka, and her meekness made me feel uneasy.

We went out onto the station road. It was about three quarters of a mile to the sea. It bothered me very much that Inka was only wearing shorts and a brassière, I think it bothered her too. We walked in the middle of the road and didn't look at each other.

'Inka, don't take any notice of anything. Just you work the way I told you to, that's all.'

'I am.'

'And don't think about that.'

'I'm not thinking about it at all.'

At the Point, the waves were breaking right over the road, and their spray had laid the dust. The shore looked flattened out, and seethed with eddies of waves and foam. Inka left the road and sat down under a bush, her back to a sandy ridge. I stayed on the road, but sat down too.

'They'll never be able to get to the shore,' said Inka.

'I'll swim out to them.'

The sea was roaring, and the wind had wiped the sky clear of its whitish shrouds. We had to strain our voices so as to hear each other.

'Why can't you go back by the evening train? It's only tomorrow you're leaving,' said Inka.

'I don't know. I expect it's impossible, or they'd never have come out in the yacht in this weather.'

'Have you been thinking about me?' asked Inka.

'All the time. That's why I came.'

'What were you thinking about me?'

'Don't, Inka! It's not something you can really talk about. I'll write you.'

Inka sat, her feet ankle-deep in the sand, hugging her knees, which were pulled up to her breast, arms tightly round them. She rested her head on her knees and looked at me, and I at her. At this distance I was able to look at her. I got up. Why? Even now I don't really know why. I got up without thinking.

'There's the sail!' Inka said, pointing. But there was no sail where she was pointing to, there couldn't have been. In such seas, you can ride with it, or against it, but never broadside on. But that didn't matter. The sail was there. Short waves with white crests broke as far as the horizon, and over them skudded the dirty-grey triangle of the sail.

'They're coming!' I said, and looked round. Inka sat hiding her face in her hands. I looked at the sea. The boat was coming towards us on the landward tack, mainsail fluttering. That was right. It must have been Vitka at the helm. In ten minutes on such a tack, they'd have to go about, or the boat would be driven onto the shore. I took off my shirt, waved it over my head, and put it on again. Then I glanced round. Inka hadn't looked up. I came down from the road. Only about two paces in front of me the surf thundered. A foaming, sandy wave surged over my feet, then sucked back, tearing the sand from under me, and I dashed forward. Five feet of water swept towards me, and at the level of my eyes, the sun gleamed cloudily through its dull-green crest. I threw myself down head foremost, chest flattened against the wet sand, arms flung out. The wave passed over me, lifting me. I jumped up, and ran, the rushing water broke round my legs, and I was down again, and a new wave went over me, and again I jumped up, deafened by its roar, to meet the cloudy-green wall. Only once I didn't manage to dive under the wave in time, but that was right at the water's edge. The wave struck my chest, heaved me up, and threw me down again, and the rushing water carried me out into the sea. A wave lifted me, and as I sank again, I saw the yacht. Sashka stood steadying himself, one foot pressing against the deck, one arm clutched round the mast, a line in his other hand. He was watching me, waiting for the exact moment to throw. I struggled with all my strength to stay where I was, face towards the yacht, so as not to miss the moment when Sashka threw me the end. He threw it just as a wave lifted me. I caught it, hung for a split-second in the air, then pulled myself towards the boat, and as another wave lifted me, tumbled onto the deck. Sashka bent over me, and I saw the anxious look in his eyes.

The boat had tacked, and was moving out to sea. Inka stood on the shore. The shore rose with her and fell, and rose again. Sashka pointed at my feet. Only my right shoe was on. I took it off and threw it into the sea. I hadn't any socks on, in summer I wore them only on special occasions.

I struggled aft and took over from Vitka. He flapped and rubbed his numbed hand. I ran up the mains'l. The waves were beating against the yacht's starboard side, spray breaking over her. The sea was roaring, and it was impossible to talk. It's good to have the spray in your face, so that it's impossible to talk, because then no one can see you crying.

We went out into the open sea, and when we were broadside on to the lighthouse, we turned for port. The shore and the town seemed to have only three colours, white, yellow and green. During the next three hours Vitka and I changed places several times, but all the same our right hands were numbed by having to hold the sheet. We never let Sashka take the helm in this sort of weather because he wasn't sensitive enough to the pull of the sail. When the harbour came into view I took over the helm from Vitka. We swept through the formation of warships, and only then realised at what a speed the yacht was going. The rating on the fo'castle of the battleship *Paris Commune* signalled 'Happy Landings' with his little flags. There could be no question of using the quay, even the barges had been stood away from it, and were pulling at their anchors. I decided to run her aground, and pointed to the place I was heading for. Vitka sat beside me with the anchor ready just in case. Sashka crouched in the bows holding the end of the towline. Standing on the shore were Pavel and half a dozen others. I went all out, and only nearing the beach itself, hauled down the sail. Sashka threw the tow line, Pavel caught it, and began to haul in quickly. The yacht flew in to the shore on the crest of a wave, and buried its keel in the dry sand. We climbed down. Everything was swaying before my eyes, and the ground kept receding under my feet. Pavel came to us. He bent towards me and shouted:

'That's half a bottle you owe me, Professors!'

I wanted to be sick, and went off into the bushes; Vitka, then Sashka went off in their turn.

'You idiot! You blithering idiot! Why didn't you warn us you were going to Inka?' asked Sashka as we were coming out of the harbour.

'Sashka, don't go on at him!' said Vitka.

'Get a move on! Quick! To the Commissar's office,' said Pavel.

He came out of the harbour gates with us, and it was only then I noticed he was in his Sunday best and slightly drunk.

We arrived at the office, our faces green. Lieutenant Miroshnichenko looked at his watch and said:

'You ought to get ten days clink for this! Sign here.'

I signed my name in a couple of registers, hardly knowing what I was signing for. Sashka was given a ration of drink for the journey, instructions and money. Vitka and I got only our instructions.

'Pereverzev has the travel documents and rations,' said the Lieutenant. Then he gave us a long look. 'I suppose the Top Brass knows best. Maybe they'll make something of you,' he said.

'Can we go?' I asked.

'Yes. Be at the station at ten hundred hours exactly. They won't hold the train for you.'

We went along the empty, echoing corridor. The working day at the Commissar's office was over, and no one was there except the duty-officer. He saw us to the yard, and locked the door behind us.

14

All I took with me was a change of underwear, a spoon, a mug, and a pair of socks, and it all went into my mother's old briefcase.

'You're not serious! Surely you've got to take more than that?' asked my mother.

'That's what it says! Check it yourself! "Two changes of underwear, outer clothing, socks (or puttees), mug, spoon,"' I read out. I was sitting on the divan holding the type-written sheet in my hands. It was headed 'Instructions'. I, Belov, Vladimir Alexeyevich, was to report for orders to the Commanding Officer, Sklyansky Red Flag Training School, not later than 28th June, 1936, at the following address: Leningrad, 3rd July Street, No: 21. Then followed the list of things I was to bring with me.

'Outer clothing—that means overcoat,' said my mother. 'I'm sure of it.'

'Who's going to wear an overcoat in June?'

'I don't know. I don't know. You should have checked the details at the Commissar's Office.' My mother looked across the table at the pile of belongings I'd thrown on the bed, and her lower lip came up over her upper one.

She got up and went into the kitchen to put the kettle on and fix the supper. I knew I ought to go and help her, but I hadn't the strength to get up off the divan; I settled myself more comfortably, stretching out my legs. The primus began to hiss, and flare up, then went quiet; probably something obstructing the flow. Over me hung the cloudy-green crest of the wave, and beside me stood Inka, telling me:

'Kick it, Volodya! Kick it!'

'In our circumstances, the best thing to do would be to run!' I answered. Inka laughed and we ran along the road. We ran, laughing, the wave chasing us, its cloudy-green crest translucent in the sun. And we would have escaped, but Yurka stepped out onto the road.

'The kids are slaving away while you're having fun!' he said. The wave crashed down on Inka, sweeping her off her feet, and foaming and sandy, carried her out to sea.

I wiped my sweating forehead with my hand. I think it was terror that woke me, but perhaps it was my mother. She was standing beside me, teapot in one hand and the frying pan in the other.

'When you were little, we could never get you into bed!' said my mother. 'You'd shout and laugh and run around the flat. Then silence. We'd find you asleep under the table, under the bed, anywhere, except in bed. Only your father could get you into bed at the proper time. I don't suppose you remember any of it, do you?'

'No, I don't.'

At supper my mother said:

'You're beginning to look extraordinarily like your father. I'm glad you're going into the Army, it'll make you more of a man.'

'D'you blame my father?'

'Your sisters thought up that one! How should I blame him? After all, he's your father. But I had a hard time with him. Volodya, you must promise me you won't drink.'

'Don't worry, I'll never be a drunkard.'

'Your father drank an awful lot. Sometimes it's hereditary.'

'Mother, who was the man who used to live with us, and where is he now?'

'D'you really remember him?'

'Yes, but not very well. If you don't like talking about him, then don't.'

'Why shouldn't I? That man was the biggest mistake I ever made as a Party member, and as a mother. I've never been afraid of admitting it. But it was *my* mistake. It has nothing to do with you or your sisters. D'you understand?'

'What sort of a person was he?'

'A stubborn and confirmed Trotskyist. When I realised, I drove him out!'

'And where is he now?'

'It doesn't matter. He's no concern of yours. You had a father, a weak but honest man, and you've got me. But that man has nothing to do with you.'

'Shall we go to bed?' I asked. 'I'll help you clear the table, then let's go to bed.'

'Don't you clear anything. Just get into bed. I'll have nothing to do tomorrow anyway.'

Then I lay in bed, while my mother sat on the divan sewing an inside pocket for my money into my trouser belt.

'You'll have twenty-five roubles in your purse, that's enough for the journey,' she said. 'This hundred you'll change in Leningrad. Not before. I won't give you any food, there's a restaurant car on the train.'

'They gave us ration money at the Commissar's office, but I don't know how much. Alyosha Pereverzev's got it,' I said.

'So much the better, then you won't need this hundred for some time.'

I tried not to fall asleep while my mother was in the room.

'What time do you have to be at the office tomorrow?'

'Ten o'clock.'

'In the Army they say ten hundred hours. Couldn't you ask them to deal with your business last?'

'That's what I'll do. I'll arrange it and come straight to the station.' My mother hung my trousers over the chair. 'That's how we used to hide our Party documents before the Revolution.'

'Wherever did you have your inside pocket in those days?'

My mother blushed and laughed.

'Go to sleep!' she said.

She turned out the light, went to her own room and put it out there too. It was raining, the windows were shut, and the water tinkled softly on the panes. I thought, I'm leaving home in earnest, for a long time, in fact for good, and I tried to imagine what the flat would be like when I was no longer there. My mother put her light on and came out of her room. I think she stood for a long time by my bed, but I was already asleep.

At breakfast next morning something peculiar seemed to be happening to her. She'd drunk her tea, and put the sugar bowl back on the dresser while I was still eating my omelette. Then she came back and took away the bread.

'Hey, Mother! I can drink unsweetened tea, but it's horrible eating an omelette without bread,' I said, jokingly.

'Oh dear, I'm so sorry!' she said, putting the bread-basket back on the table. Then she sat down and started smoothing the tablecloth with her hand. 'If I can't get a decision about the Health Department Workers' pay from here, I shall have to go to Moscow. Write me at once from Leningrad, I might be able to go over to see you.'

'Of course, I'll write.'

We sat at the table for a while in silence.

'Time I went,' said my mother, and looked at me, and all my life I've remembered the misery in her eyes.

She went out and I started looking for the briefcase. On the divan where it had lain yesterday was my mother's jacket. I didn't think of picking it up at first, when I did, I saw the briefcase underneath. My mother came into the room wearing her cap.

'Take the jacket, it might come in handy,' she said. 'If you don't need it, throw it away.' She looked all round the room, as if it were she who was going away, not I. We went through the kitchen, and it was I who locked the door. I handed her the key. She looked at it, then at me:

'But that's your key!' she said. 'No, no, you keep your key.'

The morning was cool and windy, the sun only coming through at times. My mother came with me as far as the tramstop. I got into the rear car, and as soon as the tram started, wedged the briefcase on the floor between my feet and, using my nails, unpicked the stitches on my trouser belt. I tore out the inside pocket, transferred the money to my purse, and threw the bit of stuff away. I hadn't taken the jacket of course, and my mother hadn't noticed. I knew she wouldn't.

Alyosha met me on the platform and took me to the coach to show me my seat.

'Nobody else here yet?' I asked.

'Yes, Vitka and Pavel are.'

There were a lot of people on the platform seeing other people off. Seeing people off is one of the forms of entertainment in seaside towns. Most of them were crowding round the two Moscow coaches. The morning train came in on the other track from Simferopol. Zhenya's father ran past shouting:

'Rooms to let! Lovely rooms, for every taste and every pocket.'

Sashka arrived with his parents, then Katya and Zhenya appeared. They came out of the waiting room where they must have been sitting till all of us were assembled. I waited for my mother, trying not to be seen. Our history teacher Vera Vassilyevna came up to the carriage.

'Sashka, Vitka, come over here! But where is Volodya?'
she asked.

I went up to her. I'd quite forgotten that it was the school
leavers' party today. Vera Vassilyevna had brought our
prizes. I'd been awarded a chess set, Vitka—the novel *How
the Steel Was Tempered*, and Sashka—Babel's *First Mounted
Brigade*. Vera Vassilyevna handed us each our prizes
and kissed us, and made a short speech about Sashka's
award.

'Sashka,' she said. 'Only because I believe that you are
mature enough to realise the defects of this book, and because I know how much you love this gifted writer, however
alien his ideology, did I agree to your being presented with
First Mounted Brigade.'

Sashka's mother shed a few tears, and Vera Vassilyevna
herself was very moved. She put her arm round my shoulders
and asked:

'Where's your mother?'

'At the office. She'll be here any second now.'

'Fancy even thinking about the office when your son is
going away!' said Sashka's mother.

I'd like to know for whose benefit she was saying that. If
it was for me, she was wasting her breath. I had no wish to
listen!

'It's always sad saying goodbye to one's pupils. But I can't
imagine the school without these boys! I must be getting old
and sentimental,' said Vera Vassilyevna.

'I wish all young people were like you,' said Sashka's mother.

Sashka's father was standing, his hands behind his back,
humming softly to himself.

Uncle Peter called me, and took me aside to the waiting
room window. He looked at me for a long time, so long that
I began to feel embarrassed.

'Tell me. Tell me honestly. Vitka isn't offended with me,
is he?' he asked.

278

'No, Uncle Peter, he isn't. Nobody's offended!'

'Good. Now I want to ask you a favour: Vitka's a bit green. Keep an eye on him will you?'

'Everything will be O.K., Uncle Peter. You'll see. Everything will be O.K.'

'That's fine then. I'll be glad to see that.' Uncle Peter ruffled my hair and clapped me on the back. He went back to Aunt Nastya and Vitka, while I went back to the carriage and stood opposite the entrance to the platform so as not to miss my mother. Pavel was standing at the carriage window.

'The longer I live, the happier I am I haven't any relations!' he said.

Katya and Zhenya were strolling up and down arm in arm. Sometimes they went up to Sashka and Vitka, exchanged a few words, and again strolled up and down. Everything was fine for them, in a fortnight they, too, would be leaving for Leningrad. Zhenya had got her summons to go to the Music Academy yesterday. Then both of them came up to me, and Katya said:

'D'you know what we've decided? We'll go to the party tonight, and tomorrow we'll go to Inka.'

'A good idea,' I said. They walked off, looking offended.

And there was still no sign of my mother.

The third bell went, and suddenly everyone remembered that they hadn't said the most important things, and in fact that they'd not even said goodbye! It was impossible to get near the carriage steps. Sashka's mother was standing in front of everyone, and Sashka was shouting to her from the link-platform between the coaches.

'What are you wailing about? I'm not dead!'

Very Vassilyevna shouted:

'Let Volodya through!'

She was pushing me in the back, and saying:

'You know you can *always* count on me.'

As I forced my way through to the steps of the carriage people were patting me on the shoulder, wishing me a happy journey; someone kissed me—Aunt Nastya, I think. The train jolted. I got up onto the step, and then I saw my mother. She was coming from the front end of the train. She must have realised she was going to be late, so she was coming from the front so as not to miss my coach. The train was moving slowly, and you could feel the engine beginning to pull. I jumped down onto the platform and ran to meet my mother. It was not so easy to find her in the crowd. We bumped into each other almost by chance, and hugged each other, as my coach moved slowly by me. Sashka and Vitka were shouting and reaching out their hands to me. I got onto the step. My mother walked alongside, her face raised to mine. Her damp grey hair was poking from under her peaked cap and there were trickles of sweat on her temples. We began to leave her behind as soon as the coach pulled out from under the station roof into the sun; she was still walking along, looking at me, and when she reached the end of the platform, she was ahead of everyone else. I can still remember my mother at the end of the platform, in her black strap shoes, canary-coloured socks, and long skirt. Her legs were like marble, white with blue veins.

I never saw my mother again, not even in death. . . .

At the junction further along the line, the Moscow coaches were uncoupled before the arrival of the Simferopol-Moscow train. We were already out on the platform when the engine shunted the coaches onto the siding. We stood on the empty platform. For the first time no one was watching over us; from now on, we were accountable to no one but ourselves. This experience comes only once in a lifetime, when you leave your home for good, knowing that if ever you come back it will be only as a guest.

'Well, try anything once!' said Sashka. 'So we'll aim at not dying yet!'

The day had turned fine, and we could feel the warmth of the sun-baked flagstones through the soles of our shoes. We went along to the station buffet to have a cream-soda. It was cold and fizzy. We drank so much of it that we had a job to breathe, and then, all at the same time, reached into our pockets to pay up. I took out my new purse, my mother's present.

'Let's have a look!' said Sashka. He turned it over in his hands, Vitka looking over his shoulder. Neither he nor Sashka had a purse. At the bar Pavel was having a beer, chuckling as he looked at us.

'Why not knock back something stronger?' he asked.

'In a heat like this? You can keep it! We're not ashamed,' said Sashka.

'Looks as if I'm going to be bored to death by my fellow-travellers!'

Sashka and Vitka hurried off into the town to buy themselves purses. Pavel was having a chat with the barmaid.

'Pour me a glass of vodka—neat, love, and let's have a bite of something with it.'

'Those young fellows were right to say it was too hot to drink,' said the barmaid.

'Oh, they're professors!' said Pavel. 'Listening to them—you can just die of boredom.'

Both Pavel's elbows were propped on the bar-counter. The barmaid too was leaning over it, her hands hidden under her bosom. Their heads were almost touching, and they were smiling. I got two bottles of beer for Alyosha who'd stayed in the compartment to look after our things. It was stuffy in the compartment, and empty, most of the passengers had gone into the town. I went out onto the open link-platform between the coaches, where you could feel the wind blowing, and it was cooler. I sat on the footboard on the shady side. Beyond the track, the steppe began, and the brightly glittering salt lake, whose waters flowed through the canal to the

Saltworks' basins. Vitka reappeared and looked hard at me.

'What's the matter with you? Where's Sashka?'

'There, in the next carriage. With a smart looking woman and her daughter. Did you see Inka?'

'When?'

'Just now. I thought she'd be here already. Sashka and I saw her; she was on her way to the station.'

I jumped down from the step, and went running to the station building, through the waiting room, out onto the street, and back again onto the platform. Inka was nowhere to be seen. Vitka was standing on the platform.

'Did you speak to her?' I asked.

'No, Sashka was talking to that woman's daughter. We thought we'd see her here.'

'You stay by the coach. Don't go away anywhere,' I said.

I found Inka in the little Station garden. She was sitting on one of the stone stumps of the railings, swinging her legs.

'Inka! What are you doing sitting here? Why didn't you come to the carriage?'

'I didn't want you to see me.'

'Why not?'

'Because I didn't!'

Something of what we'd experienced on the wastelands still lurked in our eyes, and because of it we couldn't look into each other's face for long. Three iron gas-pipes, one above the other, linked the stone stumps. I sat on the top one, but I was still below Inka.

'Tomorrow Katya and Zhenya are coming to see you.'

'Let them. So what! I won't complete my norm today either. Yurka sits the ones who don't at a separate table so that everyone can see them. I'm always sitting at a separate table.'

'Don't let's talk about Yurka. Let's talk about us.'

'Yes, let's.'

'I feel as if I were . . . guilty towards you. I expect I am.'

'There's nothing for you to feel guilty about. And don't let's talk about it. Don't let's talk about it till I come to Leningrad.'

'Will you be coming?'

'I'm sure I will. Didn't you hear what I shouted to you as you were going? Didn't you?'

'"There's the sail".'

'That was earlier on. I'm very glad you didn't hear!'

'What did you shout?'

'I'll never tell you that. . . . Or maybe I'll tell you if I come to Leningrad. I was so afraid you'd hear!' Inka gave me a sidelong glance from under her eyelashes. Her old, flat shoes were half off, hanging from her toes, and a rim of dust showed clearly round the damp soles of her feet. 'Volodya! I'm going,' she said, and stayed where she was.

'Wait. There's still twenty minutes till the train leaves,' I said.

'I'm not waiting for the train. I've got to walk four miles, and after that I'll still have to work. I left at dinner time.'

'Are you hungry?'

'No. But have you any money? Then buy me some cherries! When I was passing the little market, I saw some.'

We came out of the station garden.

'Sashka and Vitka saw you. Won't you come over and have a word with them?'

'No.'

At the little market by the station, I bought Inka a big bag of cherries. Then I put my arms round her and kissed her. We kissed hurriedly because we were shy of strangers seeing us. Inka's eyes were full of tears, but she didn't cry. She walked away from me, eating cherries as she went, and spitting out the stones.

'Young, but forward! They've no shame!' said a woman

283

who was selling little boxes made of cockle shells. I stood and watched till Inka went round the corner, then said:

'What's the use of shame, Ma?'

'I can see you've no use for it!'

I wasn't going to start anything with this woman who was wilting in the heat. Our train was standing on the near track. Sashka came hurtling into me on the platform, and began yelling:

'Where the hell've you been? I've been running all over the station after you!'

'Don't yell,' I said. 'I went to look at the town.'

'Did you see Inka?'

'You just dreamt you'd seen her!'

'It's enough to drive anyone crackers! I saw her with my own eyes!'

'Why didn't you stop her?'

'But she was going towards the station. Who could imagine she was going anywhere except to meet us?'

We went to our carriage; Vitka was standing outside it.

'Did you hear that? Seems we dreamt we saw Inka! Seems you and I are lunatics!' said Sashka. Vitka looked at me and said nothing. Pavel came over to the coach. His eyes were glazed and his hands fumbled the air a couple of times before he caught hold of the handrail.

'At Janko, I'll have a quick one to sober me up. Mind you wake me,' he said.

The three bells went, and the passengers rushed into the coaches. We went through to the second link-platform, and I stayed there. Sashka wanted to stay too, but Vitka pushed him into the coach. Once beyond the station the hot wind tore in at the open door. The dark-blue sea, with its white horses, hit my eyes like a blow. On the empty road I could see a tiny figure, but at that distance it was hard to tell if it was walking or standing still. I climbed down on to the bottom step and hung on by the handrail. The wind was tearing at my shirt, and just below me, the ground sped away under my feet.

'Inka, my Inka!'

The wind snatched the words from my mouth, and the rumble of the train drowned my voice.